So Horrible a Place

So Horrible a Place

MARGARET DUFFY

First published in Great Britain in 2004 by
Allison & Busby Limited
Bon Marche Centre
241-251 Ferndale Road
London SW9 8BJ
http://www.allisonandbusby.com

A catalogue record for this book is available from
the British Library.

10 9 8 7 6 5 4 3 2 1

ISBN 0 7490 8303 4

Printed and bound by
Creative Print + Design, Ebbw, Wales

MARGARET DUFFY was born in Woodford, Essex, and has worked for the Inland Revenue and the Ministry of Defence. She now lives in Devon in a one-time crossing-keeper's cottage with her husband and three cats and divides her time between writing and garden design. *So Horrible a Place* is the ninth novel to feature Patrick Gillard and Ingrid Langley.

Acknowledgements

My thanks go to Susan and Godfrey Johnstone for their help and advice concerning the making of films. Any errors remaining are my fault and not theirs.

1

'If you shoot someone in the heart and they have a gun in their hand they can fire right back at you,' Patrick said. 'You have about twenty seconds. I would aim for right there,' a long forefinger pointed between his eyes. 'But if you shoot from behind go for the brain stem.' He tapped the back of his neck. 'That's instant death.'

'And the vital organs?' asked the man he was addressing.

Patrick shrugged. 'It depends how much you hate the guy. If you go for the stomach that's the most painful. Speaking personally if you're going to kill someone I see little point in indulging in unnecessary *embellishments*.'

The other leaned back in his seat with a thoughtful smile. He was a good-looking man, tanned and dark-haired, but a little chubbier than I had imagined from his screen image. This point had been raised by the man himself, laughingly admitting to be under a ruthless regime of exercise and dieting by his personal trainer. There was not a lot of time.

Backing up the people preparing Rik Harrison – who had been plain Richard Harrison until very recently – for his rôle as a world-class assassin in his new film *Blood and Anger* was my husband, Patrick Gillard, until very recently a Lieutenant-Colonel in the Devon and Dorset Regiment, not to mention working in Special Operations and MI5, who had just resigned his commission. Danger had come too close to the family to make carrying on an option. Patrick's out of the blue job was to help Harrison, who was in his early thirties, transform himself into a convincing cold-eyed killer. He was providing insider knowledge to promote cool self-confidence, tuition in unarmed combat, knowledge in the handling of various firearms and anything else that was thought relevant. No one was criticising Harrison's acting ability, merely recognising that knowledge led to authenticity.

We were in London, in and around where most of the filming was to take place, for the start in two days' time of his proper coaching of Harrison; regarded as one of the most promising of Hollywood's new young stars and who had in the past twelve months decamped from the Shakespearean stage. In the UK he had also appeared in one low-budget film, a thriller and, more importantly, a police TV series, when he was reputed to have melted the heart of every female aged from nine to ninety. I was tagging along as, at the film company's suggestion, Patrick and I were going to make a sort of holiday of it, although I was realistic enough to wonder if this was a ploy to involve the novelist wife slightly in case she felt ignored and got on her high horse. And no, I was not numbering myself among the melted.

We remained in ignorance as to whom we had to thank for recommending Patrick for the job. The amount of money he was being paid for what would probably be no more than two weeks' work was not breathtaking but no doubt the experience would be interesting.

'Patrick . . . ' Rik began, 'Or do people call you Paddy?'

'No,' Patrick told him in a somewhat chilly fashion. 'They don't.'

Harrison did not seem to be put off. 'Right, Patrick. What about knives?' I noticed that although he had picked up an American accent in the short time he had been in the States he was now, consciously or not, starting to imitate Patrick's somewhat crisp manner of speaking.

'I can't teach you to throw a knife in such a short time but I can make you look useful with one.'

'A stuntman'll be used for the real action,' Harrison said. 'I was told they're going to do most of that kind of stuff

12

somewhere well away from the main sets in case they get it wrong and make a nasty hole in someone.'

We laughed as he had mimed extreme terror as he had uttered the last words.

A lot of water has flowed through Lydford Gorge since the day Patrick came back into my life and fainted at my feet in the kitchen. It was a fairly decorative affair as faints go but then again he was never a man to blunder through life in an ugly or clumsy fashion. The world is his stage and this undercover soldier, who has been known to reduce strong men to tears with his voice alone and crack walnuts just with his fingers at Christmas, deports himself on it with grace and elegance even when, as on that occasion, he was just out of hospital, exhausted and still in pain from injuries suffered during the Falklands War. The faint then, that boneless collapse right in front of the Aga, was a symbolic plea for mercy, an application for reinstatement into my hearth and home.

Perhaps it had not been so symbolic. What my one-time husband had in mind – this proposition revealed to me when he had recovered a little and was lying on the sofa with a mug of tea – was that I should partner him in his new career working for D12, a department of MI5. One of the reasons I weakened and agreed, eventually, was that I had an idea it would give an already fairly successful author – I write under my maiden name, Ingrid Langley – hefty chunks of utterly riveting material. In this I was not mistaken, the only snag being that I only just escaped with my life several times in order to be able to make use of it. Re-marriage to Patrick and two children later, I resigned to concentrate on them and writing. Then Patrick's brother Larry was killed and we adopted his two children and suddenly the family consisted of an alarming number of people with one of the breadwinners still likely to come home for the weekend in a body-bag.

So, after discussion, he had resigned. There had then been a couple of months during which he had disappeared for three or four days at the time, I assumed to tie off a few loose ends in Whitehall, on the last occasion returning home with a small gash on his head that had required a couple of stitches.

'What have you been *doing*?' I had asked in exasperation. 'Here's me thinking you were clearing your desk. I think I can handle you undertaking a few more small assignments and even cope if you said you simply couldn't face life without some of the old excitements but when you just disappear and then come back slightly dented . . . Patrick, we did *discuss* this.'

'The job really was supposed to be advisory,' Patrick had said, touching the healing area on his temple. 'But the Land Rover slid off the dirt road into a gully.'

I had given him my best scathing stare. 'And when did the best thing ever to have come out of Solihull slide off anything into anywhere? Or were the tyres completely bald? Or, more likely, were you ambushed, shot at, mined or generally discouraged from proceeding further by the bandits, terrorists, insurgents, guerrillas, revolutionaries, freedom fighters or Mujahideen you just happened to bump into on the way to Sainsbury's?'

'That's it. Finished,' Patrick had promised, palms outwards in a gesture of peace. 'Scout's honour.'

'I happen to know that you weren't in the Scouts,' I had responded smoothly. 'And even after all these years your father's still writhing with embarrassment because they wouldn't have you after you flew from the church tower's flag pole a very large pair of knickers that you'd pinched from someone's washing line.'

That first evening, when we met Rik Harrison at the hotel where were all staying and had dinner together at a nearby

Japanese restaurant, was a sedate and amicable occasion with no hint of the *angst* I knew would erupt when our leading man started his training. In order to make someone proficient in, for want of a better description, taking care of himself – for obviously nothing make-believe or phoney was required or they would have asked someone else – certain other basics had to be mastered first. My husband is not the kind of man to teach another potentially dangerous techniques if that person is not also trained in self-control and anger management.

Patrick would earn his money. Harrison would be shocked to discover that for the first twenty-four hours he and his tutor would be isolated in the same fairly large room together, with a toilet off, that was situated on the top floor of our hotel among other rooms that could be booked for meetings and similar gatherings. There would be no furniture, no contact with the outside world, no food, water the only liquid to drink from the tap over the handbasin in the toilet and no sleep. It was a scaled-down, customised version of the early stages of all special operations training.

I had absolutely no intention of being present during any of this initial period.

This was not to say that I was in ignorance of what would take place, for in a very minor and gentle way – although that was not how it had seemed at the time – it had happened to me. When I had first joined MI5 Patrick had taken it upon himself to teach me basic self-defence and number one lesson had definitely been keeping my emotions under control. The irony of this is that Patrick has the most incandescent temper when driven too far but he has at least learned to channel it away from misdeeds, mayhem or even murder. Well usually. The occasions when I have witnessed him fail to do so, thankfully deliberately, still give me nightmares.

I was fully aware that, as far as the pupil was concerned he, Patrick, would undergo metamorphosis from the friendly and calmly efficient ex-army officer into something that Harrison would loathe; a scathing tormentor who would pick his personality to pieces to see what made him tick and find him very much wanting. Harrison would rant and rave, he would probably weep, he would lash out and get his ears boxed for his trouble, on receipt of a little useful tuition he would try to wait until Patrick fell asleep – Patrick would pretend to doze – to enact revenge only to be punished with much more advanced moves. Torment would progress like this until he stopped resenting his treatment and started using his brain. I was hoping he was more mature than he had given me grounds to believe so far and also that Patrick would use his commonsense and adjust the training accordingly, as in this case it could not be abandoned. For after all, Harrison was not entering any kind of employment where his life might depend on it.

Fortunately he already knew some basics after his stage-work as he had received training from a fight director in swordplay and quarterstaff. He knew how to fall. He told us he could also do slaps and phoney hairpulls, fake elbow smashes to the solar plexus and knees to the groin.

'And all that was for A Midsummer Night's Dream?' Patrick asked, straight-faced.

Patrick had resigned his commission. I had to keep telling myself this because, even after all I had said, I could not get used to the idea. He was still only in his mid-forties and possessed health, strength, a higher than average experience of what life had to offer and a lamentably low boredom threshold. It was all very well being safe for the sake of a young family but if he was not happily and closely involved in something that exercised his keen intellect he would just shrivel up and die.

There was a certain sadness on my own part as well: close

brushes with death notwithstanding. Okay, we had also almost starved, lost in the Canadian boondocks, and been shot at with various firearms, sometimes effectively. People had tried to kill us in car crashes, hit us over the head with rocks and sent us flower arrangements with explosives hidden inside them. We had been doped, kidnapped, locked up and tortured. (For sheer originality though Patrick had yet to equal our DCI friend James Carrick who had been sealed up in an old boiler and left to die. Luckily Patrick had found him in time.)

But we had also had an awful lot of fun. And if I was honest I would have to admit that the *carte blanche* status under which we had operated had sometimes resulted in situations that had left us almost intoxicated with exhilaration. Like the time I had shot out two of the tyres and the windscreen of a car being used by some dedicated and utterly revolting crooks who had been unwise enough to arrive outside our cottage in Devon ... And the night when Patrick had thrown a man who had just jumped out from behind a bush and taken my photograph into the River Avon, and then for an encore had lobbed in a couple of semi-drunken yobs who had tried to interfere.

Power is like a drug: it seemed that life might be rather dull in future.

No, no, NO. Patrick would find himself a challenging job that would involve travel, planning, motivating others, tight schedules ...

My writer's imagination presented me with a picture of a stoical figure in an airport departure lounge, dressed in a sober suit, white shirt with regimental tie and carrying a briefcase. Exactly like a couple of dozen other men in that same place interspersed with scruffy Brits going on holiday. Businessmen? Civil servants from the Foreign Office? Engineering consultants? Salesmen?

No, we should have to move to somewhere where he could have a lot of interesting projects. An old manor house to renovate perhaps. No, again. Patrick is pretty lousy at things like that: he'd once made me a movable wooden plant trough that had resembled the newly-raised *Mary Rose*, only on wheels.

What *was* he going to do?

I had no choice, on the Monday morning, but to stay in the hotel for the duration of the first twenty-four hours, or however long the men stayed away, as it had been arranged, temporarily, that any visitors for Rik would be sent along to me. Having given the reception desk my mobile phone number – I had no intention of staying in my room – I had a late-ish breakfast, read the newspapers in a lounge, had coffee in a vast conservatory filled with artificial plants and then went back upstairs with a view to doing a little writing before lunch. As soon as I had switched on my laptop the phone rang.

'There's a Ms Deena O'Leary to see Mr Harrison,' the receptionist reported.

'Please ask her the reason for her visit,' I requested.

After a short pause, 'She says she's his agent.'

'I *am* his agent, for God's sake!' an angry American voice came distinctly over the line.

'You'd better send her up,' I said.

I opened the door to take a short walk down the corridor for a little exercise before she arrived – I loathe being cooped up in hotels – and had just turned from looking out of a window at a square below where a full gale was endeavouring to strip the late-summer leaves from the plane trees, when I saw a woman approaching. Something told me that here was my visitor. She walked with an affected bouncy stride, shoulder-length auburn hair flowing, a rather long nose, reminding me irresistibly of a Red Setter groomed to within an inch of its life for Crufts. We arrived at the door of my room together.

'Ingrid Langley?' she enquired coldly, without preamble, having checked the room number over my shoulder. Then, obviously having decided that it was, and giving me no chance to say anything went on, 'I understand you know the whereabouts of Rik Harrison. As you now know I'm his agent. I have something very important for him to sign.'

'Sorry,' I said. 'He's in training. They've only just started and can't be interrupted. If you – '

She had been shaking her head as though I was a slow-witted child as I was speaking. 'It happens all the time. Just tell me where he is and – '

'It's my *specific* task to repel all boarders for at least twenty-four hours,' I interrupted, feeling it was my turn to carve up. 'If you come back tomorrow night it's a pretty safe bet you'll be able to have free access to him. This was all agreed with the director.'

'I assume he's in the hotel somewhere.'

I merely smiled, probably infuriatingly.

She waved a slim Gucci document case beneath my nose. 'But this is vital!'

'I'm sorry,' I said. 'Would you like some coffee?'

'I demand to be told where he is!' she shouted in my face.

'And there was me thinking that it was only the English who were losing their good manners,' I murmured.

'I shall call David,' she promised, turning on her four-inch heels and stalking off, her hair whizzing round like it does in the TV shampoo adverts.

David Goodheim was the producer and a fat lot of good it would do her. Even if he did grant her access everyone still had to get past Patrick and the SAS has better things to do.

I discovered later that she had tried to bribe one of the young men on duty at reception into telling her Harrison's whereabouts.

During the afternoon I fended off an assistant to the costume designer; female, charming, Harrison's personal trainer; male, polite but openly resentful of not being able to see his charge, and two girls who, giggling, described themselves as friends of his but were probably fans hoping for a glimpse. I dutifully took the names and mobile phone numbers of all of these people, promising that I would give them to Harrison. I realised, belatedly, I should have promised Deena O'Leary that I would ask him to contact her if he appeared before the time I had stated but was not particularly contrite and this had a lot to do with her big mouth and voice about as comehitherish as a chainsaw.

I was getting ready for what promised to be a lonely dinner when the phone rang and I was told that a Mr Martin Longton would like to see Patrick.

'I'll come down,' I said. 'Perhaps he'd be good enough to wait in reception.'

There had been no need for me to grab the list of names I had been given as I was already aware that Martin Longton was the film's director. This was not to say that I knew what he looked like. My problem was solved for me, in rather bizarre fashion, when he recognised me immediately.

'Miss Langley! Read your latest. Terrific!'

We shook hands. He was tall, lanky, hair all standing on end from the gale and brimming with a thousand enthusiasms.

'Have they finished for the day? Is Rik about?' he asked, gazing around.

I explained.

'I hadn't realised that he was having to go into *purdah*,' was his comment when I had finished. 'God, what a hoot! Deena'll tear her hair out when she gets to know – she's a bit of a control-freak.'

I told him about that as well.

'Good for you. They made him ditch his agent over here, you know, and it was quite unnecessary. I think Deena has David by the short hairs too. Anyway, shall we have a drink?'

We made our way to a small bar Patrick and I had discovered that did not seem to get as crowded as the others and found a table. I smiled to myself when Longton caught sight of himself in a large tinted mirror on his way to the bar and raked the fingers of both hands through his dishevelled dark locks in a fairly hopeless effort to tidy them. When he returned with the drinks – white wine for me and a plain tonic with ice for him as he was driving – he asked if I would like to have dinner with him at a nearby Greek restaurant.

'We could have arranged for someone else to stay in, you know,' was his reaction to my telling him that I was hotel-bound for the rest of the day, at least.

'I sort of understand the wizardry,' I told him by way of an explanation, adding, 'and I owe it to Patrick to stick around.'

'Has he done this sort of thing before?'

'What, coached film stars?'

He nodded.

'No. Until very recently he was in the army.'

'It's a bit unusual.'

His tone aroused my curiosity. 'You sound as though you think it's *very* odd.'

Giving me one of his boyish smiles, Martin said, 'It is rather. There are quite a few fight directors, stuntmen and people like that who could have been taken on. Is David Goodheim a friend of yours?'

'I've never even met him. Nor, to my knowledge, has Patrick.'

Lowering his voice, Longton said, 'I get the idea he was involved in Special Operations and exciting stuff along those lines.'

'Yes, but I thought you knew all about it.'

'No, I just got an email from David's secretary in California saying that your husband had been hired for the job.'

I racked my brains for a possible connection and could not think of one.

'I'm famished – haven't eaten since breakfast,' Martin announced all at once. 'Will you join me for dinner here?'

I decided that it would be a wonderful idea for an author and a film director to have dinner together.

As we ate Martin Longton told me why he had urgently wanted to talk to Patrick. It was was to tell him that there had been a change of plan, and, due to a bookings mix-up that was not his, Martin's, fault, filming was now having to start at a warehouse the day after tomorrow instead of in a week's time. He had spent the entire day frantically trying to get the people, plus the the camera and sound crews, he wanted to commence work virtually immediately. Some were unavailable, working elsewhere, others abroad, several had refused on the grounds that their contracts indicated otherwise and they had important things to do in connection with their families.

'At least the problems are with folk like electricians, riggers, and set-dressers,' he told me. 'I'm home and dry with a camera operator, lighting cameraman and the focus puller as they're a team I always work with if I possibly can. Luckily they're free. I'm pretty sure I've got a sound crew. Even more luckily there's not much in the way of sets needed as it's cowboys and Indians stuff in the interior of the warehouse. Your Patrick'll now have to carry on with Rik in between shooting. I should imagine he'll be in his element.'

He seemed to have built up a somewhat gung-ho image of the man in my life. I said, 'Not wishing to make the wrong kind of comments but your leading man is going to have to starve himself for forty-eight hours. Obviously, he was under the impression that – '

'You mean he's overweight?' Martin interrupted, appalled, crashing his knife and fork back on to his plate.

'Just a bit,' I said. 'But he'll lose a couple of pounds today for sure so it'll be a good start.'

'I'll get him on a treadmill,' Longton promised darkly. 'The idiot's probably been filling himself up with junk – giant Cokes, burgers a mile high and fries. They do, you know, young actors – mostly the blokes – when they first go to the States, even if they didn't go in for that kind of thing much at home. Somehow think all of a sudden that it's cool. I'll crucify the idiot.'

'He does have a personal trainer though and said he was on a diet and exercise régime.'

'Bob Wayne. He's the one with the nails. Tomorrow morning – or whenever your husband's finished with Rik – we'll make him run ten miles instead of five, or whatever he's been doing.' Longton recommenced eating, shaking his head sadly.

Although the problem would soon have become apparent I was rather wishing I had not been the one who had brought it to his attention. Another problem was that I felt I ought to inform Patrick of the change of plan. But after thinking about it I did nothing: the most important thing right now was for Rik Harrison to undergo important training and, while doing so, lose a little weight.

'I'm really glad we had the funding organised before the British Government pulled the plug on some tax loopholes,' Longton continued. 'Most of the money's coming from the States.'

I said, 'The novel that I presume the storyline for the film's been taken from, *Blood and Anger*, caused quite a stir when it was published. I haven't read it but know it was written by an ex-special operations soldier about a mission in Northern Ireland that went terribly wrong and three men were captured, tortured and then shot by the IRA.'

'That's right. And he blamed another of his colleagues who was also involved. All the names were changed but those on the inside knew whom he meant. There was no proof but the man left the regiment under a cloud and apparently became so bitter and twisted about it that he hired himself out as an assassin – selling all his expertise to whoever wanted people bumped off. That's who Rik takes the part of in the film. But we've changed the end so that someone else comes along with evidence to prove his innocence just as he's about to undertake an assignment that will almost certainly result in his own death.'

'Do you know what happened to the man in real life?'

'No – but he's presumably still murdering people for money in lawless parts of the world. I can't ask the author, John Taylor, as he's no longer with us.'

'Oh? I don't remember hearing about that.'

'I'm not aware of the details other than that he was only in his late forties. I think Melvyn Lockyer, the scriptwriter, said something about him dying on holiday in the West Country but I'm afraid I didn't really take it in.'

After a restless night, writer's imagination in lurid over-drive as to what was going on somewhere overhead and missing a companionable warmth, no, a downright sexy man, next to me, I got up, exhausted, at six-thirty, had a shower in an effort to feel better – it failed – and then went down to find strong proper coffee. It would be disastrous if Rik was accidently injured, or resented what was going on and walked out, refusing to carry on with the part. Actors are notoriously touchy, I told myself, film stars usually in possession of a galaxy-sized vanity. Perhaps, subconsciously,

I had hoped that Patrick might carve out a new career for himself doing this kind of work. Would he fall at the first hurdle?

There were a handful of early souls having breakfast but even this number was too many for me in the mood I was in – on reflection caused by being cooped up indoors – and I took myself away to a corner and the long-suffering young waiter had quite a long walk to reach me across the deep-pile plum-coloured carpet. I ordered coffee and toast and acquired a newspaper.

A couple of minutes later there was a draught of movement beside me and someone plonked themselves down in a spare chair.

'Mornin', Ma'am,' said Rik, tracksuit-clad, breathing deeply and glowing.

I suppose I gawped at him. Finally, I said, 'When did you finish?'

'Just after five-thirty a.m. Patrick told me I was cleared for take-off. So I did. Then Bob Wayne grabbed me and we've been for a run in the park. Fantastic. But we're – Patrick and I, that is – are starting again at nine. Not in that room up there though. Somewhere else.'

'So where did Patrick go? I haven't seen him.'

Rik was still getting his breath back. 'No idea. His mobile rang and I left him talking.'

'He usually switches it off when he's involved like that.'

'That's what he said. Thought he had. Apologised.'

'Several people have been trying to get hold of *you*.'

He shrugged. 'They'll get back to me if it's important.'

'Including your agent.'

My coffee and toast arrived and he gazed at it appreciative-ly. 'She's always belly-aching about something.'

'The other thing that's happened is that shooting's starting tomorrow.'

'Yeah,' Rik said heavily. 'That's partly what Patrick's call was about.'

I called the waiter over and asked for another cup and saucer. 'No sugar,' I told Rik sternly, giving him some coffee using the crockery already on the table. 'No cream.'

'I know. Thanks. We talked about that. I'm not going to be a lean, mean, killing machine in time even if I don't eat anything at all until tomorrow. I'll have to wear corsets or something. God.'

I simply had to know. 'So – er – how did it go?'

'Okay. I'm used to being told what to do – drama school and all that – and what he was showing me how to do was fantastic. Fantastic. Saturation bombing, fast-forward teaching. I now know how to deal with a mugger, disarm someone waving a knife and other things. But mostly to stay cool, keep my temper and use my brains, although he didn't seem to think I was a hot-head. He really tried though, goaded me until I really wanted to take a swing at him. I didn't – I knew he'd have lifted my head off my shoulders. I couldn't believe how the time flew.' He took a mouthful of coffee, swallowed and grinned. 'I taught him something in return.'

'What?'

'Man-kissing.'

Slowly, I cranked up my lower jaw into its rightful position. '*What?*'

'Man-kissing. You know, Mafioso-style. Grab head, kiss on lips, slap shoulder, big hug. It's quite a cult. Everyone's doing it, especially here in London – nothing to do with gays. It's supposed to be the sign of the high-living, devil-may-care internationalist.'

With regard to the identity of his tutor I found myself enormously admiring his courage.

'You have to be very self-assured and macho about it,' Rik went on. 'Guys *never* air-kiss.'

'Patrick doesn't really move in the kind of circles that go in for that kind of thing,' I said, thinking of the effect that such a greeting would have at a regimental dinner.

'Who knows?' Rik replied impishly. 'He might meet a real Italian godfather.'

'Being nosy,' I said, 'what was your parents' reaction to their Eton-educated son telling them he wanted to be an actor?'

He drew in air through his teeth in mock horror and then gave me a quizzical look.

'I read up about you,' I explained. 'Patrick asked me to do a little research.'

'There was a bit of bad feeling to start with but they soon got used to the idea. My two sisters are the really brainy ones, both at Oxford now. Dad just made me promise I wouldn't turn into what he called a 'scummy actor': drugs, drink, the wrong sort of women and stuff like that. I can understand that, it would reflect badly on him. Not that he said anything along those lines.'

'What does he do? – if you don't mind my asking.'

'I'm not sure *exactly*. I only know that he's dead clever, speaks several languages and works for a Government department. He knows the ins and outs of world politics. Some sort of advisor. He doesn't talk about it and we don't ask so I guess it's all a bit secret. My theory, and I'm only telling you this as I know you've been involved with MI5, official secrets and that kind of thing, is that he's involved with counter-terrorism.'

This was all getting rather interesting.

2

Still looking remarkably fresh despite presumably having not slept for around twenty-four hours, Rik Harrison left me, saying he was going to his room to have a shower. I finished my breakfast and then checked our room to see if Patrick was there doing the same. He wasn't. Feeling a bit annoyed by now – it really was a lovely morning and I would have liked some much needed fresh air and exercise in the park myself – I rang his mobile number. It was switched off so I left a message of the where-the-hell-are-you-we-need-to-talk variety. Then the telephone rang and it was reception.

'Is Mr Harrison available yet? His personal trainer is here.'

Something made me cautious for hadn't Rik just completed a run with the man? 'Has he an ID of any kind?' I asked.

There was a pause. 'No, he says he has nothing on him as he's just wearing a tracksuit.'

'Please ask him his name.'

Another longer pause and I could hear voices. Then the receptionist came back on the line. 'No, I'm sorry, Miss Langley. His English was very poor and I couldn't even discover what language he was speaking in order to fetch an interpreter. I'm afraid he's gone.'

'What did he look like?'

In receipt of quite a good description I made my way to Rik's room hoping he was out of the shower by now.

Wearing a big fluffy robe he looked surprised to see me.

'May I come in for a minute?' I asked.

He flung the door wide and I entered.

'I'm probably wide of the mark,' I said. 'But has anyone been making threats against you?'

'You always get daft letters from fruit and nut cases.'

'But no actual threats?'

He shook his head. 'No. Why?'

'I met a man yesterday who said he was Bob Wayne, your personal trainer. Would you please confirm what he looks like?'

'He's a largeish sort of guy with thinning red hair, blue eyes and . . . ' Rik thought hard. 'Big feet. I reckon he takes size elevens.'

'That's whom I saw then. So the man asking for you just now in reception saying he was your personal trainer wasn't He was fair-haired, slim and rather tanned. His English was very poor and he seemed to have no identification on him. Could it have been anyone else you know?'

'Jeez. I only left the guy twenty minutes ago. Is this all part of the Gillard training?' Rik said with feeling. Seeing from my expression that this was not the case he dropped into an arm-chair. 'Well, it definitely wasn't Bob as he's from Blackpool and wouldn't fool around like that. Plus, he never tans. He lobsters. But surely the guy should have known that people in films and on TV have to be protected from idiots. Anyway, for crying out loud, Bob said that as I was involved with stuff with Patrick he wouldn't see me again until this evening.'

'I think you ought to stay in here until Patrick gets back from wherever he's gone and we'll talk about it.'

'But is it really necessary? Why are you so worried? This kind of thing happens quite a lot once you're remotely famous.'

'I don't know why Patrick was asked to do the job,' I said. 'Nor does Martin Longton. And you've just told me that your father's involved with secret government work.'

There was a faint noise within the flat somewhere. The soft-est falling sound: like someone tripping over and falling onto a pile of rugs.

I walked forward, grabbed Harrison by the arm and

steered him back into the bathroom – steam emanating out of the doorway – from which he had obviously just emerged.

'Is there anyone else here?' I hissed in his ear.

'No,' he whispered. 'I heard it too.'

'Stay here.'

'But – '

I soundlessly closed the door on him.

His accommodation was actually a suite judging from the number of doors that led off a fairly large entrance cum reception room. I guessed there were two bedrooms, one possibly with a second adjoining bath – or shower-room and another sitting room. The sound seemed to have come from one of the rooms on my left as I had stood just inside the main door. I cursed myself for not having asked Rik which rooms he had been into when he returned but people can always hide in wardrobes. Anyway it was too late now.

It was perfectly possible that what we had heard was nothing more than a suitcase falling over.

Fervently wishing that Patrick had not had to give back his Smith and Wesson I armed myself with a heavy glass vase and went for it, charged through the first door, ducked low to miss any incoming missiles and rapidly eyeballed every inch of the bedroom.

No one.

The window was closed so any intruder had not gone out that way. I quickly checked the wardrobes at the same time keeping an eye on the door. You need to work in pairs doing this kind of surveillance: right now any number of assassins could be bloodbathing Rik. I detonated into the room next door, another bedroom, and this time a knife blade thunked into the doorframe a matter of inches behind me.

'Bang,' I said, going down on one knee, all the better to see over the bed, holding the vase like a gun, my target as large as life.

Patrick chuckled and came over to re-acquire his still-quivering knife. Then he slammed the door, pulled me to my feet and gave me a mind-blowing kiss, his hands roaming just about everywhere.

I prised myself away and reopened the door, saying over my shoulder in a stage whisper, 'This isn't *our* bedroom.' Which was a real shame.

My husband uttered a dirty chuckle.

'You can come out now,' I called in the direction of the bath-room door. 'I knew it was you,' I said to Patrick. 'It's the after-shave.'

'Never assume,' said he, switching to businesslike. 'I did note that, among others, Rik uses this one too.'

'Vases aren't as good as a Smith and Wesson,' I said.

'I had to return it, you know that.'

'How long have you been in here?' Rik asked Patrick, rea-sonably, I thought. He did not seem all that put out.

'I wanted to see how easy it was to get into your room,' Patrick told him. 'Too easy. I decided the further little exercise would be a good idea after I overheard Ingrid telling you about the mystery visitor. Any ideas as to who he might have been now you've had a chance to think?'

'Not a clue.'

'We'll worry about it later,' Patrick told him. 'Right now, you and I are going to a war-games set-up I know of not all that far from here where we will get you slaughtering any number of cardboard gunmen. It will be like a film set for you in a way as all kinds of natural and unnatural disasters will befall you at the same time along the lines of floods, collaps-ing walls made of foam blocks and power cuts. But there will be . . .' He smiled like a shark, 'differences.'

'Real ammo?' Rik enquired eagerly.

'A paint ball weapon for you. Other people will take shots at you with live ammunition.' Another ghastly smile. 'Ready?'

And, halfway out of the door, 'bring a clean pair of underpants with you.'

'I've got to get dressed yet!' Rik yelled after him.

'You have two minutes,' said the already distant voice.

'He's not kidding about the real bullets, is he?' Rik asked hopefully as he headed at some speed in the direction of his bedroom, shedding the robe as he went and thereby giving me a glimpse of a truly splendid bottom.

'No.'

'Thought not.'

So he went, the pair leaving in their wake several frustrated members of Harrison's entourage, one – I discovered later – incandescent agent and me; not resenting the 'little exercise' but desperately needing to ask a few highly relevant questions.

Deeming myself released from the need to stay in the hotel I went for my walk in the park, endeavouring to banish all present suspicions from my mind to think about the plot of my next novel. This had been somewhat tenuous and to do with blackmail and murder in high places but inexorably I found myself thinking of threats and murder on a film set, an idea which somehow seemed to have a lot more going for it.

I had a good idea where Patrick had taken Rik and wondered if they might walk back across the park afterwards with a view to losing a few more fractions of an inch from around Rik's waistline. That was if the actor would be in a fit state to undertake any more exercise today. It was just as well that Martin Longton did not know what his lead was up to right now or he would probably be chewing his fingernails to the wrists.

A small café by the lake seemed a good place to have a sandwich and I sat at a table beneath a tree where I could keep an eye on the main path. I bided my time over a mug of coffee, took a notebook from my bag and jotted down a few ideas for the book. Some women might have been indulging in a little retail therapy but wandering around crowded shops looking for bargains is my idea of hell. My mind still kept coming back to the job in hand.

As Patrick had tested the security of Rik's room *before* I'd arrived with news of the appearance of the apparently phoney personal trainer he might have learned something, either from the phone call or from Rik himself. Patrick had, after all, worked for MI5 for years and probably knew about, or had even met, Rik's father. Had a man deeply involved in counter-terrorism measures received threats against himself and his family? But then again, only the most sophisticated terrorist organisations would even know of his existence and even that possibility was unlikely.

I shut my notebook impatiently and shoved it back in my bag. It was no use applying a writer's fevered imagination to real life without evidence – one just ended up with cloud-cuckoo land. And Patrick no longer worked for MI5. I told myself the situation was straightforward; a one-time soldier – who perhaps was finding it difficult to abandon his training in matters of security – had been recommended by a colleague for the job of beefing up a film-actor's skills. The 'personal trainer' at reception had probably just been a devious fan.

The fine morning had turned into a grey afternoon, and, all at once disenchanted with writing novels, hanging around waiting for other people and the ceaseless roar of city traffic, I went to the cinema and saw an instantly forgettable film. Returning to the hotel in time to get ready for dinner I found Patrick soundly asleep lying crosswise on the bed wearing his bathrobe and looking as though he had precipitantly dropped off while choosing a shirt from the wardrobe. I left well alone and headed for the shower.

'The mystery caller's been identified,' Patrick said when I

returned. Dressed, he was frowning at his reflection in a long mirror. 'This shirt's hellishly creased.'

'They get like that when you fall asleep on them,' I pointed out. 'Who was he?'

'Rik's stand-in, one Vladimir Romanov.'

'But the man was described as having fair hair!'

'Rik tells me he's had it bleached for another job, liked it too much to change back to his normal dark brown and will wear a wig for this one. Apparently he's as Russian as he sounds, has fractured English, is a really wild lad and drinks vodka like most people take tea. He was actually *looking for* Rik's personal trainer and was under the impression he was staying in this hotel this weekend. He isn't. Confusion all round.'

'He had no identification on him though.'

'That apparently is nothing new. The man abides by no known rules and is often either missing on set or late. Directors only put up with him because he has an incredible talent to move and copy the mannerisms of anyone he's able to watch for a few minutes. Not just men – women too.'

'Is Rik dining with us?'

'No, the poor sod's going to have a salad in his room so he doesn't have to watch us filling our faces with fillet steak cooked with masses of black pepper, herbs and cream. That's what I'm having anyway.' And with that Patrick progressed somewhat regally into the bathroom to slosh on aftershave.

Obviously, he had had a good day.

'How did the slaughtering of cardboard go?' I enquired when the fillet steak had disappeared.

Patrick smiled reflectively. 'I should have realised there wouldn't be a problem because of Rik's background. Grouse moors with papa, pistol shooting at school. He's a pretty good shot and doesn't rattle easily. Other than the fact that he tends to be a bit clumsy I'm quite impressed with him all round. We went through the final scenario together – you know, the storming of the tower after going through the flooded tunnel – and I showed him a few really low and cunning moves that'll be useful to him at some time or other. The technicians got a bit fed up with me.' He laughed.

'So in other words, you practically demolished their set-up. You always do.'

'*Used to,*' he corrected gently. 'We only got access because someone owed me a favour. Are you having a dessert?'

'I might. Patrick . . . '

He gazed upon me. 'Sticky toffee pudding?'

'No, thank you. What I really want is – '

'Yes, I know,' he interrupted. 'The answers to questions along the lines of what on earth are we *really* doing here? What has this celluloid piffle got to do with me? I got your phone message, by the way. If I knew the answers I'd tell you. Admittedly, we only found out today, or rather you did, what Rik's old man does for a living. I have to admit that it's not a name I've heard but he might well use an alias – as you know, some of them do.'

'Looked at sensibly though why wouldn't you be told if anything was going on? Why keep you in the dark?'

'That's the big question. So all we can do is keep our eyes and ears open and help make a film.'

'Who rang you when you were with Rik early this morning?'

'Oh, I'd forgotten about that. It was David Goodheim's secretary to tell me of the earlier start of filming in case I didn't know already. They want me to stay on the job, especially for the first phase which is all the shoot-em-up stuff in a warehouse. The original approach was from that quarter, from the States, if you remember. That does rather rule out something dodgy going on at this end. But how has the great US of A heard about yours truly?'

'You once shot and wounded a member of the Canadian secret service,' I recollected.

'I can't think the Yanks would want to reward me for that though,' Patrick said wonderingly.

I punched his shoulder.

'Early night?' he suggested.

'Why not?' I replied. I was still reverberating from the kiss he had given me earlier.

Lack of sleep finally caught up with him, however, and he went out like a light as soon as he got into bed.

A young woman who introduced herself as Cathy, adding that she was a 'runner', went on to say that she had been assigned to Patrick and me for an hour or so, in between anything else she might be called upon to do, to help us familiarise ourselves with what was going on. Not a lot was going on at the moment: those not involved with either the make-up or wardrobe departments stood around, singly or in groups drinking tea, courtesy of the location caterers, their breath and the contents of the thick pottery mugs steaming in the chilly morning air.

It was just after six forty-five.

'Breakfast is at seven,' Cathy went on to say. 'And filming will start at seven thirty. That's if the set's ready – this is a panic job really.'

She reminded me of a Bird-of-Paradise flower, all pointy bits; spiked-up orange hair, long fingernails, bony knees and battered pointed-toed shoes. She was hopelessly underdressed in a cropped top and micro-skirt and although hugging herself appeared otherwise to be ignoring the unseasonal cold.

I said, 'I thought they were just going to film inside the warehouse.' This was where all the activity was going on right now. From the outside it looked very down-at-heel and from within came the sound of loud hammering.

'Inside and with a few shots from inside looking out through the doors. But it's pretty empty in there – just the four walls and the ironwork that's holding it up. The chippies are fixing up stuff on one side that looks like overhead metal walkways, ladders and more girders. Plus a load of pallets and oil drums props got from somewhere that people can hide behind.'

'But that'll sound all wrong, won't it? When people walk on the things that aren't metal, I mean.'

She smiled at my ignorance, but not in superior fashion. 'It doesn't matter. More often than not they put the sound effects in afterwards. Together with the ricochet sounds of real bullets.' She gazed around. 'Is your husband here yet? I'm supposed to check that he's arrived.'

'Yes, he's with Rik somewhere.'

'I think Rik's in the doghouse,' said Cathy, lowering her voice. 'Martin Longton's angry with him for putting on weight. I heard him say they're going to have to use his stand-in a lot more – head and shoulders shots of Rik and full length and distance shots of Vladimir where you can't see his face.'

Someone shouted at Cathy to go and take a message to another cast member in their caravan, I did not catch the name. She had told me that runners work for a pittance wage, being general dogsbodies, hoping eventually to be given a proper job. She worked behind the bar of a pub to earn a little more money and was still living with her parents.

The hammering was becoming frenzied.

Two police cars and an ambulance arrived and I stared for a moment in surprise before I realised, when men wearing casual clothing got out of the driving seats, that they were not genuine, but from one of the agencies that provide such things for film companies. As they went off in the direction of the caterers' caravans one of the double doors of the warehouse rumbled slowly wide open to reveal part of the interior, lit like a stage set with large spotlights on wheeled stands. There were protesting shouts from within that it was draughty and it rumbled closed again.

I decided to go and get some breakfast.

In possession of more tea and a couple of slices of thickly buttered toast, I managed to elicit from a bearded man standing wolfing down sausages and baked beans the information that Rik Harrison was being made up in a caravan allotted to him, the 'army chap' with him. I picked my way across the uneven ground in the direction pointed out to me.

'Wonderful!' Patrick said, having answered my knock. 'I'm starving.'

'You can go and get your own,' I told him. But I handed over the tea.

Rik did not look too good, wan, haggard and tired. Then I saw that it was make-up. He laughed at my initial reaction and said, 'This is the part of the story where I was grabbed and beaten up by some heavies, after being tricked by low cunning to go to a place and have broken out of where they've left me locked up. I don't know it yet but it's a ruse by someone to find out how good I am at my job before he hires me for the big one and he's also getting rid of a local gang, the opposition, at the same time using even more low cunning. Anyway, I've run them to earth in this rathole,' he jerked his head in the general direction of the warehouse, 'and set about reducing them with one of their own semi-automatic weapons to what my old Scottish granny used to call mince and tatties. Martin liked that phrase so much he's going to put it in the script.'

It was on the tip of my tongue to observe that the director was at least speaking to him but I refrained: this was absolutely none of my business. Instead I asked, 'Is this episode for real? Is it in the book?'

'Lord knows,' Rik replied.

'So what do *we* do?'

Patrick shrugged. 'Like everyone else until told otherwise. Stand around waiting.'

'That's what happens most of the time,' Rik said. 'Folk think filming's so glamourous but that's what you do.' He yawned. 'Wait around. I'd get yourself something to eat if I were you,' he said to Patrick.

Patrick straddled a wooden chair and sat down, arms resting on the back. 'Sorry to bang on about it but first I want you to swear to me on everything holy that you've received no personal threats, nor, to your knowledge, has your father. You see, and not wishing for one moment to sound big-headed, arrogant or remotely bragging, you've got yourself a trainer who in his time has been a PM's minder and ridden shotgun for members of the Royal Family. I simply don't know why I was recommended for the job, or for that matter who recommended me, when a thousand other guys could do it.'

Rik was shaking his head. 'As I said to you before there's nothing like that as far as I'm concerned. But I don't know about Dad. I could try him on his mobile number if you like as he might not have left home yet. Not that I think he'd talk about things like that on an open line.'

'Please try getting hold of him,' Patrick said. 'It really has reached the stage where it affects how I play this. Meanwhile I'll ring a contact of my own.'

In order that each should have privacy Patrick and I went outside. I knew whom he would phone: his one-time boss in MI5, Colonel Richard Daws, tender of all known grapevines.

'Our Richard', as we used to call him, was at home too. In bed, grumpy, with a bad back. Patrick did a twenty-four carat grovel, established – I was standing right next to him and could hear every word – that Daws had had nothing to do with the fact that we were now in East London standing outside a dusty caravan that had a distinct list to starboard, that

Rik's father spoke seven languages fluently and, although his job was given a Restricted catagory as he liaised under an assumed name with people like Colonel Gaddafi, no one in any terrorist group would have the remotest interest in threatening him or knocking him off. And who (the expletives deleted) was *Rik* Harrison?

'From the horse's mouth,' Patrick said, stowing away his mobile. 'But I think I'll still stay within range for a bit.'

'He sounded quite surprised but I explained why it was important I knew,' Rik reported. 'No, no threats or peculiar letters. That's gospel too – if anything odd was going on I'm sure he'd have asked me to meet him somewhere to talk about it as Mum was in earshot and he wouldn't want to worry her.'

There was a knock at the door and it was Cathy with a message from Martin asking Rik to come to rehearsals. She somehow conveyed that his name was still mud with the director, which I thought was a damned cheek. Especially as, right now, Rik appeared to be existing solely on unsweetened black coffee and fresh air. I still thought he looked very tired but it could have been just the make-up.

Patrick grabbed himself a sticky bun on the way, succeeding in eating it without Rik seeing him.

I decided, right from the start, that the best contribution I could make to *Blood and Anger* was to stay out of everyone's way. This was difficult as the interior of the warehouse when we entered was like a tube station in the rush hour. What on earth did all these people *do*? But after a few minutes of standing watching it was possible to get a rough idea of what was going on.

To one side of the warehouse, beneath an overhead gantry, a gang of carpenters was fixing in place what seemed to be the last of several upright girders extra to those that were an integral part of the building. Judging by the way they were easily manoeuvreable they were made of some kind of light-weight material but the resemblance to the real ones was perfect as they were complete with rivets and had been painted to look like rusting iron.

Nearby, Martin Longton was among a group of people clustered around a camera on wheels, or 'dolly' as I subsequently found out it was called, one of them taking tape measurements from various positions to a point roughly six feet up the nearest girder. Others moved lights into place in response to instructions from a man I guessed to be the Chief Electrician, whom I already knew was called the Gaffer. Then a light was switched on somewhere high up and the immediate impression was of bright sunlight shining through a window – I turned round and saw there was no window – the girders throwing long shadows across the floor. The light was dimmed very slightly and looked more natural, as though the window was dirty. Other lights were switched on and to my mind the result was pure art; very atmospheric with a long shaft of light some thirty feet away now flung across the dirty concrete where a a small side door had been opened somewhere on the far side of a stack of pallets and several oil drums. Actually the day was heavily overcast so I assumed a floodlight had been placed outside.

'You come in the door over there,' Martin Longton came across to say to Rik, having to raise his voice above the hubbub and pointing to where I had just been looking. 'And your shadow is clearly visible for a couple of seconds. You'll have to pause fractionally. There's nothing particularly covert in this at all. You want blood. You're so mad and hurt so much that right now you're not even thinking straight and don't care a toss about saving your own skin. Then you move away from the door and go behind the stack of pallets and stuff over there. Again you pause. No one – in other words the camera –

41

will have actually clapped eyes on you yet, only your shadow, but that doesn't mean you don't have to get it right. I want to feel your murderous intent. The hairs are going to stand up on the back of my neck. Okay so far?'

'Okay,' Rik acknowledged.

'Then I want you to walk up here. You're not carrying any visible weapons but you exude the kind of malice that suggests you're going to wring the neck of anyone who crosses your path. You're utterly focused but stagger a little as you're still suffering from what the bad lads did to you. Then you come to the first girder,' he pointed, 'that real one, reach down into the shadows under the overhead gantry and take out the semi-automatic weapon, the presence of which has been made clear earlier in the plot. Then you walk forward again but come to a sudden stop and lean on *this* girder,' he indicated the one the cameraman's assistant had been measuring, 'as you suddenly come over a bit faint. But the overall impression is of true grit. Okay, let's give it a run-through.' Martin noticed me. 'Is your husband around?' he called.

'Haven't you met him yet?' I asked, surprised.

'No, but that's not his fault – I've been headless-chickening since daybreak.'

'I'm here,' Patrick said, emerging from beneath the gantry.

The men shook hands and Martin said, 'We do have a fight director cum stunt man who also advises on all kinds of things but he's been held up because of a traffic accident on his way here and will be a while yet. I'd be most grateful if, until he arrives, you could tell me about anything that grates against what you know to be correct.'

'No problem,' Patrick said.

Rik walked down in the direction of the doorway and went from sight.

The bearded baked-beans-and-sausages man, later proving to be Mike Cranley, the Assistant Director, appeared from where video monitors had been set up near the camera and yelled, 'Quiet Please! Stand by for rehearsal!'

There was an instant hush but for someone dropping something small and metallic.

'Action!' Longton called and went over to watch the video monitor.

An elongated shadow appeared in the doorway and paused before going from sight for a few seconds. And then Rik appeared and came slowly towards us. He did not look particularly menacing or suffering from ill treatment to me – in this lighting, even with the make-up, he looked simply too good-natured and chubby, albeit pale – and I wondered if all kinds of electronic trickery during post-production work would attend to that together with the addition of lots of suitably menacing music. He reached the first girder, executed a very nice little stagger, bent down and grabbed the weapon – a Heckler and Koch by the look of it – looked determined, but not grim, and carried on towards the camera. When he reached the second girder he paused to rest his forehead on it and closed his eyes in a fashion that was actually convincing and rather sweet.

The girder moved very slightly.

'Oh, bloody hell!' the director bawled. 'For God's sake fix the damned thing!' he bellowed into the fastnesses of the warehouse. And *you* !' he carried on shouting, this time to Rik, 'that was pretty awful. Do me a favour and get into the part!'

There was a delay while the girder was secured and the lighting was adjusted and I began to see what Rik had meant when he had said that there was a lot of waiting around.

The scene was rehearsed twice more with, in my view, little improvement. Martin did not calm down, apparently state normal, Cathy whispered to me, having appeared at my side. She had been told he was always like this on the first day's

43

shooting; like a cat on hot bricks from nerves. He did, however, apologise to Rik for shouting at him.

After the fourth rehearsal, when they were still messing around with the lighting and I thought Rik was going to burst into tears, Martin caught sight of Patrick talking to him – he had shown him how to hold the weapon correctly.

'Patrick, I thought you were supposed to be turning him into a *killer*.'

'I hope not,' Patrick said politely.

'You know what I mean!'

Patrick gave Rik an all-embracing professional glance. 'In my opinion his blood-sugar's too low to be able to achieve much right now. As far as I'm aware he's eaten hardly anything for over thirty-six hours in an attempt to lose weight. And as he's not an ex-undercover soldier in real life . . . ' He broke off with a smile that would have charmed Sauron clean out of his tower.

'Okay,' Longton said wearily. 'Where's Vladimir?' he then demanded to know. 'He should be here. We'll get the lighting right with the stand-in while someone fetches Rik a coffee and sandwich.'

The general reaction to the question being 'God knows' the runners were dispatched to find him.

'No, to hell with it,' Martin fretted when a couple of leaden minutes had ticked by. 'We'll do it without him. Patrick, you're about the right height and the build that Rik ought to be. Do me a big favour and just walk this through so they can deal with the shadows over there as you go by. Take it slowly and they'll get it right this time,' he added meaningfully.

'Is he a member of Equity?' a deep gravelly voice queried.

'You're not the union rep because I am, but you *are* a silly old bastard!' one of the members of the sound crew shouted, apparently another victim of nerves.

'Cool it, Len,' Longton said quietly.

Rik walked away disconsolately while Patrick went off in the direction of the doorway.

'Quiet!' the sausages-and-baked-beans man, Mike, called.

Longton checked that the lighting people were ready and then called for action.

The dark silhouette appeared in the doorway, paused and then slipped to one side behind the pallets with that cat-like grace with which I am so familiar. After a count of four, when anyone watching might have been forgiven for expecting a hail of lead, he appeared, walking slowly, for he had been asked to, and came towards us. His hands were relaxed at his sides, gaze raking the darkest corners. Here though was not a man acting, nor indeed putting on any kind of show but one strictly on auto having walked into a hundred such buildings during his career with the constant reminder that his name, and that of his wife, was on several terrorist organisations' hit-lists.

Patrick paused by the first girder and acquired the weapon and then went on to the second without indulging in any staggering or looking faint.

Martin Longton, as before, had watched all this on the video monitor. 'Yup!' he said. 'That's good.' Then to Rik, 'I want you to do it like that.'

The day wore on, several scenes were filmed – or 'in the can' to put it correctly – Rik recovering his energy.

But, hours previously, Vladimir Romanov had been murdered in a local car park, a neat bullet hole in the centre of his forehead.

3

Fortunately, or not, depending on your viewpoint, the police arrived looking for people to help them with their enquiries just as filming was ending for the day, some having already gone home. Initially, there was disbelief among the film crew that they were genuine, everyone assuming they were merely extras turning up for a scene that had had to be postponed at the last minute to the following day. It transpired that the officers of the law had discovered the deceased's union card in his wallet quite late in the day when the body had been moved, noticed the film company's vehicles clustered around the warehouse not a hundred yards away and made the deduction. No one was going to be allowed to leave until we had all been interviewed and at this stage the police were not revealing the manner of Romanov's death or even where he had been killed.

'Wake me up when it's my turn,' Rik said wearily, heading for a chair and adding as an afterthought, 'Poor old Vlad – I wonder what he's been up to?'

Finally, after two and a half hours, we got back to the hotel. Patrick had tied the young constable interviewing him into a few silken mental knots, thus obtaining all the relevant details.

'Romanov had been shot with what appears to be great precision,' he reported. 'That doesn't happen a lot even with murderers who are passable marksmen. No one who's been interviewed so far who was in the vicinity around the time of the shooting had heard a shot. So even taking into account things like vehicle backfires – and these days they don't happen very much either – we're talking about a long-range weapon and not necessarily just an ordinary hunting rifle. I intend to do a little investigating, as if the killer *is* a professional, the scenario moves on from the late lamented having merely taken the last packet of cornflakes off the supermarket shelf under a madman's nose. If indeed, he was the intended target.'

I said, 'You mean you're worried about Rik as Romanov was his stand-in and Rik might have been the real objective? But Romanov didn't look very much like him.'

'He did today. He had a dark wig on and when the fuzz arrived they saw that Rik was dressed identically so obviously Romanov had been all ready for work. I've no idea whether he would have been made up to look even more like him when he arrived very late as it happened but from what we've heard about him he was like that.'

'Yes, but surely someone could camp out forever on the top of a building waiting for his target to come within range,' I protested. 'You do have to undertake a bit of research on your intended victim's movements. Anyway, I was given to understand that film companies always hire cars or mini-buses to convey the main members of the cast to and from their hotels – as we were with Rik today.' This was all rather along the lines of teaching grandmothers to suck eggs but I thought Patrick was way off-beam.

'I'm only exploring possibilities,' he observed mildly.

'Although the author of *Blood and Anger* died rather young not all that long ago,' I recollected.

Patrick's eyes blazed. 'Who told you that?'

'Martin Longton. His name was John Taylor – although that could have been a pseudonym – and he died on holiday somewhere in the West Country. One would need to speak to the scriptwriter – Martin didn't hoist in the details.'

'Do you think you could do a little digging?' Patrick asked winningly. 'That kind of thing's right up your street.'

I'd had an idea he would say that.

*   *   *

It turned out to be exceedingly easy to contact Melvin Lockyer, who had dramatised the novel, as his address, in a village near Bristol, phone and email numbers were all on the director's copy of the shooting script. He even had his own website. After getting the information from Longton I phoned him.

'I only met him once initially plus a few telephone conversations while I was doing the work,' Lockyer said. He had not seemed annoyed at being rung at ten-thirty at night. 'Are you writing a book about the guy or something?'

Patrick and I had already agreed that we would tell him the truth: nothing would be gained by concocting a story. Not only that, writers are perceptive people who can usually see through cock and bull stories.

'I suggest you read *Blood and Anger* before you do anything else,' Lockyer said when I had explained. 'He didn't actually come across as a particularly nice guy and I actually found myself questioning some of his allegations as the evidence seemed very thin and circumstantial. There was a lot of resentment in the man and I wondered if that was as a result of what happened to his chums or something entirely different. The Ministry of Defence vehemently denied just about everything in the book, if you remember, and insisted that the mission had gone wrong because of some IRA informer. But then again, they would.'

I thanked him but he had more to say.

'It would be very difficult to discover the truth after all this time, it all happened nearly ten years ago, and some of those involved are dead now and the rest scattered around the world. I did see on the TV news tonight that someone connected with the film had been shot and I have to say that it made me feel a bit uncomfortable.' He laughed but it was a trifle forced. 'D'you reckon I ought to take myself off to Antarctica for a while?'

'We'll keep you posted,' I promised. 'And if we learn anything that points to anyone else being at risk I'll let you know. But I really don't think you need be too concerned. Can you give me a few details of the circumstances of Taylor's death?'

'He bought a holiday cottage in Cornwall with some of the proceeds of the book and then when there was a lot of flak coming in his direction from various sources he sold his main home in London and went to live there. Three months ago, I think it was, I got a phone-call saying that he'd been found dead – he'd fallen down the stairs, the woman said, and brained himself on a cast-iron doorstop. I got an idea she was a relative but she didn't say or give me her name. In view of all the publicity, she said, they were going to keep the funeral private as they didn't want the media turning up in droves. She asked for my co-operation. I could hardly refuse so I didn't tell anyone connected with the film or otherwise until afterwards. I have to say I did find it all a bit strange.'

'Strange?' I queried but wondering about the odds on men in their forties falling down the stairs. Perhaps he had been drunk.

'Nothing I could put my finger on – except that she spoke in a whispery sort of voice as though she hadn't wanted to be overheard. But you get these gut feelings sometimes, don't you? I can give you the address of the cottage, if you like.'

This he did and I thanked him again and rang off.

'He was sort of saying that he thought it stank,' I finished by telling Patrick, having repeated the conversation for his benefit. I had found him in our favourite bar rapidly sinking a well-earned pint.

'Where is the place?'

'Tredennis. I have an idea it's near Port Wrinkle.'

He pondered for a few seconds and then said, 'I think it's

worth investigating and I'm not too sure the the police will make the link – if indeed there is any kind of link – at least, not until they've exhausted all ideas at this end. It might be worth while giving James a bell in Bath and finding out if Romanov had any form before you go charging off down to Cornwall.'

I gave him a not amused look.

'Look, I'd really appreciate it if you would go as it actually affects everything on this job. I can't leave: I've signed a contract.'

'And there's every chance that you'll be taken on as Rik's stand-in as well. Can't the stuntman do it?'

Patrick shook his head. 'No, hardly. I know enough about making films to be aware that stuntmen are regarded as quite superior beings and are often the fight director as well. As far as those scenes are concerned what they say goes. Stand-ins do the kind of thing I did this morning.' He saw that I was still not happy. 'Don't you want me to do it?'

'Rik's stand-in's just been murdered,' I reminded him.

I caught our old friend Detective Chief Inspector James Carrick as he arrived for work the next morning, and, as he put it, 'I've just blown the dust off my phone,' going on to explain that the nick was undergoing major building alterations. Then someone apparently started to drill a large hole in the wall of his office and we arranged, shouting, that he would phone me back. A couple of minutes later he rang me on his mobile from the car park.

'Vladimir Romanov,' I said, getting down to business after the initial pleasantries. 'Does Central Records have anything nasty to say about him?'

'Ah, the East End murder. Well, as you know I'm not permitted to give ordinary members of the public that kind of info,' James said. 'But on the grounds that neither you nor

Patrick has ever come into that particular category I might just bend the rules a little. I do have to ask your interest though.'

I related the facts.

'It was a bit odd Patrick being offered the job in the first place surely,' James commented.

'Absolutely,' I agreed.

'And even odder how the pair of you keep getting mixed up in police cases.' He uttered a hollow chuckle. 'I always run the names of the victims of serious crime through the computer to see if there's any connection with this neck of the woods. Other than being fined several times for being drunk and disorderly plus a conviction for drunk-driving – all in the London area – Romanov doesn't seem to have got himself into any real trouble. But, and it's quite a large but, when he was done for being over the limit and had been caught driving like a lunatic in a built-up area, he was behind the wheel of a motor belonging to a local Russian bad-boy, one of those imports from the old Soviet Union that everyone can do without. Apparently Romanov had been hired as his driver between film-work – or that's what he said at the time – and there was no evidence to the contrary. The normal chauffeur was on remand on a charge of handling stolen property.'

'So what was this Russian into?'

'All the usual stuff. Extortion – in other words, running protection rackets – drugs, armed robbery, suspected of being behind the stealing of big limos to order, by shooting their owners when they had stopped at traffic lights . . . There's quite a list.'

'Romanov could easily have been involved more deeply,' I said. 'And fallen out with them in a big way and now someone's caught up with him.'

'It would have had to have been something pretty serious for such drastic punishment – hired killers with long-range rifles don't come cheap. It's much easier to knife someone or beat them up in a dark alleyway.'

'The author of the novel that the film story was taken from died in Cornwall not all that long ago. I'm thinking of going down there.' Okay, the man in my life had as good as told me to go down there.

'Well, at least leave Romanov's death to the Met. And if you *do* get a sniff of anything remotely suspicious please let me know straightaway. If only so at least one copper on this planet can blow his whistle if you get into trouble.'

'Yes, James,' I said meekly.

However I was hanged if I was going to batter off, to coin a Scottish's friend's phrase, to Cornwall without a little preparation, mental and otherwise. I succeeded in tracking down a copy of *Blood and Anger* in a small bookshop in Ilford, went back to Rik's caravan, having obtained his permission – Patrick and I had not been assigned any on-site accommodation but for the use of a nearby church hall that had been hired for the extras – and immersed myself in it.

The odd thing, right from the start, was that the author of a novel about special operations soldiers, having served as one himself, could come across, in quite a subtle fashion, as small-minded, self-centred and weak. The book was fact, written in the first person as fiction, all names changed, I reminded myself, reading a paragraph again, the facts in themselves highly controversial and thus leading to the book's success. And yet although there were very vividly written passages when I felt that here, indeed, was a man recording his memories, the characters were wooden, almost stereotyped. Was it just badly written or had the author not been what he said he was?

I tried to remember more details about the furore publication had engendered. The Chief of the Defence Staff himself had waded in to the fray, no doubt on behalf of the Commanding Officer of the regiment involved, who had, for professional reasons, made no comment. Past senior officers had not been so reticent. It was no surprise that Taylor, or whatever his real name was, faced with such big guns had, as they say, done a runner.

The betrayal was blamed on a man referred to as Jack – all the soldiers involved were just given first names – the reason for it being that another of the members of the troupe, Phil, had allegedly raped his girlfriend. There were pages of obscene dialogue: rows between the two had been 'reconstructed from memory', according to the explanation in the short foreword but which really served to pad out the story. I skipped through all this, together with the accounts of laddish nights out followed invariably by oceans of purely gratuitous, and highly improbable, sex.

It was fairly obvious that the author had loathed both Jack and Phil. Jack was accused of having made a phone call just before a particularly difficult mission and tipped off the local IRA commander, the idea being, Phil in command, that he would be shot. Taylor hinted that some kind of 'deal' had been made. But both Phil and a man by the name of Barry had been captured after a shoot-out, together with the youngest member of the group, David. All three had been tortured before being shot, their mutilated bodies discovered in a country lane near the border a week later.

The evidence that Taylor presented; that Jack had sworn he would get even, he had behaved oddly during the twenty-four hours or so before the mission, he was seen in a call-box looking very furtive, that a local 'snout' had said he knew he was to blame, to my mind was as flimsy as Melvin Lockyer had indicated. Obviously aware of this and that he needed to beef up his testimony the author raked up something from Jack's past to which he had himself admitted; how he had arranged to have his brother-in-law beaten up for calling him an oaf.

The last few chapters went on to describe how Jack – who one had to admit had made no attempt to sue the author for libel – had left the country and become a hitman. He had even assumed a false identity on a couple of occasions and returned to the UK to undertake assignments for criminal bosses. Various shootings and murders were sensationally described, none with any real evidence to back them up and for all the reader knew the whole thing was a complete fabrication.

Angrily, I threw the book aside.

As a result of what Taylor had alleged, and despite denials from people in high places, a man had been forced to leave his regiment and, embittered, had turned himself into an assassin for hire. Was *Blood and Anger* merely a bad book with a grain of truth in it or was the entire thing a fabrication as Taylor had a grudge against the man for another reason? My own feelings tended to favour the latter as the foul-mouthed morons in the story bore no relation to the several personable young men whom I knew were involved with Special Services I have met since marrying Patrick. And the next question, of course, was why had he, by depicting his colleagues thus, libelled *them* as well?

I was allowed into the warehouse as they were between takes. It was hot from the lights and noisy and a bunch of some of the most villainous-looking men I had ever clapped my eyes on were near the doorway, sweatily getting their breath back. Then I noticed that there was a camera high up on the gantry, on a kind of jib, technicians draped all over it. Farther along it a deadly *pas de deux* was going on in strange slow-motion; a man who could only be the fight-director and Rik rehearsing fight moves. On the floor beneath where they were standing was a pile of mattresses. I went closer to enable me to hear what was being said and as I did, careful and complicated handholds resulted in Rik's sparring partner ending up half over the railings of the gantry. He pulled himself back up.

'No, I'm supposed to go right over. You must lift me.'

'You're heavier than me,' Rik said. He was out of breath too.

'You should have got yourself fit. But it doesn't really matter, if you grab me where I showed you my momentum will help when we do it at speed.'

'Then do it at speed,' Patrick said, and I detected impatience. 'Otherwise he's going to put his back out.' I had already spotted him up on the gantry a short distance away. He was dressed exactly the same as Rik; black jeans, black leather jacket and his normally wavy hair had been ruthlessly flattened down with water or gel.

'He hasn't got the holds right yet either,' the man persisted.

Patrick approached the two. 'The whole thing would be easier for Rik, and a lot more impressive to look at, if when you run at him with the iron bar – pick it up, would you? Okay, now run at me,' he went on in his best army intructor's voice, 'Yes, come on. I duck as you swing, get hold of you thus – and – thus,' a quick grunt of effort, 'and relieve you of the iron bar as you go over.'

The man soared over the railing and landed neatly on the mattresses.

I left them to it and turned to see Martin Longton waving me over.

'We've got a bit of a glitch with the camera,' he said, without going into details. Lowering his voice he continued, 'The police were back this morning. Apparently Romanov had a criminal record. Nothing really serious but a while ago he was loosely involved with a criminal gang that operates not a million miles from here. The inspector in charge of the case asked me if any dodgy people had come looking for him. All I could say, of course, was that we've only just started filming and Romanov must have been shot as he arrived for work. It was a very professional job, by all accounts.'

'But how would anyone know he was going to be here?' I said.

'That's a good point. Anyway, I told this copper how worried I was that someone else might be targeted and that I was arranging to hire some security guards but he didn't seem to think there was a problem or danger to anyone else – he was pretty convinced some kind of score had been settled and he could nab someone in this gang. I rather got the impression that he was going to pulverize someone until they confessed – but for God's sake don't quote me on that.' Longton had been gazing anxiously upwards at the efforts to fix the camera but now looked at me directly. 'I'm going to have to use your husband in the way I was going to utilise Romanov. Rik's overweight and it shows in the distance shots and we can't just shove him in some kind of body-belt or he won't be supple enough for the fight scenes. Even then I think I'll ask Patrick to do the one they're working on now as he obviously knows what he's at. If Rik strains something it'll be a disaster so we'll just use him for the fight close-ups.'

I decided I would not concern him further with news of my impending trip to the West Country. But he had not helped to alleviate my own worries – unarmed security guards are no match for professional criminals.

Several people were urgently waiting to talk to Martin and I felt very superfluous and left. I waved to Patrick but he was concentrating on rehearsing a different, more complicated, move and hardly responded.

Part of the car park where Romanov had been killed – on the far side from where I was standing – was still cordoned off by blue and white incident tape, a single vehicle, guarded by a constable, obviously the murder victim's, remaining. The driver's door of the white Audi was still open, suggesting that the shot had been fired before Romanov had had the chance to close it. From where though had the murderer taken aim?

I scanned the surrounding buildings, thinking that the person who ought to be making knowledgable guesses about this was right now playing gangsters. No, I pulled myself up sharply, that simply was not fair: Patrick had a job to do. Surely I did not resent his obvious enjoyment of what he was doing? I concentrated on the office blocks, high-rise flats, and what looked like a hospital chimney, while turning slowly through three hundred and sixty degrees. There were any number of suitable vantage points. It would help to know more details: the direction that Romanov had fallen, not necessarily exactly the opposite one to which the shot had been fired as he might have slumped against the car and then slithered down.

The car park was unusual in that it did not belong to the local authority – no pay and display machines – and was presided over by an elderly man who issued tickets ensconced in a little wooden hut. When I got closer I saw that he was making a brew of tea on a picnic stove balanced precariously on a narrow shelf that was already overloaded with magazines, packets of biscuits and a pair of Wellington boots. Grizzled, not very clean but giving every indication of being highly astute, he watched my approach.

'You look like a reporter,' was his dour greeting. 'I'm fed up with talkin' to the press.'

'Almost right,' I said with a big smile. 'In actual fact I'm a crime writer. But don't worry, I'm not going to ask you about gory and sensational details so that I can use them in one of my books.'

'No?' He looked a bit disappointed and then gestured towards his battered metal teapot. 'Cuppa?'

'Thank you very much.'

'Everyone calls me Joe.'

It was all very domestic and cosy within the hut, despite the hazardous state of the shelf, if a trifle grubby, and I wondered if he was on his own in life. The mug he selected for me was assiduously wiped on a tea towel, the condition of which would have driven members of the Health and Safety Executive to ply one another with smelling salts. I found myself hoping that my immune system was up to scratch.

'I'd only given the geezer 'is ticket a coupla minutes before he got shot,' said Joe over his shoulder as he stirred the pot. 'Not one of the regulars. 'E didn't seem too keen on parkin' 'ere at all. Asked about security cameras. I told him I was the security camera and if I saw anyone messin' around with the motors I'd bash their brains out with my knobkerrie.' At this point, having got to his feet and fought his way through waterproofs and other coats hanging behind the door, he produced a ferocious-looking thick knobbed stick and brandished it under my nose. 'My old Dad brought it back from South Africa. By the time you've farted around diallin' 999 the bloody car's ten miles away. Besides, all the young tearaways know Joe and they stay well away from 'ere. But 'e still parked as close to the 'ut as 'e could.' He waved his arm in the direction of the Audi, some fifteen yards away.

'They tell me there's a Russian mobster round here who steals cars,' I murmured, in receipt of my tea and having taken a sip. It was scalding hot and tasted like boiled leather.

'I don't tangle with the likes of 'im,' Joe said dismissively. 'And nor will you if you've any sense. He doesn't bother with the kind of motors what normally get left 'ere although I do get the odd posh one. Nah, 'im and 'is boys go for the big stuff, Porsches and the like, pinch 'em to order – usually from their owners' driveways and when they're still sittin' in 'em. A real bad lot, if you ask me.'

'You don't think the man who was shot might have been involved with him – he was Russian too?'

Joe shook his head. 'No idea.'

'Did you see it happen?'

He gave me a stern look. 'I thought you said you weren't goin' to ask that kind of question.'

'Not to put in my books. It's just that my husband's involved with making the film too and I'm worried about his safety.'

Joe then had to come out of his hut to deal with a customer and I saw that he walked with a bad limp. When the car had driven away he said, 'Well, whoever the bastard was he got his man, didn't he?'

I just shrugged.

'No, I didn't see nothin' and didn't hear the shot. You don't have to get close these days, do you, with these weapons what terrorists use? Bloody cowards, I call 'em. The first I knew of it was a lady running over and asking me to call an ambulance. I told 'er I didn't have a phone and another woman who had just arrived got on 'er mobile. I went over and had a look at the bloke but he was as dead as mutton – too late for an ambulance.' He glanced across towards the lone car. 'They're taking it away soon, thank God. That'll get rid of the gawpers.'

'How had he fallen?'

'Like a tin soldier, flat on 'is back with 'is head pointin' towards us 'ere. Nasty hole in the back of it judgin' by the blood and brains on the ground but the one between 'is eyes was as neat as ninepence. Real professional job, if you ask me.'

'The shot could have come from that building over there then.' I pointed to a block of flats.

'That's where the cops went. Not a chance of catching 'im. Not a chance in flippin' 'ell. He was probably back home in Shitsville by the time they got 'ere.' Joe uttered a rasping laugh, setting himself coughing.

I finished my tea, with an effort, thanked him and made my way towards the flats, of necessity, and design, walking quite close to the car. The bored and cold-looking constable standing by it glowered at me and I decided against trying to get any further information out of him. There was a very clean area of concrete near the car where it had been scrubbed to clear up all residues after scenes-of-crime officers had taken samples and that was the only sign that the murder had taken place.

I paused, looking at the flats. As with so many such developments there were balconies on each floor running all along each side where residents gained access to their front doors having climbed inner stairs or used lifts: any number of good vantage points from which to use a high-powered rifle. But also, of course, there was every risk of being detected with potentially dozens of witnesses. I wondered if someone, whom circumstances suggested was a professional killer, would choose such a public spot.

Where then? The roof? I again wished that Patrick was with me to give me his opinion.

Thought about, it seemed unlikely that whoever it was had set up shop, so to speak, with a view to taking out people working on the film, even if he knew who they were. Surely, Romanov had been specifically targeted. But how had the killer known he would use this car park? The answer to that might be that the man with the rifle had been in some kind of contact with his victim, or with his friends, and was aware of his movements. That rather gave credence to the Local Russian Bad Boy theory.

But on the other hand, how the hell had Romanov himself

known which car park he would use on that particular morning?

I mentally groaned. Perhaps the killer – 'Jack' in the novel – had decided to shoot Rik Harrison in protest at a film being made that he assumed would blacken his name even further, and to be sure of it had planned to pot at everyone who looked like him. This theory seemed downright silly as actors taking lead roles in film don't normally arrive in a seven-year-old Audi and leave it on what had almost certainly been a wartime bombsite.

What made more sense was that Jack, who had at one time, one must not forget, been a supremely trained undercover soldier, had somehow got to know Romanov. He could not have lived too far away if he had worked for a local crook.

'Are you all right there, madam?' asked the guardian of the car.

I started and realised that I had been standing as a woman turned to stone. I turned. 'Yes, sorry. I was just doing a little mental sleuthing.'

He seemed to find this amusing. 'Like reading whodunnits, do you?'

I decided to go along with this. 'Oh, *yes*. Miss Marple, murders in libraries and that kind of thing. Only that's all rather old-fashioned these days, isn't it? Here we have the complete opposite of folk staying in a country house for the weekend: a man shot in a public place by someone anything up to a mile away. Did you find any evidence of the killer over at the flats, by the way?'

'Not so far,' he replied cagily.

'I find it hard to believe that no one saw him if he did fire the shot from that building.'

'We're still conducting house-to-house enquiries.'

But the conversation was curtailed: a low-loader had arrived to collect the vehicle.

I decided to give the flats a miss.

The large double doors of the warehouse had been opened when I got back and vehicles; two police cars, a van and an ambulance of the non-genuine variety, were being positioned nearby for a take. My return was unplanned for originally I had intended to go straight to our hotel, collect the car and head for Cornwall.

Patrick was sitting talking to Rik and when he saw me he said, 'I thought you'd gone.'

Tersely, I replied, 'I just thought I'd share with you my idea that the killer is doing what you're so good at and is here, right beneath our noses.'

I was aware of making a good exit, just like they do in films.

4

The colour of the sea below me matched the sky; seal-grey, the wave-tops whipped into driving spray by the gale. I had parked the Range Rover in a lay-by on the cliff-top road to look at the map and the vehicle was being buffeted and rocked by the force of the wind. On the horizon to the south-west lay a murky darkness that promised rapidly approaching heavy rain, an incentive to fold my map quickly and set off again.

The next signpost I came to, on the outskirts of Port Wrinkle, indicated what the map had already told me; that Tredennis lay three and a half miles to the north. I turned right and followed a country lane uphill as the first spots of rain appeared on the windscreen. By the time I reached the village it was pouring down.

I had not driven all the way in one day, spending the previous night at home on Dartmoor, not far from Tavistock, to catch up on family matters and attend to any post. Matthew, Patrick's brother's eldest, had torn a ligament in his left foot during gym and was off school for the rest of the week as it was too painful even to walk on; our youngest, Victoria, was fretful and difficult because of teething; Justin, our other one, was fine, if his usual stroppy self, and Katie desperately wanted to talk to me about the possibility of her having a pony. I had made suitable noises to everyone including Carrie, the nanny, written cheques to pay a couple of bills and left early in the morning feeling very guilty at abandoning them when I ought not to.

I was driven by a deep sense of foreboding.

Tredennis – twinned with Arguille sur Brotte (*where?*) – was unremarkable; small stone cottages, quite a few drab little bungalows, a post office cum village store, a pub, a run-down car repair workshop, a chapel and a butcher's shop, the last long-closed. Having driven from one end to the other to discover all this I turned round and parked where the road widened outside a wooden building that had at one time, many years previously, been tea rooms.

Melvin Lockyer had told me that the house, Primrose Cottage, where John Taylor had lived, and died, was next to the post office. I was grateful for this as there was no name on that particular property at all now and it had to be the right place as the shop was bordered on the other side by a lane.

It was just after nine-thirty in the morning but not a soul moved. There was no sign of life behind the curtained windows of the double-fronted cottage either and the whole place looked neglected with litter and foot-high weeds in the tiny front garden. Then I spotted the For Sale sign lying in the long grass by the front wall. The estate agent's office was in Liskeard.

I went into the shop, bought a newspaper and some chocolate. There wasn't a lot else to buy; some loaves on a shelf in the window, dusty tins of carrots and peas, a few toilet rolls and boxes of tissues.

'Do you know where Mr Taylor next door moved to?' I asked casually as I turned to leave.

The whey-faced woman behind the counter pursed her thin mouth. 'He died three or four months back. You a friend of his?'

'No, I've just read one of his books.'

The woman did not say, 'Well, that's all right then,' but her expression did. 'He tripped and fell down the stairs, I understand,' she said unsympathetically. 'He didn't come from the county so perhaps wasn't used to the steep stairs some old houses round here have. They won't sell it for what they're asking, that's for sure – Cornish people can't afford those kind of prices and it's too far from the sea for townies who want a second home.'

I said, 'I might go and ask the estate agent if I can have a look round. My sister's after a holiday cottage.' This was perfectly true and explained any nosing around I might do but Sally would not have places like Tredennis on her 'to die for' list.

'Oh, I've got a key. He rented it off sometimes in the summer when he went abroad and I used to keep an eye on it. And it'll save you the bother of going all the way to Liskeard, won't it? Anyway, there's nothing in there worth pinching.'

I persuaded myself that I was not offended and murmured, 'How kind of you.'

She rummaged in a drawer and handed over two large, old-fashioned keys and one smaller more modern one tied together with fraying string. 'Use the biggest one – that's the back door key. The front door's stuck.'

On my way over to the door I asked, 'Who found him – do you know?'

'The woman who cleaned for him, Ellie Wright. She went in on the Monday morning as usual and there he was at the bottom of the stairs, dead. They reckoned he'd been there since the Saturday night. No doubt he'd been drinking, by all accounts there was no lack of that in the house.'

'Something tells me he wasn't liked. Was that why? Did he get drunk and unpleasant?'

'No, well . . . it wasn't so much that he wasn't liked as he kept himself to himself and didn't speak to anyone. Just had people coming to see him sometimes. Drink being taken in by people who looked over their shoulders all the time, if you get my meaning.' A phone rang in the back somewhere and she went off to answer it, calling over her shoulder, 'June 24th it was, I've just remembered.'

I rang James Carrick from the even more overgrown back

garden; a wooden greenhouse collapsing in on itself, overgrown conifers twisted by years of strong winds like the one blowing now into tortuous, tormented shapes, an apple tree still with a few scabby fruit clinging to its otherwise bare branches.

'I know this wasn't your case . . . ' I began.

A sigh came over the ether.

'That author of *Blood and Anger*, John Taylor, whom I told you about,' I persisted. 'It's probably not his real name. He was in his late forties and was found dead at his home, Primrose Cottage in the village of Tredennis, on June 24th, according to a woman I've just spoken to. He'd fallen down the stairs and bashed his head on a cast iron doorstop. Did the police just go along with the local view that he drank too much and his death was nothing more than an unfortunate accident? If so, why?'

'There must have been a PM,' James said, protest writ large in his tone after my cheeky implied criticism of brother officers.

'Please would you find out for me?' I pleaded.

'I'm really busy right now but I'll try to do it this afternoon,' he promised wearily. Judging by the racket in the background the building work was all around him.

'I might know a bit more myself by then,' I told him. 'I have the keys to his house.'

'Now don't do anything silly,' came the swift response.

'Like what? There's no one there – the place is empty.'

Except for three dead bats and perhaps a ghost.

The woman's statement that the house contained nothing worth pinching was definitely a matter of opinion for the first thing I saw as I stepped into a quite large and otherwise empty kitchen – even the sink had been removed – was a good quality Welsh dresser. It had been painted white at some stage in its life and was very dirty but even as it stood was worth several hundred pounds. Anyone who wished to make off with it though would have to take it to pieces to get it through the door.

One by one I opened the drawers. They were empty but for a few blank sheets from old exercise books, loose pins and a knob that had come off one of the lower cupboards. I looked in those too and beheld rusting cake tins, iron weights for kitchen scales and a pile of yellowed knitting patterns, the top one of which had been cut from a page of a magazine dated March 4th 1956.

The downstairs layout of the cottage held no surprises; sitting and dining rooms at the front, and the kitchen, which had a walk-in larder, and a scullery off to the rear. The front rooms were empty of furniture but, as I had already seen, with the curtains left at the windows. The decor was seventies-style, probably genuine judging by the grime on the wallpaper. There were drawing pin holes everywhere in the room to the left of the front door and blobs of Blu-tack where posters, fragments of which still remained in places where they had been torn down, had been fixed. Had Taylor started writing another book? To one side of the chimney breast – the fireplace still had ashes in it – was a built-in cupboard. Oddly, it was locked but I left it for a moment and went back into the hall.

This then, according to available evidence, was where the man had died.

I have a theory that dreadful happenings in houses; murder, violence or even just years of hatred, leave behind 'vibrations' that sensitive people can detect. Although I have never claimed to be such a person my father always used to say that I possessed 'cats' whiskers' and it is true that on several occasions certain intuitive feelings I have had have borne fruit. Nothing manifested itself at this spot in particular, the only sound the gale howling in the chimneys. Like the rooms I had already entered it merely resonated with a kind of dreary squalor.

There was nothing hazardous about the stairs themselves and they were not as narrow and steep as my own at home, this house being built, at a guess, around a hundred years later at the turn of the nineteenth century. The carpet on them was old but not worn to the point of being dangerous, neither slippery nor torn. But a drunk can fall down any stairs. I went up.

The dead bats were on the landing, sad little bundles of fur and dried up papery wings. Such creatures hold no terrors for me but the less said about eight-legged, web-spinning creepy crawlies the better . . .

There were two bedrooms, a tiny boxroom, the latter of which contained a wooden chair and a plastic laundry basket, and a bathroom. I appraised the bathroom only from the entrance and then firmly closed the door. The other rooms were dirty, evidence of dried vomit in several places on the carpets which had been wisely left behind by whoever had cleared out the place. The unpleasant stale smell went without saying.

That left the locked cupboard and the loft.

The cupboard door yielded, without damage, to a small tool I keep in my handbag that Patrick presented to me a few years ago with the promise that it would open any bottle, can, jar, coffer, chest, amphora or ark. It was empty but for an old jam jar.

Worried about staying too long and thereby arousing the suspicions of the woman in the shop next door I ran back upstairs, grabbed the chair from the boxroom and placed it beneath the hatchway to the loft. Luckily the ceiling was low and I am fairly tall but even then, when I had pushed the hatch up and back, the wind sounding really loud now, I could only just see into the space above by standing on tiptoe.

There was a tiny roof-light casting what can only be described as a dirty glimmer on what was within; nothing but a water tank and thick black cobwebs all waving in unison to a cold draught of air. And bats: seven of them hanging up like mis-shapen black puddings.

All very disappointing unless one was a naturalist.

I had been unrealistic, I suppose, to imagine that I would find anything of interest. After a struggle to shut the hatch and ending up having to hook it with a wire coat-hanger I found and re-designed for the purpose I left the house and locked up. Then I turned and received a terrific shock as someone had silently come up behind me. He was, I felt, relat-ed to the deceased owner's neighbour insofar as his face was the same colour, that is, of putty. That was where the resem-blance ended for he was at least six foot four and horribly obese and although there weren't actually a couple of bolts through his neck and staples across his forehead, he definitely seemed to come from that stable.

'Mum says you've been a long time.' This was uttered in a flat monotone.

'I looked in the loft for signs of the rain coming in,' I said. Ye gods, there was only eighteen inches between us and my back was hard-up against the door. 'And woodworm, dry rot, that kind of thing.'

'Mum says you've been a long time,' he repeated.

Obviously, I hadn't made myself quite clear. 'Shall we give her back the keys?' I suggested brightly, dangling them beneath his nose. His breath smelt like a dog-kennel, probably on account of the bad teeth.

'People do as Mum says.' He came even closer.

'You too?' I asked, determined to keep looking him in the eye. 'Yes.'

'Well, do as your Mum says and come with me so I can give her back the keys.'

'You don't go in there.'

He was leaning over me and our faces were only a matter of inches apart now.

'Why not?' I gritted, drawing myself up to my full height.

'No one goes in there.'

'It's not your house.'

'No – one – goes – in – there.' Each word had been ground out as though uttered by something mechanical. Only robots don't have spittle.

'Because he's dead?' I asked, preparing to slid sideways and make a dash for it. I had one murder suspect already and could already feel his hands around my throat.

A look of surprise. 'No. But he is dead. There was blood in there.'

I then did something that I recognised as being downright stupid. Somehow, I turned my back on him, unlocked the door and went in again. 'Show me,' I said. At least I now had room to manoeuvre.

He came in, thankfully going over to the doorway that led into the hall, and began to pick at a piece of loose wallpaper, keeping an eye on me in between.

'Well?' I said, preparing to make like a springbok should things become really awkward.

'Men,' he said, slowly tearing off a tiny strip, fascinated, giving it all his attention. 'Girls,' he shot a quick glance in my direction and then smiled slyly. 'Drinking. All on the floor.' Another smile.

'You saw them,' I said, deliberately not making it a question.

A lot of slow nods. 'No clothes. I saw them.'

'And when he fell down the stairs? Did you see that too?'

'He didn't fall down the stairs.' He released the piece of wallpaper when it became detached, watched it float down, started on another and I suddenly saw him for what he really was: an overgrown and neglected child with a brutal, homemade haircut.

'No?' I whispered.

'There was blood on it so I washed it.'

'What did you wash?'

'The heavy metal thing. A metal chicken. I liked it. I like chickens. It had fallen on his head – in the bathroom. I washed it when Mum was out and put it back where it should be.' An arm was waved vaguely in the direction of the hall.

I went a little closer. 'You took it *home* and washed it?'

'When Mum was out. Then I brought it back, dried it like I do the dishes and put it back where it should be.'

'So why was it in the bathroom?'

A shrug.

'But Mr Taylor was found dead at the bottom of the stairs with his head against it.'

'He was dead in the bathroom. I didn't like him and I didn't want to get into any more trouble. I just liked the chicken – I washed it.' A fierce look at me. 'You'll tell them and I'll get into trouble.'

'No, you won't, not if you didn't hit him on the head with it. Did you?'

Lots of slow head-shaking.

'The blood was in the bathroom?'

'A bit.'

'Did you wash that too?'

'No, just the chicken – I liked it.'

'So you didn't tell your Mum he was dead in the bathroom?'

An emphatic shake of the head. 'I would have been in trouble. I'd been in trouble before – for looking through the window. He caught me and there was a lot of trouble. Mum hits me with a big spoon when I get into trouble. It hurts.'

'I won't get you into trouble. Did you see anyone else come to the house that day – after you left?'

'A man. I saw him from my window. I didn't like him and didn't look at him again in case he saw me and told Mum.'

'So you don't think he did see you?'

'No.'

'Can you remember what he looked like?'

'No. He had a tracksuit on with the hood up.'

'Big, small, thin, fat?'

'Big, strong. He looked horrible. I didn't like him.'

'We'll go and give your Mum back the keys now. I'll tell her you helped me lock up.'

And, God help me, he gave me a big hug.

Now, of course, I was in a huge quandary. The doorstop would have been taken away by the police, no doubt as Exhibit A, and because my large friend had washed and dried it – I could imagine him giving it a final loving polish after he had replaced it in the hall thus removing his own fingerprints as well – there would have been little, if any, forensic evidence on it. This should have caused suspicion. What I really needed to do was to talk to James Carrick before I unleashed any police investigation on the unfortunate lad next door.

I had not wanted to go into the bathroom even though it had been comparitively clean. Had that been because my cats' whiskers were right on target? Had someone scrubbed it clean?

There is a large hotel above the beach at Port Wrinkle where in the past the family has enjoyed very good cream teas. Their lunch menu was on a par and I practically had the whole restaurant to myself as I sat at a window table gazing through the rain-streaked windows at the high tide pounding onto the shingle beach. I felt strangely shivery after the morning's work. Perhaps I needed something hot to eat: I had only had a cup of tea and a piece of toast before I set out.

My mobile rang when I had just finished my bowl of soup.

'Hi,' said James. 'I haven't really had time to dig into this but it would appear that the PM found that Taylor had zillions of milligrams of alcohol in his blood, his liver was definitely on the way out and he had a pretty thin skull. Not many question marks *there*.'

A couple of serving staff were within earshot so I merely thanked him, explained that I could not talk now and said I would contact him shortly. As soon as I had replaced the phone in my bag it rang again.

It was Martin Longton. 'I don't want to worry you,' he began carefully. 'But we've had another problem. It looks as though someone took a shot at Patrick as he was crossing the area outside the warehouse. It's all right though, he's fine, just a couple of small wounds in his neck where the slug ricochetted off the wall and some bits of brick hit him. He was taken to hospital to get them removed and for a check-up but they're only minor flesh wounds and he should be okay very quickly.'

'Which hospital?' I butted in.

'St Thomas's. Ingrid, please don't kill yourself getting there as I've a feeling, knowing the guy a bit now, that he'll discharge himself later on this afternoon. We had a hell of a job getting him in the ambulance in the first place.'

Which would figure. 'I'll drive carefully,' I lied.

'I'm shifting us out of here,' Longton continued. 'It's obvious there's some kind of lunatic around. David Goodheim's flying over tomorrow and is insisting we shoot the rest of those scenes in a more secure venue even though it means recreating the inside of the warehouse inside a studio complex. The important thing is there'll be security people on gates. It all costs more but he says he has the funds. I intend to

73

postpone the warehouse work for a while and get on with all the other interior stuff where I can do without a stand-in and Rik says he'll do all the rehearsals. Oh, and Rik's getting an official minder. Deena O'Leary, his agent, has arranged it. It'll give Patrick a few days to recover – that's if he wants to continue as stand-in. I'd be really grateful if you'd let me know about that ASAP. We can't carry on here, that's certain – it's too open and too public.'

'Not wishing to worry you either,' I said, speaking as quietly as possible. 'But something I've found out this morning suggests that the author of *Blood and Anger* might have been murdered.'

'Oh, Lord! Still, I'll worry about that another time. And don't you worry about Patrick – I'm sure he'll ring you himself any time now.'

But Patrick did not ring me and, several hours later, was still in hospital. Longton's rather breezily optimistic prognosis was not quite borne out for one jagged sliver of brick had only just missed Patrick's jugular vein, the other had lodged near his windpipe. Although both had been successfully removed, together with some smaller fragments, it had had to be done under a general anaesthetic and for the rest of the day, at least, he was going nowhere.

He was awake but still a bit whoozy when I reached his bedside and talking hurt so I just settled for giving him a cuddle.

It was understandable in the circumstances perhaps but I forgot to phone the scriptwriter, Melvin Lockyer, and warn him about the latest developments.

I felt I had no choice but to talk to whichever policeman was handling the cases of the two shootings: not to say that I necessarily intended to stop my own investigations. This proved to be a DI by the name of Nathaniel Foster. Fiftyish, dark-haired and untidy with a desk overflowing onto the floor with paperwork he gave the impression of being overworked, world-weary and even ill.

'Your husband was very fortunate, Mrs Gillard,' he began by saying. 'Now, why did you want to see me?'

I told him about my findings in Cornwall.

When I had finished he said, 'You know, it really isn't a good idea for – '

I interrupted him with, 'Get on the phone to DCI James Carrick in Bath and ask him to explain. It'll save wasting a lot of time and you from uttering a lot of silly, ploddish platitudes.'

There was a short silence and then Foster said, 'I knew a James Carrick when I worked undercover for the Vice Squad.'

'I'm sure he said he once did. He's fair-haired and someone once described him on a bad day as looking as though he'd be far happier skinning sheep on the Faroes.'

'That sounds like James. He's in Bath these days, you say?'

'Yes.'

'And he's a good friend of yours?'

I nodded.

He tried to stare me down but I won.

Foster left the room to phone and was away for rather a long time. When he returned I detected a more businesslike attitude. 'This lad you spoke to in Cornwall . . . ' he said, reseating himself. 'We have to describe him these days as having profound learning difficulties. In view of that why did you believe what he said?'

'I have a four-year-old at home,' I told him. 'You can read them like a book at that age and I don't think he was lying.' I leaned forward in my chair. 'Look, I don't want him bullied. His mother hits him with what he described as a big spoon and having met her I'd say it's probably an old iron soup ladle.'

'I have contacted Devon and Cornwall Police but please give us a little credit,' he remonstrated gently. 'I emphasised that he was vulnerable and they're sending along someone who's worked in Child Protection. Mind you, they weren't very happy at possibly having a murder case on their hands. '

'Someone must have moved the body and cleared up in the bathroom *after* – I don't even know his name – after he left the house. And, as I've just said, he saw a man later that day wearing a tracksuit with the hood up. If he's telling the truth that could have been the murderer.' I had the copy of *Blood and Anger* with me and placed it on the table between us. 'Do please find the time to read that. Parts of it are badly written, other sections read as though they have been taken directly from someone else's account of events. The man who's referred to as Jack, the one Taylor alleges tried to take revenge on a member of his troupe and in doing so was prepared to sacrifice all the others, could be Romanov's killer. His career and life were ruined by the allegations although nothing ever seems to have been done since to discover the truth.'

Foster said, 'We have no way of knowing if one word of this book is true. The author might have done the dirty deed himself and shifted the blame.'

'I agree, but one way or the other the damage has been done and it's fact that Jack, or whatever his real name is, became so bitter and twisted that he took to a life of serious crime. Patrick's insisting that he wants to carry on as Rik Harrison's stand-in. Obviously, I'm worried for his and Rik's sake for it might be the star of the film that this person's really gunning for. He probably doesn't know they've changed the ending either.'

'Changed the ending?' asked Foster, baffled.

'Of the film. In the film he's exonerated, I suppose to make a happier conclusion – more of a family movie.'

'I'll do a deal with you,' the DI said with a case-hardened

smile and after due thought. 'Leave the police to catch this bastard before he kills anyone else, while *you* exonerate him.'

'Have you found out where the shot that almost hit Patrick was fired from?'

'Not yet,' Foster replied heavily.

'And I take it any pulverizing of local hoodlums hasn't paid off yet?'

He just glowered at me.

'Well, what did you expect him to do?' Patrick said. 'Give you a bloody medal?'

A few more adjectives that he did not normally utter in my hearing had been rammed into the remark, a sign that his disposition was less than sunny. Given the situation, this was to be expected but it did not mean I had to put up with it.

'Sorry,' he said in response to the look.

Communicating, but of necessity not over-chatty as his throat, lightly bandaged, was still very sore, Patrick went back to reading the *Daily Telegraph*. I had collected him from hospital, taken him back to the hotel and we had been in our room for no more than fifteen minutes. Then, suddenly, he stood up, hurled the paper into the far corner and crossed the room to face the window, hands tightly clenched. I waited a few seconds and then went over to him.

'Do you want to go home and forget all about it?' I asked his taut profile. He has been on the receiving end of more than his fair share of malice aforethought in his career and there is such as a thing as the last straw. Then I realised it might be nothing to do with this but a form of grief: the knowledge had finally hit home that what had been a way of life for him was really over.

He did not look at me. 'No.'

'Shall I go away and leave you alone?'

'No.'

'What do you want to do?'

'Cry.'

I squeezed between him and the window and put my arms around him. Tears were already spangling his eyelashes. 'Sorry,' I whispered.

'What for?'

'Giving you a look for swearing. Patrick, I spoke to Elspeth last night, explained what had happened and she suggested that if you were fed up and a bit under the weather we could go and stay with her for a couple of days.'

'It's not a bad idea,' Patrick muttered.

'I think she might be a bit lonely – your father's gone on some trip abroad with the Mothers' Union to look at Old Testament ruins. There was a straw poll among the members of the clergy team as to who should lead the group and he won.'

'And isn't himself a terrible traveller?' Patrick said under his breath with an Irish accent. 'He lost. Sick as a dog on trains, planes, boats, sulkies with fringes on top, camels, you name it.' He started to laugh softly, then shed a few tears into my shoulder and afterwards we packed up and headed for Hinton Littlemoor.

'I resent that cop Foster's sarcastic suggestion that we leave catching the killer to him while we set about exonerating him,' Patrick said. But the gaze that came to rest on me was amused and zephyr-light, a change of demeanour that had an awful lot to do with his mother's cooking, a large plateful of which was before him. Elspeth had gone to answer a ring on the doorbell.

I said, 'There might not be any exonerating to do if the allegations made in the book are perfectly true.'

'That has to be borne in mind but I still think we ought to investigate and find him before the police do, even though whoever grabs him it will have the same effect – take him out of circulation.'

'I really want to see his face light up when we tell him the good news that the end of the film's different from the book,' I said sarcastically.

'It might save lives if we find him first,' Patrick stated matter-of-factly. He returned happily to his steak and kidney pudding for a minute or so and then said, 'I too served in Northern Ireland and have the added advantage of having been in a more senior position with a better overall picture. It shouldn't be too difficult to get to the truth and there must be several people who know only too well what really happened.' He glanced at me. 'I wasn't necessarily suggesting that this character would survive our meeting should he prove difficult.'

'Foster's team are still crawling over the warehouse site – I just happened to pass by there before I picked you up.'

'He has to rely on different types of detection work, and also forensics. Today I shall get on the phone which will mean, hopefully, that tomorrow morning we'll be able to go and find someone's neck to threaten to wring unless they spill the beans.'

'You're not supposed to be doing *anything* for at least a week. Not even drive.'

'You can drive and I'll do the wringing. Besides, I'm on contract now to do this stand-in job for Martin Longton. That'll flash up again in a couple of days.'

'I still think Jack, or whoever he is, has somehow got himself inside the production unit and knows everything that's going on and even knew Romanov's movements that day.'

'Actually, I'm beginning to think you might be right.'

'Then the target is the making of the film generally and not anyone in particular.'

'Romanov was hardly an important player though and

quite a maverick character by all accounts – people never knew when or even if he was going to turn up. Why not Longton, or one of the actors taking the other leading roles whom we haven't met yet?'

'The killer knew Romanov and he was an easy one to start with?'

'Could be. Change of plan then. Tomorrow we go and find this East End Russian hoodlum and ask him a few questions about his staff.'

'Please give yourself another twenty-four hours to recover.'

'It's only wasting time.'

Elspeth returned. A still attractive woman in her mid-sixties she is the only person on the planet under whose scrutinising gaze Patrick actually wriggles. 'What did I hear about you going somewhere tomorrow?' she demanded to know of him.

'The day *after* tomorrow,' he corrected humbly.

'You haven't yet told me how you managed to get those bits of brick embedded in your neck. Ingrid said you were involved in some film but we were both on our mobiles and you know how bad the reception is here. Is this an army television film or a recruitment thing that they've dragged you back to do for a while?'

'No, it's a feature film and I'm working as Rik Harrison's stand-in.'

Her eyes round, mother surveyed son. '*Really*? What, *the* Rik Harrison?'

'Yup.'

'What's he really like?' she asked eagerly.

'Overweight,' I declared. 'Patrick's much more attractive and a far better actor than he is.'

Elspeth beamed at the pair of us. 'The key to a happy marriage,' she said. 'A wife who knows how to flatter her man.'

5

'How are we going to play this?' I asked, hearing the tenseness in my own voice, the four-hour drive from Somerset almost over.

Patrick looked up from the street map he was perusing. 'You don't have to come with me.'

'Coming with you is better than waiting for you to be returned in instalments.'

'I have absolutely no intention of starting any trouble,' he protested. 'Besides, things are different now. I'm not even going to adopt an alias. Just be myself.' He pulled a gargoyle face at me, grinning, which I did not get the full benefit of as I was trying to concentrate on driving.

Patrick went back to the map. 'According to James – whom I apologised to profusely after waking him at six-thirty this morning on his day off – the place to go in the East End of London with a view to tracking down the ungodly is The Anchor pub in North Road, West Ham. Which, as it's only a couple of miles as the vulture flies from there to the warehouse where we were filming, is promis-ing.'

'Funny name for a pub there,' I muttered.

'Not really, as according to the map there are wharves at Bow Creek on the River Lea nearby. Anyway, James, as Foster said, once worked for the Met. No doubt due to the fact that I'd ruined his lie-in he seemed to relish the idea of my tan-gling with London mobsters, but in all fairness he did urge caution. His view is that since the demise of the Kray twins everything's gone downhill and the days of big gangs ruling whole areas are over. But he still suggested I went armed to the teeth.'

'I simply can't believe a policeman said that to you!' I exclaimed.

Patrick shugged disarmingly. 'Perhaps he doesn't want my demise on his conscience. Anyway, I've brought my knife.'

Under the circumstances the knowledge that he is more dangerous with that than most men armed with a meat-cleaver was not particularly consoling.

'I've absolutely no right to carry a gun in public now,' Patrick continued, correctly registering my silence as disapproval.

I still said nothing even though thinking that those who have our names on their extermination lists – terrorist organisations, criminals he has helped put behind bars and people like that – were hardly likely to have crossed us off, dewy-eyed with fellow-feeling, even if they knew Patrick had left the job, rather the reverse.

Patrick said, 'Take the next left, would you? According to this it's near the London Gas Museum.'

'D'you you know what this man calls himself?'

'Not a clue. It's likely he's one of those with a different name every week. Second right – by the lights.'

'You do realise that this character is rumoured to be behind an operation that shoots the owners of cars he wants when they're parked in their own drives or stopped at traffic lights? And here we are rolling up in a Lichfield conversion Range Rover!'

'No, I don't remember your mentioning that,' my husband said evenly.

'Sorry, I got it from James.'

'What else does this character specialise in?'

'Drugs, protection rackets, the usual mobster stuff.'

The traffic lights went red and I had to stop, my overactive writer's imagination responsible for the cold shudders going up and down my back. I told myself that we were in a busy thoroughfare in broad daylight, with just as expensive cars all around us and there was absolutely nothing to worry about.

Patrick glanced at his watch. 'It's getting on towards lunchtime. I suggest we leave the car in a multi-storey car park, where it will be as safe as anywhere, and make like tourists looking for the seamier side of London life.'

No iffy bits there: I knew we would find it.

The Anchor appeared not to exist anymore so had either undergone a name-change or the people we asked immediately decided that their consciences would not allow them to be responsible for sending us there. There were pubs of the mock-Irish, wine bar and sort-of-bistro varieties but Patrick ignored all these and plunged down ever more dreary side streets in the direction of the Thames. There was one almost certain near-mugging when three tall youths, hoods up on tracksuit tops to hide their faces, approached from different directions all at once. Patrick countered the situation by pausing, knife in extended hand, and springing the blade – I have never got used to that ghastly slicing click – just before they were actually upon us. They veered away and then ran off.

Then we came to – nothing. A vast expanse had been cleared of buildings and all that remained were piles of bricks, tangles of reinforcing rods, some still with chunks of concrete attached, and smouldering heaps of rotten-looking timber. A group of children who ought to have been at school were lugging rubbish, anything that might burn, to one of these obviously with a view to getting it to blaze up again. On the far side of the huge open space there appeared to be a street market. I turned and saw a noticeboard which carried the information – just discernible through the multi-coloured graffiti – that the area was soon to be developed, courtesy of the European Union and other organisations – to provide shops and affordable housing. The lucky inhabitants would have a choice of views; large oil storage tanks, what looked like a sewage works and a scrap yard.

I realised that the building immediately to our right on a corner and fronting directly onto this temporary desolation was one of those tile-hung Victorian pubs with etched windows that have all but disappeared except where they have been 'restored' almost out of recognition. It was called The Boatman. I nudged Patrick.

'It's not quite the kind of thing we're looking for,' he said after a cursory glance. 'Most of the customers will have gone with the houses they lived in.'

'Leaving it as a perfect watering hole for those who favour the possibility of fewer visits from the police.'

'Okay,' he agreed dubiously. 'We'll give it a try.' He pushed open the door into the Public Bar and went in.

All was rather dark within and no one seemed to be around. Patrick wandered over to a dart board, idly scored three twenties in a row and then came over to where I was studying some of the old framed photographs on the wall. They depicted a time long gone; Thames barges tied up to wharves, dirty children playing hopscotch and skipping in narrow dingy streets, dispirited horses harnessed to carts and wagons lined up in a railway yard. The all-pervading impression was of smoke-filled poverty.

There came the sound of footsteps laboriously ascending stone stairs and a man of considerable girth puffed into view. 'We're not open yet,' he snapped.

'We didn't break down the door,' Patrick pointed out politely.

'Nevertheless – '

Patrick interrupted with, 'I'll have a pint of Marston's, my wife will have an orange juice with lemonade, no ice, and then we would like two rounds of beef sandwiches, brown bread, one with mustard, the other with horseradish. Would you like me to pay you now or afterwards?'

Glaring at us but probably suspecting we might be connected to the local Licensing Authority, 'mine host' poured the drinks and then grabbed a notepad, wrote down the food order, ripped off the page and thrust it at a girl who had appeared from the rear somewhere. I had an idea she might have peeped at us through a small internal window when we had entered, just a fleeting movement I had seen, no more.

Patrick gave me my drink – obviously I would be carrying on doing all the driving – and leaned on the bar. 'Tell me, was this place once called The Anchor?'

Eyeing the speaker grimly the barman said, 'No, that woz up near the old gas works. They pulled it down.'

'Where did everyone go then?'

'Some went to The Greyhound just round the corner, a few came 'ere. Most got rehoused 'cos all the streets woz razed up that end too. It gives yer the bleedin' pip – ripped the 'eart out of the place.'

'So if I wanted to find someone who might have frequented The Anchor . . . ' Patrick left the rest of the sentence in the air, smiled like a shark and added, 'He's Russian – bit of a lad, him and his boys.'

'He don't come 'ere,' said the other, jowls flailing as he shook his head emphatically. 'There's nothin' for him 'ere. You the bill or somethin'?'

Patrick laughed at such an absurd suggestion. 'No, not at all. I'm hoping he can help me find the bastard who killed someone I've discovered is an associate of us both and who,' he gestured at the bandage around his neck, 'as you can see, also took a pot shot at *me* the other day.'

'He don't come 'ere,' the man said again. 'You'd need to ask in nightclubs 'n' places like that. Folk like that aren't around in broad daylight.' He glanced up when a group of elderly men came in, realised he had a good excuse to escape the questions and moved across to serve them. He then left the bar and the girl brought our food and took over.

'Gone to make a phone-call?' Patrick wondered in an undertone.

'I shall have to wash my hands,' I announced, not speaking particularly quietly.

'It's round to the left past the door to the other bar,' said Patrick, who, from professional force of habit, always upon entering a premises immediately notes the location of all entrances and exits.

I duly paid a visit to the Ladies and on my return nipped up the stairs I had guessed might be somewhere in that area – there was a Private notice strung on a piece of string tied to the bannisters but you never get any results by obeying bits of cardboard – and had a quick look around. When I got back to the bar Patrick had several visitors, five to be precise. There was something familiar about three of them so I went over to the bar. When things like this happen my role is that of reserve.

'People don't come into my patch waving knives,' a badly dressed man with a dreadful complexion was saying to Patrick, who had risen to his feet but was still munching on a sandwich.

'So you're one of DI Foster's sidekicks?' Patrick asked, giving every impression of puzzlement.

The man spat on the table in the direction of Patrick's beer.

'Only this is *his* patch,' Patrick said, speaking very crisply, having swallowed his mouthful. 'Or was when he last arrested me for shoving my knife up the arse of someone who spoke out of turn. Someone just like you actually.' And he went on to elaborate at length on the parentage, appearance and sexual habits of this unfortunate in gut-wrenchingly obscene fashion, all the while poking the shirt front of the one he was talking to with the liberally mustard-daubed sandwich. When Patrick stopped talking, having perhaps run out of ideas, everything went quiet, nobody moved in this eyeball-to-eyeball confrontation and I braced myself to wade in and kick a few goolies should the need arise.

Then, it became apparent that the newest arrivals had decided they ought to be elsewhere. This was manifested initially by the henchmen beginning to inch backwards towards the door but soon turned into a full-scale rout, mustard-blobbed shirt and all.

All the old-timers applauded.

'He couldn't even spit straight,' Patrick said disgustedly, garnering the remains of his pint. 'Did you see those boys? Not one of them was over seventeen.'

'Still criminals though,' I said.

'I know, but I hate having to swear like that in front of young people, whatever they are.' He muttered something further, the only bit of which I caught referring to 'a modern-day Fagin.'

'Do we go and find some nightclubs?' I enquired.

'Yes. Like the dog that barked, in the night time.' He chuckled.

'There's a large room upstairs that's obviously used for meetings,' I told him, voice lowered.

'Don't you want that sandwich?'

'I don't fancy it somehow.'

Patrick swapped my plate for his empty one. 'You'd be useless in a real war.'

'I seem to remember being lost in the boondocks with you in Canada and existing on worms and raw fish and hare,' I countered, a bit offended.

'It's not the same,' he said with a gentle smile. 'What's this about a room upstairs?'

'It's used for meetings. Or even as the HQ of some kind of club. There's a street map of Moscow on one wall, an old

Bolshoi ballet programme on the floor in one corner and a cupboard full of Kalashnikovs, Molotov cocktails and canisters of Sarin gas in a little room off to the side.'

He gazed at me, sparks of – what? anger? amusement? deep in his eyes. Even after all this time I sometimes don't know what is going through his mind. But one thing is certain; he hates it if I am flippant when we are working.

'It's just as well I know when you're having me on,' he murmured, at last.

'The ballet programme's there though.'

'Ingrid, it's such a long shot it's off every scale!'

'Please yourself.'

'All right then,' he sighed. 'We'll come back tonight if we draw a blank everywhere else.'

This was not to say that we were idle for the rest of the afternoon. We toured the district on foot, including the area immediately adjacent to the warehouse, went in all pubs that promised a certain seediness and casually introduced the subject of the Russian. No one admitted to knowing anything about him, or even an awareness that such a person existed: only in The Boatman had the barman given us that satisfaction.

'We can do no more until tonight,' Patrick said a couple of hours later when we were going in the direction of where we had left the car. 'God, why am I so tired?'

'Because within the past few days you've had an operation to remove several chunks of wall from your neck,' I said.

'Oh, is that why?'

Asking around had obviously worked. They were waiting for us by the car, casually, yawning, all too aware that this particular multi-storey car park was not equipped with CCTV cameras. Again there were three of them but that was where the resemblance to the day's previous events ended: these were in their twenties or early thirties, one black, two white, fit, tanned, wearing suits and giving the impression they had plenty of thought-provoking attitude.

We were observing their presence courtesy of the small but powerful binoculars I keep, together with a few other useful bits and pieces, in my bag, from a window-side table in the third floor cafe of the departmental store across the road, Patrick having chosen the parking space for me. There were large plants all the way along the sill beside us, which was useful in concealing our surveillance of them.

'No one takes me,' Patrick said stonily, lowering the glasses. 'I shall decide where and when we meet. He's only a two-a-penny crook after all. But it's important to make contact with that lot in order to share those views.'

'You simply aren't fit to take on all three of them if they turn nasty,' I told him.

He shrugged. 'Needs must.'

'Patrick,' I hissed. 'Where is the intelligent undercover soldier who would never start a fight if he could outwit the enemy instead? You say you're never taken but you will be – bundled ignominiously into a car and carted off to this bloke's personal Kremlin. I repeat, you've several stitches in your neck and are not fit to win any fight with those three.'

'You know perfectly well that I never use brute strength – just know-how.'

'All I perfectly well know right now is that I'm talking to pig-stubborn male pride,' I retorted.

The stubbornness though had meant he had never entered into discussions on this subject and was not about to start now. He finished his tea and sticky bun in silence, had another long, careful look at what was happening over the road and then stood up to leave.

'What do you want me to do?' I asked, feeling like bursting into tears. I can't bear it when there is any kind of rift between us and this was all my fault. But I have never been one to stand by while others offer themselves as cannon fodder.

'I can't promise anything,' was all Patrick said before heading for the exit.

No, dammit, the man was not infallible and I had no right to expect him to be. I went after him, using rather regrettable language under my breath.

We used the multi-storey car park's stairs; lifts are too confining and restrict the view as you leave them.

'I think it would be better if you just observed,' Patrick said just before we reached the level where we had parked. 'I'd rather you weren't taken, if that's what happens, although I'm not too sure we're in any particular danger as word has probably got round that all I want is information. Any difficulty will arise if this character has anything to hide with regard to Romanov's death. And of course if he's the one behind the sniping that's been going on since . . . '

In our days with MI5 we had rehearsed this kind of thing many times and I turned sharp left at the top of the stairs and did not look back. These men were not necessarily expecting anyone still to be accompanying the one they were, presumably, after. I walked until I reached the last row of vehicles parked close to the outside wall – this level was pretty full but soon it all would start emptying out when the nearby shops and businesses closed – and then made my way along them so that I was parallel with but slightly to the rear of Patrick whose head and shoulders I could just see above the car roofs several rows over to my right. I could tell that he was strolling naturally like a man with not a care in the world. The Range Rover was some thirty yards away practically dead ahead of him.

I shivered and this had little to do with the cold wind that always seems to blow through these ghastly structures, winter or summer. A car passed me on its way out, a toddler throwing a temper tantrum in the back, the woman driver yelling at it from the front. It became quiet again and still I walked, but more slowly now as I did not want to overtake Patrick along the rows of cars. Then, by a pillar and using it as cover, I stopped. Patrick, ahead of me now, had also stopped. I went on again, on silent feet, to the next pillar. Then, on the strong breeze, came the sound of voices and the mixed scents of expensive male fragrances.

I walked a little farther over to the right, squeezing between the cars, and took refuge behind a Japanese four-wheel-drive vehicle, peeping at what was happening only a matter of yards away from me around the corner of the windscreen. There seemed little risk of being detected: they were far too intent on eyeing up each other.

It was a war of nerves all right. The three immaculately dressed bodyguards, stooges, whatever, whom I could see quite clearly, were displaying a kind of macho and sneering patience – you could almost see the testosterone boiling off them. This patience faded quickly and was replaced by wide-eyed wariness. Patrick was sideways on to me but even in that position I could see that he was swaying a little on his feet, slowly from side to side.

I had a very good idea what was going on. It is quite useless to be all balls and horns when faced with someone giving every appearance of being intellectual but somehow at the same time as mad as a spanner. I knew from past experience that Patrick's eyes were resembling living, crazy, polished pebbles. The men were holding that stare, unable to look away, not even to watch the knife that was in his hand.

Weasels hunting rabbits do it too.

'Put the knife away,' called a voice, right behind me, making me jump. Something jabbed between my shoulder blades and then he said to me, 'Keep quite still or I shall kill him from here.' And again to Patrick, 'I have your woman. Put the knife away.' He pushed me forward with a hand on the shoulder and Patrick turned so that he faced us but could still see the other three. He put the knife back in his pocket.

'See, I trust you,' said the newcomer, leaving me and approaching him 'I don't want your knife and I trust you not to use it. But as you see I myself am armed and guns are faster than knives.'

He was about five feet six in height, of slight build and dressed all in dark-blue; slacks, polo-necked sweater and leather jacket. His hair was bleached blond, past shoulder length and unkempt. He was pale – no doubt spending most of his life indoors – and had neat, crafty features.

'Not always,' Patrick said, smiling just a little.

The Russian, for that, surely, was who he was, also smiled. 'We do it one day and one of us, I certainly, will live to tell my grandchildren.' He made a point of noticing his three, fidgeting, employees. 'You, you and you, bugger off. Tomorrow I hire myself some people who earn their wages.' He turned his back on them. 'I understand you want to talk to me. This is your car?'

'You know it is,' Patrick answered.

'You will drive me somewhere where we can talk in private. Your woman can leave.'

'Ingrid is my wife. She drives.'

The hapless three, who were still hovering, were treated to a contemptuous glare. 'You have no ears?' the Russian bellowed. 'Get out of my sight!'

They went and he watched their retreating figures for a few moments before saying, 'We can't stay here, people are coming. All right, you drive,' he said to me. 'Nothing silly or I shoot him.' Turning to Patrick he said, 'Are you the Gillard who was shot at who I read about in the paper?'

'That's right,' Patrick said. 'I understand Vladimir Romanov was a friend of yours.'

'Get in the back. I shall sit in the front by your wife and watch you both.'

Obediently I went over and took hold of the handle of the driver's door. 'I like to know who I'm giving a lift to,' I said. 'Or do you want us to call you sir?'

'You may call me Alexei,' the man said regally.

I gave a good yank on the handle.

All hell was let loose. The alarm is very noisy, made in the US and different from most as Patrick had insisted he wanted to know exactly if it was ours going off. After it was fitted we had tried it out once to see if it worked and thereafter left it severely alone. It sounds exactly like a steam-powered destroyer whistle, a kind of rising whoop-whoop-whoop, and had the desired effect, the Russian finding himself overpowered.

I unlocked the car, de-activated the alarm and the few souls who had frozen in their tracks carried on towards their cars giving us filthy looks.

'You see Alexei, old chum,' Patrick said quietly to him, pocketing the Russian's hand gun and mobile phone, having frisked him. 'Ingrid and I used to work for MI5 and it takes more than a handful of hoodlums to spoil our day. Now get in the back and I shall sit beside you – with the knife and gun of course – but don't worry, I won't use them, for if you give us any trouble I shall merely wring your bloody neck.'

Words upon which to ponder when you are already rubbing a badly wrung wrist.

We drew up at deep dusk on a track running through an Essex salt marsh and all got out into the strong north-easterly wind. It was cold, the only sounds distant motorway traffic and the dry rustle of the reeds. Patrick pushed Alexei on ahead of us, without saying anything, in the general direction of the North Sea. The man walked for several yards and then turned to face us, arms wide.

'Why have you brought me here?'

'I understand you get your morons to kill people when they've stopped at traffic lights so you can steal their motors,' Patrick said. 'Keep moving.'

'No, that is not true. I steal cars, true, but I never kill.'

'Funny, you said you would kill us a short while ago. Keep going.'

'That was just *words*!'

'And of course you peddle drugs and run protection rackets and kill any previous employee who gets in the way. I expect the bodies of those three you gave the sack to will be found on waste ground somewhere tomorrow. By the way, what *did* Romanov do to upset you?'

The Russian stopped and turned again. 'Look, I tell you, he did nothing to me and I did nothing to him. I only joke with my boys. But I will tell you nothing else out here. Take me to – '

Patrick grabbed him by his lapels and shook him. 'There are no conditions. Uncomfortable out in front, are you? Those who expect a bullet in the back have usually done the same to other people.'

In case we were followed I had driven a very convoluted route to what I regarded as a suitable venue to ask someone delicate questions. My teeth were chattering and, to be honest, I would have preferred to stay in the car. Patrick was now dangerously tired: he had tripped on the uneven road surface a couple of times and, worryingly, was likely to lose his temper. When that happens he is capable of doing anything, speakable and otherwise.

'I am a powerful man,' Alexei said, I am sure sensing Patrick's physical weakness but unaware that he was metaphorically putting his head in a noose. 'No one treats me like this. I shall have you hunted down and – '

He stopped speaking for Patrick had swayed and then collapsed.

Swiftly, I stooped and removed the gun from Patrick's limp fingers. 'Whoopee!' I chortled, my heart nevertheless thumping like a pile-driver. 'You do keeping changing your tune, you know. And here we are, the top-ranking author and the shitty little crook and I'm going to shoot you in self-defence with no one to stop me. To hell with Romanov, he was a shitty little crook on the quiet too. I get quite worked up about law and order, and in my books the shitty little crooks always end up behind bars – or dead. This'll be terrific material.' And, stepping back a little from him and holding the gun two-handed, just the way I had been taught, I took careful aim at a point between his eyes. 'Just like poor old Vladimir, eh?'

I was actually quite shocked when he flung himself face down and snivelled, 'No, no, no! I did not kill him! I liked Vladimir. We came from the same region of Russia and spoke of many things together.'

'Keep talking,' I said when he paused and peered up at me.

'He worked for me sometimes but would never drive cars on a job. He said his film career meant a lot to him and he would be finished if he got into real trouble with the law. There was a time when he was driving my car and had had too much vodka and was stopped by the police. He was fined and it frightened him. I did not kill him. He was my friend.'

'Who did?'

'I don't know.'

I put a bullet into the track near one of his outstretched hands.

'I tell you the truth! It was a professional,' Alexei wailed, snatching the hand close to his chest. 'From outside the area. That is all I know.'

'What about your own bunch of gangsters?'

'They would not have dared harm him. I would know if it was one of them. But there was no reason. No one hated

Vladimir and if I knew who killed him I would take care of them myself. I tell you, Vladimir was my friend.'

'Did he have any other friends?'

'Women no. He was gay. No, no, not me too. I am married with lovely children. We were friends because of Russia.'

'Did he have a partner then?'

'No.' He quickly pulled his other hand towards him, adding, 'I do not think so. He was a loner for most of the time. But he recently spoke of someone he had met in a pub some-where. This person – I do not know if it was a man or woman – wanted to get into films. He had been coaching them or some such thing. Vladimir did not sound too interested.'

'When did you last see him?'

'About two, three weeks ago. We talked of Russia and drank vodka.'

'Did this person have a name?'

'He only spoke of them once. As I said, it bored him. Sam. Is that a man or woman?'

Samuel or Samantha? Heaven only knew. I said, 'Get up and start walking. No, not back the way we came.' I pointed ahead into the gathering darkness. 'Keep going. I've very good night-vision and hearing and if you even slow down I shall start shooting.' Out of the corner of my eye I could see that Patrick was weakly trying to rise.

I waited until Alexei, probably not his real name come to think of it, had completely vanished into the gloom and I could no longer hear his footsteps and then heaved my hus-band to his feet, bundled him into the car and wearily drove back towards the city.

I have always hated salt marshes.

6

'Stand by for a take – everybody quiet please,' the assistant director, Mike Cranley, shouted.

Then, when the order had been given for the camera and sound recorder to be switched on and they were up to speed, someone banged down the clapperboard.

'Action!' Martin Longton called.

The set was of a large, stylish living room, the 'view' through the window that of a panorama of city lights. This, of course, was also a mock-up. The actor Jonathan Fortune sat in a large leather swivel chair smoking a cigar and oozing fat-cat malevolence, an armed minder standing to one side of the room between him and the door. Fortune, who was playing the part of an international gangster whose name I had forgotten the instant someone had told me, removed the cigar from his mouth, smiled grimly and pressed the button on his desk intercom.

'You can send him in now.'

After a short pause Rik Harrison entered warily, registered both men's presence, especially the minder, and walked a couple of paces forward.

Fortune gestured towards a spare chair. 'Sit down.'

But Harrison merely tossed a small object in the direction of the desk and exited, fast.

'Cut!' Martin called. 'Can we do that once more please with slightly longer pauses, the first just before Rik comes in and then between the invitation to sit down and throwing the grenade. Give him a nice smile and make him wait to die, Rik.' He consulted the camera and sound crews and they had no problems with the take.

'First positions please,' the assistant director said.

97

I now knew that the explosion, flames, dismembered bodies, guts and other devastation would be seamlessly added after further takes somewhere else and in the post-production stages together with special and sound effects.

None of this caper was in the book.

I went away to the side of studio, found a chair and sat down. Working in a studio complex after being in the warehouse was luxury indeed: Patrick and I even had our very own small room. This was not to say everyone felt completely secure: the jumpiness and slight apprehension of those on the set was evident especially when there were any sudden loud noises. It was rumoured that the producer, David Goodheim, was going to look in later on a morale-boosting exercise.

Patrick was working somewhere with Rik, the fight director and others rehearsing a complex sequence, no doubt the ubiquitous violence that was all this film seemed to consist of. Typically, he seemed to be enjoying himself but I was rapidly losing interest and yearning to go home and write, probably because my rôle right now was mainly that of stand-in's camp-follower.

My resentment was tempered by the fact that Patrick was still not very well, his neck too sore for him to drive. As before, transport was available – we had moved to a different hotel – but we preferred to be independent. At least though Rik now had an official bodyguard so Patrick no longer felt that this was his responsibility.

My mobile phone rang and I went outside the studio to answer it.

'It's DI Foster, Miss Langley.' There was a short silence and I wondered for a moment whether the signal was bad but he must have been rallying his thoughts – or in hindsight, choking on humble pie – for he went on, 'In view of the fact that your husband was injured the other day and the trouble you took in coming and see me with your findings I feel duty-bound to tell you that Devon and Cornwall Police intend to exhume John Taylor's body and conduct another post-mortem. They've interviewed Teddy, the young man you spoke to, and his mother, and it would appear that she saw what must have been the same person he said he did on the Saturday night that Taylor probably died.'

'Wasn't she questioned at the time?' I asked.

'The person I spoke to didn't say but I gather from other house-to-house enquiries that have been carried out in the village that it wasn't unusual for strangers to be seen at that cottage at the weekends so perhaps she would have thought nothing of it at the time and did not mention it. I also got the impression – which fits in with what you told me – that she isn't a particularly pleasant person so probably didn't care.'

I thanked him for telling me.

'Is your husband well enough for me to have a chat with him? He left hospital before I could spare someone to get down there and then you weren't at your hotel and I lost track of you.'

'Yes, he's here – working but shouldn't be.'

'What time does he finish?'

I explained that I did not know and was not sure of his exact location so could not go and ask him. Which all sounded rather feeble but Foster seemed undeterred and it was arranged that he would call in to our hotel later that evening on his way home.

'And you're absolutely sure you didn't see anyone suspicious just before the shot was fired?' Foster asked.

'No,' Patrick replied. 'But I wouldn't have done – it came from well outside the warehouse perimeter, almost certainly fired by the same weapon that killed Romanov. Have you found the slug?'

99

'No, it ricocheted off and could be anywhere. We're still looking.'

'I *think* I heard it though, unless it was just noise from the nearby building site – which incidentally would have been a good position. Have you asked the crane-driver if he saw anyone suspicious?'

From Foster's expression one assumed that, so far at least, no one had.

We were sitting in the hotel bar – Foster was now off-duty – and from his routine questions, which could have easily been dealt with over the phone and his somewhat diffident manner, I guessed they might not be the real reason for his presence.

'Lieutenant-Colonel . . . ' he began hesitatingly.

'I'm just plain mister now,' Patrick said with a smile. 'I've resigned my commission.'

'It was actually because of your rank and service experience that I wanted to talk to you,' Foster went on. 'I understood from James Carrick when I rang him the day before yesterday that you've occasionally worked together where his cases nudged, as it were, matters of national security.'

'That's true,' Patrick said carefully. 'But please remember that was when I was acting in an official capacity.'

Well, sort of and some of the time, I thought.

'I really could do with some insider information on this undercover unit stuff,' Foster said fervently, with a glance in my direction. 'I read the novel that your wife gave me and it would seem there are grounds for investigating the background to it – but it's a different world to the one I live in.'

'When's the PM on the late author?' Patrick asked.

'Tomorrow, all being well. A Home Office pathologist is doing it. I'll let you know the result.'

Patrick relaxed back in his seat and took a sip of his drink, his favourite single malt, and said, 'I've made a few phone-calls during the past couple of days and it would *appear* that this Taylor character, whose real name was Rundle, was never in the army, the Light Brigade or Uncle Tom Cobbley's Rifle Volunteers.'

'That's amazing,' Foster said. 'But, unfortunately, not hard evidence that can be used.'

'Special operations units tend to be like that,' Patrick told him. 'However, it's as gospel as it's likely to get. And we're not talking about a cover-up by those in authority in case that's what you were thinking. The incident did take place, some kind of information was passed to the enemy and three members of the unit were taken prisoner and subsequently found murdered. The MoD said at the time that an IRA informer had been responsible but that wasn't true. Rundle appears to have been a relative of one of the soldiers who survived from whom he could have got his authentic background to the story. I then made a call to someone else and it all started to get a bit murky. The character referred to in the book as Jack – and I have to admit here that I haven't read it, this info has come from a pretty safe source – the one who was alleged to have betrayed the others and subsequently went off the rails, can't have had anyone rape his sister because he didn't have one. He was actually an orphan as the rest of his family were killed in a car crash. So much for his motives against the one called Phil.'

I said, 'According to the book Taylor loathed both Phil and Jack.'

'This is getting terribly complicated,' Foster lamented. 'Who were the other two who were killed with Phil?'

'Barry and David,' I said. 'David was the youngest and regarded by his chums as a bit of a mascot. But it still gets us nowhere because all the names were changed.'

'The other thing is it's unlikely anyone would be able to get my source into court to testify,' Patrick said. 'Even if they did again there's no real proof, only the certain knowledge of one particular person...' And when Foster carried on looking at him he added, '...who was the commanding officer of the regiment at the time and now holds court in Whitehall plastered in gold braid and medals.' He laughed. 'That's a bit of an exaggeration but I'm sure you get my drift.'

'I don't think your phone calls have helped a lot,' I said to Patrick, getting my revenge for not being told about them. 'In fact they've merely muddied the waters. Let's go back to basics. The Oracles of Murder; motive, means and opportunity. It all points to Jack. He's still bitter and is now outside the law so has the means and the opportunity. Whether he's guilty of what happened in Northern Ireland isn't actually very relevant now. Who *is* Jack? That's what you needed to have asked your source.'

Somewhat po-faced, Patrick said, 'I was just about to point out that what I'd discovered wasn't really a lot of use to this police investigation and that we needed to go back to square one. And in answer to your question I did and his name is Samuel Whitaker.'

'Sam!' I gasped. 'Romanov was coaching someone with that name.'

'Who told you that?' the DI said.

'A local Russian hoodlum who said his name was Alexei,' I replied. 'Romanov had worked as his chauffeur.' I related the rest of what the Russian had told me.

'We picked him up yesterday and left him somewhere in the Essex marshes,' Patrick said insouciantly by way of an explanation.

I gave him a lifted eyebrow together with a look that said, 'And who faded away and as good as left his wife alone with a dangerous criminal?'

Foster said admiringly, 'Carrick did say you got results and would be able to help me in certain matters.'

'James probably said that because you once put his name down for a bungee jump and he doesn't like heights,' I commented a little later when the DI had left.

'Look, I'm damned if I'm going to do Foster's investigation for him,' Patrick replied. He frowned. 'But having said that, and assuming that your theory the killer has infiltrated the making of this film is correct, has it been discovered if anyone who should have been working on the set at the time of Romanov's death was absent?'

'And should have been inside the warehouse when you were shot at and was absent,' I said. 'No idea – but I would have thought it's pretty basic police procedure on Foster's part to find out. He should have done it already but I would rather have a good snoop around Romanov's house, talk to the neighbours and find out with whom he associated. And now, of course, there's Sam.'

'Doing that is a hell of a sight easier then making a list of just about everyone working on the movie and eliminating them one by one,' Patrick agreed. 'And frankly, I'm sick to death of all these aliases.' He reached for the phone. 'Okay, Foster wants us to assist him from our own particular angle but first we'll get his permission for a little investigating that could be seen as trespassing on his authority. MI5 can't wave a magic wand and smooth things over for us now.'

The permission was instantly forthcoming.

'James has actually done us a favour,' was Patrick's wry comment at the end of the call. 'Foster said his team has conducted house-to-house enquiries in the neighbourhood but we can do whatever we think is necessary.'

'He must be really desperate to say that,' I said. 'And I can't think his boss would approve if he knew.'

'No, but poor old Nat isn't a well man, is he? You can see

that a mile off. He'd get his milkman on the case if he thought it would help.'

'Look, I hate being negative but we won't have a leg to stand on if it all goes pear-shaped. Foster'll deny ever having involved us in order to save his own bacon.'

Patrick smiled peaceably. 'Oh, yes. So we stay ahead of the game. By the way, what did you do with Alexei's handgun?'

'I locked it in the cubby box in the car.'

'It ought to be handed over to Foster. I've never carried an unauthorised firearm and I'm not going to start now. Besides which, we don't have any more ammo for it.'

I countered with, 'What about that small cannon you once took to Wales and ended up almost demolishing a house with?'

'You know as well as I do that that was the most desperate situation we've ever been in and a complete one-off,' Patrick replied infuriatingly. He had not known the situation would become desperate when we had started out, cannon and all.

Having promised, once upon a time, a long time ago, to love, honour and obey the man sitting by my side and suspicious that I would shortly be finding myself the sole investigator due to his pressure of work, I brooded about this. The wording, I felt, was not actually an instruction to me to scurry along to the nick with the neat little Swiss automatic and hand it over, weeping with remorse at the oversight, but a statement setting out an ideal situation. And taking into consideration the fact that I was never officially authorised to carry any kind of weapon in the course of my work with D12 but more often than not had the Smith and Wesson residing darkly in my handbag – all my bags still smell of gun oil – and Patrick had instructed me on how to handle several different kinds of firearms in the name of self-defence, such flawless ideals seemed misplaced. If we were about to tackle a crazed one-time member of a second-to-none special service it was sheer stupidity.

This thinking was being trotted through my conscience for the second time as I had foreseen the dilemma when I had put the weapon in the secure hiding place, actually a small safe with electronic locks, in the Range Rover. Also to be taken into consideration was that I had made Alexei empty all his pockets, in case he was carrying another weapon, before sending him off into the gloom. Besides his car keys, which I had tossed into a nearby pool out of sheer bloody-mindedness, I had acquired sufficient ammunition to partici-pate in a small uprising.

Romanov had lived in a terraced house in Shepherd's Bush – Foster had given Patrick the address – not far from the under-ground station from which I emerged the next morning into heavy drizzle. There was now a certain urgency: in two day's time the production unit would start work on the outdoor shots at Wrotherly Hall in Surrey, the date having been arranged months previously. Patrick and Rik, plus others of course, would find themselves, as Patrick had put it, 'scam-pering around in the open with bull's-eyes painted on our backs'. A security firm was being hired to patrol the grounds of the Hall, which apparently were very extensive with woodland. It sounded to me like the sort of place in which you could easily hide an army.

As I had predicted, my partner in endeavouring to solve crime had been called for duty on account of his svelte outline for medium distance shots in 'smoky' corridors. Watching him work with Rik it was apparent there was now a strange, to me that is, rôle reversal. Patrick had had to learn to move and walk like the leading man and copy the mannerisms he had adopted for the part he was playing. So while the Gillard cat-like grace was much in demand for some scenes, for other closer shots, where obviously his face was still not visible, he had to be someone else. In the latter part of one scene where

105

real thunderflashes were thrown the stuntman would be taking over, this more a matter of insurance than the need for rock-steady nerves.

After consulting my London A to Z, I plodded through the rain in the direction of the road where Romanov had lived – it was not worth taking a taxi – pondering on all this. Okay, Patrick was getting paid rather a lot of money for what he was doing, but was it worth the danger? I ruefully came to the conclusion that the question was easily answered from his point of view: yes, getting shot at was just like old times.

I had wondered if the house would still be under some kind of police guard and, sure enough, a constable was stationed outside the front door. It occurred to me that I had no credentials but introduced myself anyway. It immediately transpired that Foster had let it be known that two criminal profilers, Gillard and Langley, would visit the home of the deceased so all I had to do was say that my partner was working elsewhere, perfectly true, and show my driving licence as proof of identity. Promising not to touch anything – even though SOCO had completed their tests the CID team had still not finished their search for evidence – I went in.

If I could not poke and pry what chance had I of finding out even the smallest detail about Samuel Whitaker? He appeared to be so confident that he had used his real name. I already knew that no one openly calling himself that was involved with the film because first thing this morning and in confidence, Patrick had asked Martin Longton to check. Everything was beginning to point to my theory being wrong and that Whitaker had merely befriended Romanov to learn his movements in order to make him target number one. Now, point being made and having missed his next victim, the killer may very well have taken himself off to carry on shooting other people for money and/or to drink himself to death.

Right now, I was rather hoping it was the latter.

My dark mood was instantly banished when I beheld the icons in Romanov's living room. Most were quite small, some four to five inches square, but exquisite and, although I am not knowledgable about such things, looked as though they might be worth a great deal of money. But it was wrong to think of monetary value when gazing upon a beautiful Virgin and Child. I went from one to another; saints, apostles, forgetting for a moment the reason for my visit.

Here then was an insight into the character of a man I had never met and of whom I had only seen a black and white photograph in a newspaper. As soon as this happens, and I had experienced it before, the murder victim ceases to become merely a media story in one's mind or a crime statistic but an entity who had listened to the Tchaikovsky, Rachmaninov and Mahler CDs stored in racks in an alcove while perhaps sipping a glass of wine as he had admired his collection of icons. This man had left his home one morning very recently and never returned.

I walked slowly from room to room and then went upstairs. There was really not a lot that I could do.

Everywhere was very clean and fastidiously tidy, the decor tasteful and unfussy, and there was no sign that the police had rummaged around and removed anything in their quest for evidence although the whole place had been dusted for fingerprints. However, an empty table with an adjacent chair, a multi-socket extension lead on the floor nearby in a third bedroom suggested that a computer may have normally been *in situ* and that it had been taken away for examination.

Despondent, I went back downstairs and into the kitchen. This was high-tech; stainless steel, black polished granite worktops and a bright red tiled floor. It did not look as though anyone had ever so much as made a piece of toast in it and I decided that Romanov had habitually eaten out.

I lingered again by the icons and then made my way out with a view to asking questions in all the nearby restaurants and cafés.

'I'm sure all the right people know about this,' I said to the bored man on the doorstep. 'But in case they don't and it comes to light later I feel I should tell you that I think one of the icons might be missing. There's no actual gap but above a row of three there's a tiny hole in the wall where it looks as though another little brass pin could have been and there's a small square of very slightly darker wallpaper. He could have given it away or moved it of course but I should hate you to think I had made off with it.'

He accompanied me indoors to have a look.

'I reckon they're the Evangelists,' he said after due consideration. 'You know, Matthew, Mark, Luke and John. You wouldn't give away or move one of a set, would you? Thank you very much, Miss Langley. I'll tell the boss.'

Well, they hadn't taught him that at Hendon.

Two hours later, and dosed to the ears with caffeine as I had drunk so much coffee, I had made modest progress. Romanov had regularly eaten breakfast, usually black tea and two croissants with jam, at The Cat's Pyjamas, a bistro only a matter of thirty yards from his front door. This establishment opened at 7 a.m. and according to the Greek waiter to whom I spoke, who was agog to talk about the crime, they were always very busy right from the start. Romanov had not been talkative, if anything the opposite, and my informant had never seen him with anyone else. He often read a Russian newspaper. Sometimes he would turn up in the evenings for a light supper with which he would order a bottle of red wine, drink half of it and then take the rest away with him. The waiter had never seen him in the middle of the day.

It appeared that Romanov had often dined at Browne's,

again not far very away but in the opposite direction, a restaurant set to one side of a small courtyard that one approached through a gated archway. He had been quite well known here and the place was much frequented by people who worked in the film and theatre industry. Not one to mix much though, a word here, a greeting there, the manager informed me, eager to speak to someone as exotic sounding as a criminal profiler. (Foster having handed me on a plate such a useful guise I was sticking with it.)

Then, having almost ruled the place out as it looked decidedly scruffy from the outside, I had descended a flight of steps to a basement where a sign over a door indicated that I had arrived at Shrieking Freddie's. This, I realised shortly after I had walked through the door, was a gay coffee house cum bar. One might be forgiven for wondering, such was the crush of people so early in the day, whether it was the only such establishment this side of Bletherbury-on-Trim.

'You want to know about Vladimir Romanov?' said the man behind the bar, obviously a stand-in for The Incredible Hulk, when I had stated my business. 'Sure, he used to have a drink here sometimes. But I only got to know his name after his picture was in the paper. He was quiet, like.'

'So he didn't have any particular friends?'

'No, not really. He wasn't part of the gay scene round here, if that's what you mean. And he wasn't ever in the business of picking someone up. I think he just felt comfortable here.'

'Did you ever see him *with* anyone?' I had asked, and risked adding, 'A man called Sam?'

'What does he look like?'

'That's what I need to find out,' I had responded tersely.

'No, I didn't. But I'm not here all the time. Try Fanny O'Riley's just down the road. He once told me that's where he went with business acquaintances. He seemed to be a private sort of person – perhaps he didn't like just anyone in his home.'

True to its title Fanny O'Riley's was an Irish-themed pub with a restaurant on one side. Presiding over a plethora of shillelaghs, harps, gruesome resin leprechauns of different sizes peering out of a jungle of greenery, plus a stuffed donkey, complete with cart, in the entrance had been a large lady who could have been created by Beryl Cook. Summing her up I had immediately decided to abandon my 'new' profession as it would obviously cut no ice.

'If you're not the bill I ain't answerin' any more bleedin' questions,' proclaimed the woman. 'They were clutterin' up the place with their big flat feet half of yesterday lunchtime and trade was bleedin' awful.'

'You may not have heard of me,' I had said diffidently. 'But crime writers sometimes visit real-life places, like pubs, to get a little background colour.' I gazed around admiringly. 'And in search of interesting characters.'

'Wot did you say your name was?'

'Ingrid Langley.'

No, she had never heard of me.

'So why do you want to know about this geezer who got shot?' she had stridently asked after a pause.

'Because he was Russian and had worked for a Russian gangster in the East End. That's meat and drink to a crimewriter.'

'It didn't say anything about that in the papers.'

I had smiled in conspiratorial fashion. 'No, well it wouldn't, would it?'

'Look, we don't get dodgy types in 'ere,' she had said, bridling.

'Well, of course not! It's just that if I'm going to plan a novel based around this man I need to know who his law-abiding friends were so I don't accidentally lump them in with the crooks and someone sues me.' Would she swallow this codswallop?

There had been another silence and then, possibly because she had just realised she might come under the heading of 'interesting character' and be immortalised in print, she had said, 'I told the coppers I'd seen 'im a few times but when yer rushed off yer feet yer don't necessarily notice who the customers *are*. They showed me a picture,' she had shuddered blancmange-style. 'Not the same one as was in the papers but one that'd been took after 'e was dead. They tidy 'em up, comb their 'air an' all that but yer can always tell, can't yer? Yer could tell where they'd put stuff over the 'ole in 'is 'ead – right between 'is eyes.' A podgy be-ringed finger had pointed to the spot on her own forehead.

'Horrible for you,' I had murmured sympathetically.

'But all I could say is wot I'll tell you: 'e'd bin in 'ere with different bods over the months but only one I really noticed, a bloke I saw 'im with two or three times recently. I only noticed because he seemed to be tellin' him somethin', teachin' 'im sort of thing and the bloke was takin' notes, bits of paper all among the plates 'n' stuff.'

'Did you catch this man's name?'

'No. And they both paid cash so no credit card signatures to check.'

'Can you describe him?'

'I only noticed that he was bigger and broader than the Russian bloke. And scruffy, 'air all over the place and stubbly chin. 'Is clothes looked as though he'd slept in 'em.'

'What about the colour of his hair and eyes.'

But she had shaken her head to a tinkle of dangly earrings. 'Dunnow, really. Sort of brown, I suppose, but it could have been anything as it looked greasy or wet. Rainin' more'n likely.'

Untidy hair darkened by water or gel, together with scruffy clothing and the need for a shave can be easily arranged. And the fact that he was taller and broader than

Romanov was fairly useless information too as the Russian had been of slight build. Which left the possible killer quite unremarkable.

I returned to the house with a view to talking to the neighbours but no one was at home.

7

As DI Foster put it, 'The new post-mortem on John Taylor shoots very large holes in the original finding of accidental death.' While it was true that the deceased – the name Taylor was being retained to avoid confusion for the purposes of the investigation even though at one time he had been called Rundle – had a thin skull it was not abnormally so and the crushing injury it had sustained was much more severe and therefore not consistent with falling down the stairs and hitting it on a cast iron doorstop. It was more likely that the object had been wielded as a weapon by a strong person, probably male as it weighed just under two kilos, four pounds four ounces. The pathologist did go on to make the point, however, that Taylor could well have been thrown from the top of the stairs to the bottom, the doorstop having been deliberately moved from its normal position against the wall by the front door in order to cause injury. He thought it highly unlikely though as the murderer would have no guarantee that such an action would result in death or even mortal injury unless repeated several times. Bruising to the rest of the body, which was well-preserved as bodies tended to be these days on account of the treatment process all wood goes through, even that used for coffins, *was* consistent with the deceased having fallen down the stairs, in the pathologist's view shortly before death. Other findings, which had been discovered at the first PM, were that Taylor had not been a healthy man, poorly nourished and with some liver damage due to alcohol intake. There was some evidence that he had taken drugs.

As far as other, new, police work was concerned, some of the bathroom floor of Primrose Cottage had been taken up and detritus scraped from the sides of the floorboards, the upper surfaces of which were much cleaner than the rest of the house and appeared to have been scrubbed. Blood and what was described as 'cerebral matter' had been found in with the dirt, the DNA of which matched Taylor's.

'You can read all the technical stuff if you want to,' Foster ended his phone call by saying. 'But you'll have to come to the nick to do that, I'm afraid, as so far I've only the one copy.'

I thanked him and told him we would return the call when I had shared the news with Patrick, whom I found on the corridors set. Close-up shots were being taken of his right hand holding a Luger pistol and firing blanks.

I gazed around me. If my theory that the killer had infiltrated the making of this film was correct – and I was beginning to doubt it – there were any number of people whom it could be. Discounting those whom I now knew well there were still dozens of others; the production manager, the art director, costume designer, set dressers, electricians, VT operator, riggers, the lighting cameraman, camera operator, focus puller, grips, gaffer, sound recordist, boom operator and clapper/loader plus runners, assistants and secretaries, a couple of whom I had been told were men. Where did one start?

'Patrick's hands are more photogenic than mine,' Rik explained to me a couple of minutes later.

Having found a chair away from the action, although the bangs were still very loud, and settled down to wait I turned to him as he sat with a baseball cap tipped over his eyes. 'You must get a bit fed up with it,' I said. 'Not being regarded as utterly perfect, I mean. Surely what your hands look like doesn't matter a toss on the stage.'

'No, but you don't get close-ups in the theatre, ma'am,' he replied with old-fashioned gravity.

'Where's your minder?'

'Gone to have something to eat.'

'Is that wise? Shouldn't he be eating it right here?'

'The guy has to have a proper break. Okay, I was getting a bit twitched when we were out at the warehouse but as Deena organised this before she went back to the States I feel safe, especially now we're in the studio.'

I gazed at him in asperity. 'Well, I'm going to spoil your complacency. They've just done another PM on the author of *Blood and Anger* and discovered he was murdered. Romanov, your stand-in, was murdered. Someone tried to murder Patrick, your replacement stand-in. And the star of this film, which no doubt is costing millions, has sent away his body-guard and isn't even keeping the most basic personal surveillance.' Regrettably, my anger then really got the better of me because I could have been a widow right now and had just caught sight of his mid-morning snack on the floor by his side; a large pink milkshake and a cream bun with icing on the top. 'You're just lounging there – a fat, self-satisfied sitting duck,' I yelled at him.

I had thought we were out of earshot what with all the bangs but Martin Longton called 'Cut!' and Mike Cranley came over. 'Look, mates, I know we're going to post-synch this but – '

'She's telling me off,' Rik interrupted. 'Correctly, as it happens.' He garnered the offending thousand-and-one calorie snack from the floor, stood up and thrust plate and carton into the assistant director's hands. 'There we are, old chap,' he said in a very upper-class English voice. 'Have another pound on your hips on me.' And walked off.

Patrick appeared. 'Everything okay?'

'Here,' said Mike. 'You're thin. Have some elevenses.' He passed it over and said over his shoulder as he went back to the set, 'Do me a favour and ask your good lady not to beat up the leading actor.'

'Taylor was murdered,' I reported bullishly to Patrick,

taking a large bite from the bun and slapping it back on the plate. 'Plus blood and brains between the bathroom floor-boards.'

'Can we have another take, please?' Longton called. 'Only a bit quicker this time?'

Patrick quirked an eyebrow, took a swig of milkshake, a bite from the bun, gave me a sticky kiss and a big smile and went back to work, leaving me to finish both.

David Goodheim arrived about five minutes later with a very beautiful woman on his arm. This I soon realised was the American co-star of the film, Jaquie Lauderdale. Somehow I had imagined the director would be big, blond, bumptious and noisy with a perennial cigar, but he was almost exactly the opposite, grey-haired and clever-looking, which just shows how wrong you can be. Jaquie was instantly recognis-able from myriads of images of her in the media; all smiles, glowing, not remotely jet-lagged. With raven-black hair, tall and graceful, she was faultlessly dressed in a cream trouser-suit and coral-coloured accessories. I suddenly felt dead scruffy, not to mention the sticky mouth and fingers.

'Well, here we are,' said Goldstein quietly, all preparation for the next take having come to a complete standstill. He intro-duced Jaquie to Martin Longton as though presenting him with a great treasure. Out of the corner of my eye I saw Mike Cranley send Cathy away at the run, presumably to find Rik. The three stood talking, Goodheim no doubt asking about the shootings and then Longton beckoned Patrick forward where-upon he received sympathy from the visitors: body language is a great revealer. One of Jaquie's elegant and bejewelled hands lightly stroked the bandage that was still around Patrick's neck. When he gave her the kind of look that until that moment I had assumed was for me alone, I discovered that my sticky hands were now clenched into extremely sticky fists.

116

I went away and found somewhere to wash them.

When I returned an early lunch break had been called, and nobody but a few technicians were in sight. I rang Foster's office number to tell him that I thought Patrick's new commitment to the film would make it difficult for him to do much investigating and also to ask if he knew of my suspicion that one of the icons was missing. I was told that he was now in a meeting.

I then remembered that I had still not contacted Melvin Lockyer as I had promised should there be any alarming developments and rang his number. It was unobtainable.

Everything was getting decidedly bloody awful.

I made my way to a canteen and had a salad to offset the effects of my earlier refreshment and pondered. Who was the woman who had contacted Melvin Lockyer to ask him to keep the details of John Taylor's death from the media until after the funeral? He said she had sounded as though she had not wanted to be overheard. Had Taylor had a wife? A girlfriend? Why had it been necessary for her to whisper? Had she phoned from Primrose Cottage while the police were present? And, setting aside the possibility that the local press might know exactly who the deceased had been, why had she not merely waited until after the funeral to tell Lockyer? Had she come upon his name and address among Taylor's papers and the call had been a ploy to discover exactly who and what he was? If she was an accomplice of the murderer this was not a particularly comfortable thought.

I wondered how this latest development would affect Foster's investigation for now, presumably, he would have to liaise with Devon and Cornwall Police. I was actually going to have to amend what I had been about to say to Foster and tell him that it was difficult to see what both Patrick and I could do to help further as events had gone beyond the ins and outs of special forces units. Unless the DI still wanted to have pretend 'criminal profilers' on the peripherals. I rather felt he needed genuine ones.

Patrick appeared by my table. 'I've been looking everywhere for you. We're in the restaurant and David said he'd like to meet you because – '

'Wow-ee,' I butted in in a bored voice.

He pulled out a chair and sat down. 'What's the matter? Why did you go off like that?'

'Nothing's the matter. I was all over sticky bun – quite unsuitable to be ushered into the presence – so went to wash my hands. When I got back you'd gone.'

It is very difficult, in fact almost impossible, for a man to think like a woman and some never even give it a try but –

'That wasn't very tactfully put, was it? What I should have said was – '

'Why don't you go back so she can stroke your neck some more?'

'She made it hurt,' he said. 'May I say another four words?'

'You still went all squidgy,' I argued stonily, made even more furious by the knowledge that I was being downright childish. 'But do go ahead.'

'*A Man Called Celeste.*'

'That thing I wrote years ago? I seem to remember you took it to the States when you went on business – I'd sacked Alan my agent – showed it to some producers and sold the film rights. But after someone made a complete hash of adapting it for the screen and I did it myself nothing happened. So?'

'You look wonderful when you're angry,' he said. 'And you've been bawling everyone out all day. Ingrid . . . '

'What?' I barked.

'Sorry I went all squidgy.'

I can never remain in a bad mood with the man in my life for very long: the magic works both ways. 'What about this wretched novel then?' I said but then burst out laughing at the hangdog look on his face.

'David Goodheim has it now. He's wondering if you'd be interested in rewriting the screenplay to bring it up to date.' Patrick stood up. 'Come and talk to him. Oh, and I've solved the riddle in the sands.'

'Which one?'

'Why we're here. He's got this daft idea you'd based the book on your husband who would be just the guy to give Rik a few pointers. Quite ironic really.'

'But I did.'

'I thought Celeste was a bit of a nutter.'

'He's like you without the nutter bit.'

This, while gratifying of course, was a distraction and I was not even sure that I wanted to undertake the work. But David Goodheim was persuasive and, as it seemed that this time something might come of it, I promised to dig it out when I got home and give it proper consideration. It represented quite a lot of work as the novel – which had never been submitted to a publisher – existed as just a typescript, hailing from the days before I had bought a computer.

Patrick was not required for filming the next morning and in a way we had the day off. But the director had asked us to go to Wrotherly Hall where work would commence the day after to enable Patrick to give his reaction from a security point of view to the areas chosen for the exterior filming. For some reason he appeared to value his opinion over that of the man in charge of the group he had hired.

'I can't see how this place won't be even more hazardous than the warehouse,' I said, after our names and vehicle registration number had been checked by security staff at the imposing entrance gates. Patrick had decided to see how he got on with driving so we had changed over and were proceeding at the mandatory fifteen miles an hour down the long, tree-lined drive.

He gazed over the acres of parkland. 'No, Longton's being a bit overconfident in thinking that with patrols being carried out by various bods some kind of acceptable level of safety can be attained. Bearing in mind that a modern sniper's rifle can have a range of anything up to a mile, I shall have no choice but to tell him the truth, what you said, that it's wide open. But the cameras must roll and with a bit of luck the location people will have chosen wisely. Somewhere in the woods will be border country in Northern Ireland, by the way.'

'They're going to recreate the actual raid?'

'I understand it comes right at the beginning of the film.'

I wondered aloud how it would be handled and Patrick laughed.

'Oh, there won't be any of the background story, true or otherwise, at this juncture. Just a lot of shots using night-time filters of blokes crawling through the undergrowth, shooting a million rounds of ammo, huge flaming explosions, the usual crap you see in films.'

'You sound a trifle jaundiced,' I commented.

'It was always going to be load of crap though, wasn't it? Films involving the armed services nearly always are.' He added, almost to himself, 'Except *Master and Commander: The Far Side of the World*. That was bloody wonderful.'

We had been provided with a sketchmap and a short history of the house and grounds by the man on the gate. Wrotherly Hall was privately owned and the house, with collections of pictures, furniture, family silver and Wedgwood black basalt and jasper items, was open to the public only on a few weekends in the summer months in aid of various charities. The estate was otherwise run as a business including being hired out for functions and sporting events.

'Excellent facilities for your conference, seminar or wedding in sumptuous and historic surroundings,' I read out. 'The main garden behind the hall contains a National Collection of Roses, and superb plants from around the world that give year-round colour. There are also formal gardens reckoned to be the finest in the south of England. The grounds, which were designed by "Capability" Brown, extend to one hundred and fifty acres and include extensive woodland with an informal arboretum, a hidden valley and a lake. Designated areas are the perfect venue for carriage-driving trials and other equestrian sports. An outdoor activity and sailing centre situated on the southern end of the lake can be booked by groups.' I looked at the map, which someone had marked with three crosses. 'According to this we're heading for the hidden valley, an area near the lake and adjoining woodland.'

'It had to be the hidden valley,' Patrick said. 'With nettles and thistles. And the lake'll be filthy black water with loads of aquatic beasties that set up home in your underpants should you be unlucky enough to fall in. Longton'll make sure we all fall in. God, just like old times.'

I hide my smile but his next remark slew it dead.

'I think you ought to know that I *may* be required to do some soft focus somewhat naughty shots with Jaquie.'

'What on earth for?'

'Despite Rik's efforts – he really has been working out and living on fresh air, except for the occasional lapse – he's still a bit flabby. So it *might* mean,' here Patrick gave me a big, brave smile, 'that yours truly will have to do some of the honours. Just back views, you understand, and not close-ups.'

'Your back's still quite scarred where those Hell's Angels beat you,' I said, forcing myself to be practical and dispassionate.

'I told them that but apparently the scars can be hidden with make-up.'

'So you're going to be doing simulated sex with her.'

'Only if required. It might not happen. I just thought I'd mention it, that's all.'

I wanted to say to him that I would not have minded some of the real thing during the past few days but it was hardly fair after what had happened to him.

There was an awkward silence until we crested a rise and the house came into view. I had read in the leaflet that a medieval dwelling had once stood on the site, remnants of which survived in the kitchens and cellars, but its successor was a Palladian mansion. The house stood at the northern end of the lake with the aforementioned gardens bounded by highly ornate wrought iron railings and then lawns separating it from the water.

Patrick stopped the car. 'It makes you feel that your own place is a peasant's hovel.'

'Hovels cost less to heat,' I said.

He gazed at me earnestly. 'I'm serious in a way. We've lived in the cottage, your cottage actually, just about since we got married. And there's quite a lot of money in the bank. Wouldn't it be the right time to think of moving to somewhere bigger what with the children growing up? We've done a few alterations but we can't keep on cramming everyone in.'

I suggested we talked about it when we got home, adding, 'I'd really miss you hitting your head on that beam by the bathroom door.'

I did not want to move.

'The crosses on the map are so big they actually represent an area around a quarter of a mile in diameter,' Patrick complained twenty minutes later as we crossed the muddy ground near the lake. We had parked and then walked, thankful that we always keep boots in the car. He paused and surveyed the area. 'Any one of a hundred trees could be used as a vantage point for a sniper. I'd go for that *Wellingtonia*, they're huge but quite easy to climb if you have the right gear. With a lot of people in this vicinity it would be more difficult to pin-point one particular person, even with telescopic sights, but patience is usually rewarded. Ah, there's the lane that'll have to be used to get everything in here.' He set off again in the direction of the next location, the nearby woodland.

I asked, 'How many people are being given these maps with the crosses on?'

'No idea. I get your point: if they're handing them out like confetti to all and sundry heaven help us. As I said, we'll be as good as running about with targets painted on our backs.'

I began to feel very out in the open and vulnerable and was then ashamed of my ignoble thought that it would be unlikely I would be the one targeted.

There were broad rides through the the trees nearest to the house, the widest avenue deliberately created so that the spire of a church served as a focal point. But where we now were, at the farthest end of the lake, the trees had been left to grow more naturally and as we went up a gentle slope away from the water, our feet crunching through leaf litter, the going became quite rough with patches of brambles and the occasional fallen branch.

We arrived at what appeared to be a small stone-built barn.

'This must be the bothy they were talking about,' Patrick said. 'Well, it's far less open here than the previous place and I suppose you could ring-fence it with security guards but . . . ' He shrugged.

The building was not genuine but consisted of a cleverly constructed wooden frame over which canvas of some kind had been stretched and then painted to look like weathered, moss-covered stones. Real moss, carefully arranged bracken at the base of the walls and leaves scattered on the 'roof' added to the authenticity. There was nothing at the back but supports fixed into the ground to stop the whole thing blowing over. The wooden door was real though and opened on ancient-looking hinges. I assumed that any interior shots would be done on a set in the studio.

'On to the hidden valley,' Patrick muttered, looking at the map.

There was a loud report close by and I threw myself flat on the ground. Pigeons and crows rocketed up from everywhere.

'Watch out!' Patrick shouted but was not addressing me but somewhere through the trees in the opposite direction to the lane. He glanced down at me. 'It was a shotgun,' he said in more conversational tones. 'Stay right there for a minute.'

I watched him walk towards where the sound of the shot had come from and then disappear from sight into what might be a hollow. It became strangely silent: not even a twig moved. Then, after a couple of minutes or so, I heard feet brushing through leaves and Patrick returned from a slightly different direction.

'Whoever it was made off at the run which they wouldn't have done if they worked here and were after vermin,' he said as I got to my feet. 'Anyway, I don't think they were firing at us and it was probably just a poacher but you wouldn't really expect people like that around here. Security must be fairly lousy. It'll be interesting to see if anyone arrives to investigate.'

'There must be miles of boundry walls to watch,' I pointed out.

'Yes, I suppose one mustn't expect too much.'

We waited for a little while but no one came so we started off again heading for the third location, the hidden valley. This was also accessible from the lane, which according to the information we had been given was historic and originally one of three linked carriage drives which connected all the entrances, two of which had subsequently been closed.

Roughly half a mile farther on, the ground dipped steeply on the left hand side of the lane and we turned off onto a wide sandy path that led downwards, curving between the pines. It was very sheltered here and the sun was hot on our backs. Quite soon the trees gave way to scrubby birch and willows and then petered out altogether and we stopped, gazing out over what had once been a quarry or gravel pit. Pools of water, coloured a poisonous greeny-blue, lay between heaps of stones and round boulders, the latter looking as though they might have been dislodged and rolled down from the steep sides. The whole area, probably some twenty-five acres, but that was a guess as the piles of rocks could screen other parts, was quite barren; scarcely a stunted plant or blade of grass grew.

'Well, I suppose they had to call it something that sounded interesting,' Patrick commented.

'It's a horrible place,' I said, reminded of the 'so horrible a place', the Great Grimpen Mire on Dartmoor that Sir Arthur Conan Doyle wrote about in *The Hound of the Baskervilles.*

'It's going to be used for the bit in the story where the three captured soldiers are tortured and then shot,' Patrick explained.

'In graphic and revolting detail, I suppose,' I said.

'Fraid so. I heard someone say he was thrilled to bits with the echoes for screaming.' He let out a terrible yell, making me jump out of my skin for the second time that morning and again sending up all the birds. It resounded eerily off the cliff faces and its perpetrator provided a full stop by lobbing a large stone into one of the pools. Water fountained upwards and I half expected to see a slimy nameless *thing* emerge from the depths.

'This is my not kind of place at all,' I said. 'Shall we go?'

Soberly, Patrick surveyed his surroundings. 'You know, if those location bods had been assigned to find a sniper's idea of heaven they couldn't have done better. I mean, look at it. From the map it would appear that the lane runs most of the way along the rim on that side, so there's good fast access, with thick vegetation to provide cover. You'd need all the King's horses and all the King's men to provide any kind of security net. I know what'll happen: I'll give it nought out of ten from a safety point of view and Martin Longton will simply say the film must come first. We'd better go shopping on the way back and buy everyone a bullet-proof vest.'

'Romanov was shot between the eyes,' I recollected.

'I suppose we could all make like Ned Kelly,' he said gloomily.

'No, sorry, tell Foster I'm not prepared to pretend to be a criminal profiler,' Patrick said. 'I'm quite happy to lend him any assistance I can in my particular field but that's all. Besides, as you said yourself, I don't have the time now, especially as it looks as though I'll be back here tomorrow. But I'm fit enough to drive now so if that's what you want to do then carry on. You're good at ferreting out things that policemen miss.'

We were on our way back to where we had parked the car.

'Lunch?' I suggested.

'Absolutely. A pub that has homemade steak and mushroom pie with a big pile of chips followed by sticky toffee pudding and cream. You know something? I think I've lost weight since starting this lark: I had to do up my belt on a tighter hole this morning.'

'There's a car parked next to ours,' I told him, stopping and taking the little binoculars from my bag.

In the distance the two vehicles could clearly be seen, my concern only because there were just the two cars in the large car park, and the juxtaposition seemed a little odd.

'Can you see the reg?' Patrick asked.

'No.' I gave him the binoculars. 'It's a silver hatchback of some kind.'

He took a look. 'Someone's sitting in the driving seat.'

'They've probably spotted us by now.'

'Okay, we won't get too silly about this and break out the culverin. Behave naturally but be on your guard.'

We carried on for a short distance and then Patrick's mobile phone rang. It was James Carrick, who told us he was sitting in his car next to ours and watching out for us through small binoculars.

'It's business, I'm afraid,' he said after we had met and greeted one another. 'It took about thirty phone-calls but I've finally found you.'

Patrick made a play of examining his tax disc and the tread on one of his tyres.

The DCI laughed. 'If I'd wanted to arrest you I wouldn't have come alone. No, I'm here because there's been a serious crime on my patch that appears to tie in with what you're doing here. A man called Melvin Lockyer has been found murdered. I understand he was the film's scriptwriter.'

My ears roared and I must have looked a bit strange for I was taken to James's car and made to sit in the front passenger seat.

'D'you feel faint?' James asked.

'I'm all right now,' I said, trying to believe it.

'You're not the fainting sort,' Patrick worriedly. 'Come to think of it the last time you fainted you were pregnant with Justin. You're not – '

'No,' I said. 'I promised I'd warn him if anything else happened and I didn't.' The words were somehow strangled in my throat. Then the tears flowed and I could not remember feeling more wretched in my whole life. Someone had died and it was my fault.

I discovered later that the men had not been able to make

out, initially, what I had said but had both come to the same conclusion, that the stress of the overall situation had been too much for me. Their pragmatic response to the immediate problem was probably what I would have done myself in similar circumstances; a sympathetic and rapid removal to a warm environment, a small bracer of brandy followed by a hot meal.

'Better?' Patrick enquired gently when I had been able to eat most of my lunch. The pair had demolished huge portions of the longed-for steak and mushroom pie while James had done his best to take my mind off his news with an account of the various disasters the building alterations had caused at the nick.

'I'm feeling sickeningly guilty,' I whispered. They both looked blank so I repeated what I had said earlier.

'Ingrid, you mustn't blame yourself,' James said. 'This case has been widely reported in the national press, including someone taking a shot at Patrick. It was up to the man himself whether he stayed put or not. And of course I have yet to establish there is a connection.'

The use of the personal pronoun caused Patrick and me to display an even deeper interest.

'That's why I'm here,' James explained. 'It was you two, or Ingrid rather, who first suggested a connection between Romanov's death and that of Taylor. Oh, and now there's been a murder in three different police authorities the boss has fixed it that I should be in overall charge. It'll make a change from trying to work in the middle of a building site.'

'That's good news,' Patrick said. 'The first thing you really have to write in your little black book is that someone let off a shotgun while we were doing a recce and, as far as we know, not a soul from security came to check up what was going on.'

'I shall raise hell,' Carrick vowed.

'Have you been to see Foster?'

128

'Yes, on the way in. God, he's a changed man. Looks really ill to me but I didn't like to ask.'

'Where are you staying?'

'Nowhere yet. I've only just got here.'

'You'll need somewhere to work from too.'

'Nat's offered me all the facilities I need. To be frank I think it would be better if he left the Romanov side of things entirely to me and got on with his other work overload.'

'I suggest you stay at our hotel near the film studio,' Patrick said. 'Then we can have regular exchanges of ideas in the evenings you're free. Not only that, if you interview people, film crews and so on, you'll have an excuse to keep a presence at the filming of *Blood and Anger* without travelling a long way – and Wrotherly's only just down the road.'

'You think that's important?' Carrick asked.

'There's every chance this character has infiltrated the set-up.'

Carrick looked thoughtful for a moment and then said, 'Well, I sincerely hope not but Joanna *has* asked me to get Rik Harrison's autograph should I get within a mile of him.'

8

As a professional writer the expression 'eaten up with guilt' had always struck me as being a cliché to be avoided but now it was happening to me, a real sensation of gnawing despair and misery at the knowledge that I had failed Melvin Lockyer. We had not met but I had warmed to him during our telephone conversation and he had genuinely tried to help me. The thought of him being cold-bloodedly gunned down by an unseen and unknown enemy when a phone-call from me could have saved him was more than I could bear.

The true circumstances of Lockyer's death were far worse, something I discovered for myself the next morning when I picked up a newspaper. The latest killing had caused a sensation in the media and there were strident calls for the film to be abandoned. David Goodheim was adamant he would do nothing of the kind and was on record bellowing, 'I don't care whether this guy was guilty or not of what happened in Northern Ireland but he's a goddamned serial killer now!' Quite a few would agree with this sentiment for Melvin Lockyer's body had been found in his garage at home, hanged and disembowelled.

Patrick, who later told me he had already been in possession of the full details courtesy of Carrick, removed the newspaper from the breakfast table – I had been merely staring at it sightlessly after reading the first couple of paragraphs – saying, 'Do you think it would be a good idea for you to go home?'

I focused my gaze on him. 'Do you?'

He made a helpless gesture with his hands. 'I think you ought to decide.'

'I did try to ring him,' I said. 'I've just remembered. The day before yesterday. The number was unobtainable so he must have already been dead and his phone had been damaged in some way.'

'I should mention that to James.'

'More coffee?'

'Please. Ingrid . . . '

'I'll stay,' I whispered. 'You can travel to the ends of the Earth but your mental baggage always goes with you.'

He smiled. 'Good, I'd rather you were here. Especially if you come with me and hold my hand when I have my stitches out in – ' he glanced at his watch, ' – three-quarters of an hour's time. We must move.'

He was only half-joking: this soldier of mind has no affinity whatsoever with splinters, stitches and needles generally. 'Then to Wrotherly Hall?' I enquired.

'I shall have to check. You know, I'm really glad James is on the job. It's just what this investigation needs; a bloody-minded Scotsman with real clout.'

Carrick, who must have realised that his appointment was partly political but no doubt was as keen to prevent another death as catch the murderer, arrived at Wrotherly Hall later that same morning, all bells and whistles, just as filming was about to start. It was impossible to tell what was going through Martin Longton's mind as he watched the arrival of two squad cars, one van and a Land Rover towing a trailer that looked as though it contained four-legged representatives of the Mounted Branch. But when the racket had died away he collapsed in a chair with a resignation that was terrible to behold.

The half dozen men in muddy combat gear – I had thought this was supposed to be an undercover mission but who was I to query it? – who had been rehearsing sneaking through the reeds by the edge of the lake now floundered to a standstill and stood around waiting for everything to resume. One of them pretended to pot an over-flying pigeon with his dummy rifle. The camera crew worked on, someone making last-minute adjustments to the rails that the camera dolly was to travel along. I noticed that the VT operator, who would normally tape rehearsals and takes to be played back through the director's monitor, had turned his video camera on the visitors and was busy recording everyone getting out of the vehicles and the unloading of the horses.

Carrick went straight over to the director, a feat similar to that when Joan of Arc unerringly found the Dauphin after he had deliberately concealed himself in a mêlée of French nobles. 'Good morning, Mr Longton. I'm Detective Chief Inspector James Carrick and I've been put in overall charge of these cases. I don't intend to interrupt filming but would be grateful for a word later. Meanwhile we'll have a look round and talk to those people who are free.'

He had been, I have to admit, well briefed by us.

The two men shook hands, Longton looking hugely relieved and everyone went back to work. One of the muddy 'soldiers' gave Carrick a Gilbert and Sullivan salute and received an even better one back. Rik Harrison was not feeling very well today with a slight stomach upset and was only doing close-ups so it was the lot of his stand-in to get amongst the dirty stuff.

The security plan seemed to be working and there were some twenty-four people patrolling the grounds, not counting the police. Tomorrow, work would continue up in the woods in the vicinity of the 'ruined bothy' and the day after that, weather permitting, everything would be transferred to the Hidden Valley for another one and a half to two days' work. Other exterior shots involving helicopter chases and yet more shoot-outs would be filmed somewhere up in Lincolnshire but Rik's presence was not required there as an area of the quarry had been earmarked for those scenes involving him and Jaquie and the whole thing would be married up during post-production work.

My self-imposed job was that of closely watching everyone for the slightest clue that they might not be all they should be. I could not stare at people all the time though and not too openly and the tedium of the endless waiting between takes, while lighting was adjusted, equipment moved into position or because of technical glitches, could only be countered by reading a book or going for a short walk.

Patrick had to eat his lunch, a sandwich, without being able to change out of his by now soaking wet uniform and then had to wait while Rik did a stint in front of the camera. It went without saying that the fragrant Jaquie Lauderdale did not appear in any of these scenes. She was probably somewhere in the West End having her nail extensions seen to, I surmised bitchily. Silly, I know, but the thought of Patrick being in intimate scenes with her, even simulated, was not doing much for my already overwrought state of mind. A hug and perhaps a little sympathy would have been a great help the night before but Patrick had fallen asleep as though pole-axed the moment he had got into bed.

During the lunch break Carrick had spoken to quite a few members of the film crew, Longton included. Neither Patrick nor I were involved, we would see him later that day anyway and had already told him everything we knew.

The day wore on, Special Effects exploded what was supposed to be a mine for several takes and the half dozen, who had worked their way out of the reed bed and up the hill, acquired corresponding layers of mud. Then at last, at around four-thirty, Longton called, 'It's a wrap!' and the long job of packing up everything began. Hot showers, of a sort, were available for those who had been in close contact with the scenery but I saw Rik being whisked away by car with his minder. He was still not very well and had had to keep dashing to the Portaloos.

Patrick had a shower on site, a hot bath back at the hotel followed by a tot of whisky and then felt considerably warmer. James arrived in the bar and bought him another, just to be on the safe side.

'Anything worth reporting?' Patrick enquired of the pair of us.

James said, 'I didn't get to talk to everyone and certainly didn't turn up any suspects. The rest will have to wait until tomorrow. Sorry, ladies should have been first. Ingrid?'

I had kept a small notebook inside the hardback novel that I had been reading on and off during the day and had brought it with me. 'Nothing concrete,' I said, 'and you must appreciate I know hardly any of these people's names and if I ask I'm sure it will arouse suspicion. There are a couple of technicians who seem a bit dodgy, a youngish one with red hair, who is unmistakable and creeps around like something only half alive and an older man with hardly any hair at all and a red nose who is always in a filthy temper. We don't have any kind of description of the suspect, do we?'

'No,' said Patrick and James together, the latter adding, 'I think your youngish zombie can be crossed off on the grounds of his youth. The man we're looking for must be around Taylor's age or older.'

James said, 'The one with no hair is Joe Billings. According to Central Records he gets any job he can get his hands on when he's not helping the police with their enquiries concerning greyhound racing scams. Anyone else you didn't like the look of?'

'The sound recordist, who I think is called Len, seems a bit – well – weird and the man who takes video recordings was getting you and your team on tape as you arrived. I can't think why he should want to do that.'

'I can,' Carrick said with a laugh. 'To flog it to the media and make a useful buck or two. But, thank you, I'll check up on both of them.'

'Can you remember if Len or the other bloke were around or not when Romanov was shot?' Patrick asked me.

'No. It was the first morning and everything was really manic. But someone must have been doing those jobs. How about you?'

'No, as you say, there was too much going on.'

'And how were you to know a crime was about to be committed?' Carrick said. 'What about the blokes you were with, Patrick?'

'We swapped notes between takes and I discovered that they were, without exception, professional actors, young men, taking the roles of the soldiers mentioned in the book. I was the odd one out – an ex-professional soldier trying to be an actor. Nothing of interest to you there, I'm afraid.'

James looked at me. 'I was going to share with you both the initial findings in connection with Melvin Lockyer's death. Would you rather Patrick and I went somewhere else to talk about it?'

'Not really,' I lied.

'Neither do we want you to feel obliged to listen to harrowing details,' Patrick commented.

I said, 'Thank you for your concern but the important thing is to catch his killer.' This sounded a bit trite and pompous but what else could I say? Inwardly, I was already writhing.

'Okay, but I'll keep it brief. Well, as you might already know, Lockyer lived in Nunstone, a village south of Bristol but actually more of a suburb these days now the city's expanded so much. He appears to have been quite successful in his work but lived modestly in a small, semi-detached Victorian house. Neighbours say he was quiet and pleasant but did not mix much especially since his wife, Sonia, left him

135

for another man at the end of June this year. She was the sociable one apparently and there might – *might*, this is hearsay – have been a drink problem. We haven't traced her and her new partner yet.

'As far as the scene of the crime's concerned there's not a lot of evidence to go on. No one had seen Lockyer for a few days but this was nothing unusual for when he had a job to do – I understand he was writing a screenplay for a new TV series – he worked all hours in his study, the third bedroom of the house, and only went out to buy groceries and sometimes for a pint at the pub. But his next door neighbour did call round three days ago – something to do with the promise of the loan of a lawnmower – and found the front door ajar. Apparently it's not visible from the road because of an over-grown hedge. There was no sign of Lockyer but as he'd already said to this chap to help himself to the mower when he wanted it he went into the garage where it was kept and found the body.'

'Were there signs of a struggle in the house?' Patrick asked when Carrick paused.

'Yes, but only upstairs where the neighbour didn't go. The study was smashed up. So there was nothing to warn him of the state of affairs when he opened the garage door.' James cleared his throat. 'Obviously, I wasn't the investigating officer at that stage but I've seen photographs. I'll spare Ingrid the details but it seems that he was strung up from a big hook in a roof beam and disembowelled after, or very shortly before, death. There's one footprint in the blood on the floor made by some kind of training shoe, probably a size ten and several others leading away to the side door of the garage and they then peter out. As far as fingerprints go Lockyer's are all over the house, which wasn't all that clean, and the garage was like most people's – dusty and greasy and with the junk of ages – so no joy there either. There was so much stuff in there his car was parked in the drive. Just enough open space in the middle to – well, commit the crime.'

'Size ten feet and strong enough to lift someone up to hang them,' Patrick mused. 'He's a big man then. Or had the victim been made to stand on something that was kicked away?'

'There was nothing at the crime scene like that,' Carrick answered. 'Unless the murderer took it away with him.'

'And the hook – was it the kind of thing someone might use to help lift an engine or gearbox out of a car?'

'I would say so. Lockyer couldn't be described as heavy-weight though at just over eleven stone.'

'To get him down the stairs without leaving any evidence of a struggle means he must have rendered him unconscious first.'

'Or the victim got away from the inital attack and ran down-stairs under his own steam. Or he could have heard someone on the ground floor and then fled back upstairs to get away from a threatening stranger and was followed and overpowered.'

I said, 'You don't run upstairs and into a theoretical dead-end unless you have a weapon of some kind there.'

'There was nothing found that with any stretch of the imag-ination could have been used as a weapon,' Carrick said. 'I reckon someone sneaked up on him. The neighbour said that none of the doors ever seemed to be locked when he'd gone round there on previous occasions. I get the impression he was always borrowing tools.'

'Had no one spotted a strange car parked nearby?' Patrick wanted to know.

'It doesn't look like it but house-to-house enquiries are still going on. Our only hope at the moment is the piece of rope used which is being examined to see if the killer left any fibres from his clothes or DNA on it. Who knows, he might have taken a bit of skin off a finger or something like that.'

'Any old rope?' Patrick said.

'Any old rope,' Carrick confirmed. 'The killer could have found it chucked into a corner of the garage.'

'Yes, but would he have taken his victim in there and then searched around for something with which to dispatch him?'

'I get your point. No, that's unlikely. He could well have had a snoop round the garage first though.'

'Do you know the name of the man his wife went off with?' I enquired.

'Unfortunately not.'

'Lockyer told me that a woman rang to tell him that John Taylor was dead and asked him not to make it known to the media until after the funeral. He said she did not say who she was and whispered as though she had not wanted to be overheard. Do we know if Taylor had any female relatives? Or a wife or a girlfriend? Whoever it was doesn't appear to have lived with him.'

James asked for a page from my notebook and wrote this query down. 'Why did she phone Lockyer?' he asked himself aloud. 'I appreciate that he was the scriptwriter but were he and Taylor in regular contact?'

'Lockyer said he'd met him just once and had spoken to him a few times over the phone,' I told him. 'He hadn't liked him very much so the answer to that question must be no.'

James gave me the full benefit of his chilly Nordic blue eyes. 'Ingrid, I have the distinct feeling that you're endeavouring to lead me somewhere.'

'Suppose the woman who rang Lockyer and did not give her name or her relationship to Taylor, which is really strange when you think about it, and also whispered, was disguising her voice because she was Lockyer's wife.'

'That is a very large leap in the dark,' said the DCI after a long, thought-filled silence. 'But I have to say it deserves consideration. You think the murderer could have deliberately set out to seduce Lockyer's wife?'

'Perhaps hoping to get all kinds of insider information on other people connected with the film,' I said, thinking on my feet. 'It's possible.'

James took it a step further. 'Everything would then point to her knowing he killed Taylor.'

'So is she bad, mad, or just plain stupid?' I said and there was another contemplative silence.

'Romanov was shot,' Patrick said, ticking off on his fingers. 'Taylor had already been beaten to death with a heavy doorstop and now Lockyer has been hanged and drawn. Our man seems to favour variety.'

'And has enormous vanity,' I added.

'I thought you said you weren't a criminal profiler,' Patrick said with a smile.

I had a sudden blazing thought. 'Rik's been ill all day with a stomach upset.'

Carrick grabbed his mobile phone. 'Do you have a number for him?'

But Harrison was on the mend, dosed with Imodium, and spoke to Carrick personally, blaming his problem on a seafood Chinese meal he had eaten the evening before. He would, he said, be absolutely fine for work the next day but would arrive a little later as he had to do a promotional photo-call first thing in the morning arranged by his agent.

Patrick groaned when told of this and said, 'That means he's going to ring me very shortly and ask if I mind getting muddy all over again.'

Sure enough, a couple of minutes later, his mobile rang.

The next morning was rather wet but, due to the nature of the filming, the circumstances enhanced, rather than detracted, from what was going on even though shooting did not take place while it was actually raining. As it was there were filters on the cameras which would make it look as though it was

139

night-time with a bright moon. Patrick did point out that no one in their right mind would undertake an undercover military raid under such conditions but was told that that was how films were made.

By two fifteen that afternoon and when Rik Harrison had still not put in an appearance – it mattered not at all as those being filmed were completely unrecognisable due to mud and camouflage cream – the six raiders had almost reached the bothy where they would be taken by surprise and some of them 'captured'. Enter seven or eight armed ruffians pretending to be members of the IRA. During rehearsals, with the fight director still working on the choreography, the ambushers got a trifle over-enthusiastic, a couple of punches were thrown and, suddenly faced with an orchestrated counteroffensive they found themselves arrayed in a neat row, hands and feet tied together with their own bootlaces.

'Not like that?' I heard Patrick say innocently, to laughter.

He was, I felt, trying to take everyone's mind off murder.

Quite a while later Harrison's presence was vital as close-up shots of him engaged in hand-to-hand fighting were required. I saw Martin Longton pacing up and down agitatedly while Mike, the assistant director, tried to get hold of him.

'Do you know what this promotional photo-call that Deena O'Leary arranged was all about?' I asked the script supervisor, or continuity girl, Hayley. She and I had become quite friendly.

'Not a clue,' she replied. 'But it does happen. I worked on a film once where the female lead disappeared for three days to model sexy beachwear for a top Italian fashion house. Completely in breach of her contract of course but when it comes to the crunch you can't touch them or they might go away and never come back. Actors have walked out of films before and they're rich enough to pay any penalties. She always insisted on champagne and fresh flowers in her caravan every day too, the bitch.'

'But Rik's a comparatively new boy.'

'Not taking it too seriously though, is he?' she responded crisply.

Thought about like that, no, he was not.

Carrick had spent the day collating evidence from all three murders, mostly by sitting in front of a computer screen and talking to people over the phone. He was continuing to send a contingent to Wrotherly Hall in the interests of crime prevention for which David Goodheim, still hovering fairly nervously on this side of the Atlantic, was grateful and delighted. The grapevine indicated that he was highly impressed with the Scottish policeman but less so with the security company he had hired and had offered to pay for the police presence. Carrick told us himself that evening that he had conveyed his appreciation of the gesture but reasoned that, as filming was fairly soon due to end at Wrotherly, it would not be necessary.

'What time did Harrison finally turn up?' he now asked Patrick, who had been giving him an account of the day's events.

'At three-thirty,' Patrick said. 'He said something about being on a boat on the Thames and there was a mistake with the time of the tide and it took much longer than anticipated to get back. I think Longton got what he wanted though, which is the important thing. How have you got on?'

James pulled a wry face. 'Well, I think I've got most of it inside my head now. One thing at least has been achieved today. We discovered that John Taylor did have a wife but they were divorced six years ago and she went to Australia to help look after her mother who had gone to live with her sister and brother-in-law. Mum eventually died but she stayed over there and I understand has never been back, has no intention of doing do and has never contacted her ex. So we can rule her out – she wasn't the one who rang Lockyer. It's more difficult to find out if there were any other women in Taylor's life as, before going to Cornwall, he lived at various addresses in London, mostly rented accommodation. Sometimes he used the name on his birth certificate, Rundle, and other times Taylor, under which name, as everyone knows, he wrote the book, although Patrick has also discovered he was never in the armed services and probably got the details from a relative who was.'

'Sorry, I couldn't find out who it was,' Patrick said.

'It probably wouldn't have helped much,' Carrick said and then continued, 'I've made it a priority to trace Lockyer's wife, Sonia. It may well be that she's completely uninvolved but I'm half hoping that she is and it'll give us a lead. I've sent my new sergeant Lynn Outhwaite to talk to the Lockyer's neighbours.'

'What happened to Bob Ingrams?' I asked.

'He retired early on health grounds. Heart trouble. Despite his doctor telling him to diet, and some success a while back, like Morse's sergeant he seemed to live mostly on egg and chips.'

'Is Lynn gorgeous?'

Patrick glared at me, scandalised by my insinuating nosiness.

James gave me a cool smile. 'I know I once did have an affair with my sergeant but at least I eventually married her. But this one's off-limits: she's the Deputy Chief Constable's daughter and I do have a mortgage.'

'Can we get back to business now?' Patrick said heavily.

'I just like to know what's what,' I told him defensively.

'She writes books,' Carrick said to him in a stage-whisper. 'Writers have to know everything and it's why she's been so good at solving some of my cases for me.'

I blew him a kiss.

We got back to business, Carrick saying, 'There's still no real evidence, other than the obvious one of the victims all being connected with the film, that they were killed by the same man. We've established, or Patrick has, that the so-called baddie mentioned in the book is one Samuel Whitaker. Someone called Sam was involved with Vladimir Romanov. Surely there must be a photograph of this character somewhere in his regiment's records even though the outfit's all about covert operations. I have to say I've tried to obtain one but get referred from pillar to post. Seeing the guy is now supposed to be a copper-bottomed hitman what the hell's going on?' The last couple of sentences of this had been addressed to Patrick.

'I'll phone a few contacts,' he was promised.

'Thanks. It's imperative to build up a description. Okay, we know he has size ten feet, or thereabouts, and is strong. One assumes he's tall. The man Teddy and his mother saw in the twilight at Taylor's home in Tredennis was big and strong-looking. Teddy said he didn't like him and that's interesting. I've noticed before with people like Teddy who have child-like minds that they also possess child-like intuition. I've no doubt that this person he saw was up to no good.'

I said, 'The murderer must have had second thoughts. He'd killed Taylor earlier with the doorstop and then came back later to move the body from the bathroom to the bottom of the stairs, after which he cleaned the bathroom. Did he do that to try to cover his tracks? Taylor was the first victim, after all.'

'He could have seen Teddy go into the house,' Patrick suggested.

'That means he was still very close by,' Carrick said.

I said, 'He could have merely gone away to get some cleaning materials and was coming back when he saw Teddy. That's why he then waited until dark.'

'But surely, not knowing that Teddy was terrified of getting into trouble for going next door when he'd been forbidden to, he would have expected him to have raised the alarm,' James said.

'There would have been nothing to indicate that Teddy had actually been indoors,' I said. 'The front door was stuck and you had to go round the back.'

'Would Whitaker, or whoever it was, have the brass neck to go into the shop next door and buy cleaning materials?' Patrick said. 'For all anyone knows, the woman there might have come face to face with him.'

'She *was* interviewed at length again,' Carrick stated. 'Nothing like that came out of it. I don't know about you but if I'd done someone in I think I'd hop in my car and go and buy a bucket and scrubbing brush somewhere else, not next door.'

'If I did someone in I'd make sure there wasn't any mess,' Patrick muttered.

'It figures that there wasn't much in the way of cleaning materials at the cottage,' I commented. 'The place was pretty dirty.'

'All this to-ing and fro-ing with buckets and mops that no one in a small village seems to have noticed,' Carrick fretted. 'Bloody hell.'

'It's one of those places where nearly everyone's out to work all day,' I said.

Patrick asked, 'Did anyone see the man who shot Romanov?'

'Nope.'

'That's incredible!'

'If he was pretending to be a window-cleaner . . . ' Carrick said with a shrug. 'More buckets and cloths.'

'Not only that, these long-range weapons break down into small parts which can be quickly assembled and virtually transported in your coat pockets. We're talking about someone who merges perfectly into his background, which is exactly what an undercover soldier is supposed to do.' Patrick struck a clenched fist into his other palm. 'Finding this man is my speciality and should be down to me instead of which I'm obliged to ponce around in front of film cameras.'

'Talk to Rik,' I urged him. 'Explain the problem. Anyway, there's no reason why he can't do more of the work himself now that he's better.'

'Including of course the bedroom scenes with – who is it? – Jaquie Lauderdale? Lucky sod,' said James and then seemed to sense a certain atmosphere between his two companions and, as it was his round, went over to the bar.

With regard to Sonia Lockyer, it transpired that the people who lived directly across the road from them were able to give the police quite a lot of useful information. Henry and Isobel Kent had both taken early retirement from an art print and picture-framing business in Bath and were in the process of selling their house as well and moving to northern Italy. At one time, the two women had been close friends but Sonia's job as headteacher of a primary school in a deprived area of Bristol had proved too stressful for her, culminating in a nervous breakdown. She had started drinking, partly, Isobel thought, because Melvin was unsympathetic and not at all supportive. He could, she said, be selfish and was really only interested in his work. There were no grown-up children or relatives living nearby who could have helped Sonia either.

Isobel maintained that Sonia had changed completely from a fun-loving person into someone she hardly recognised. She had returned to work but vandalism by children from other schools, violent parents and a disastrous Ofsted report had driven her to resign. She had stayed at home, drinking. Isobel had tried to help her but this had been classed as interference by both Melvin and Sonia and the friendship had come to an end. Then, shortly afterwards, Sonia had left, putting suitcases into a car driven by a man, someone Isobel did not know.

It was only quite by chance, Mrs Kent told Sergeant Outhwaite, who sent an email to Carrick containing this information mid-morning the following day, that she had witnessed her one-time friend's departure. She had been keen to emphasise that she was not a woman who peered around curtains at her neighbours' comings and goings. It was a Friday and the man who had a round selling fresh fish from a van was later than normal and Isobel was getting a little agitated as she did not want to miss him but had a dental appointment. Henry, as usual, she had grumbled, had been out playing golf. In an effort to see if the fish-man was on his way she had opened an upstairs window wide, leaned out to look up the road and been just in time to see a car arrive at the house opposite. Sonia had hurried from the house, as well as she was able with the cases she was carrying, put them in the boot and been driven away without a backward glance. The driver had not got out to help her. He was quite a big man, Isobel was sure, and appeared cramped in the driving seat but she could not give a proper description of him as the window had been wound up and all she could see were mostly reflections. She had not noted the vehicle's registration or make and could not remember the colour.

'It's not much to go on but better than nothing,' James finished by saying when he rang me with this news.

'Do we know exactly which Friday this happened?' I asked.

'She thought towards the end of June this year.' James uttered a vibrant Gaelic expletive. 'It was Saturday the 24th when Taylor was murdered, wasn't it?'

It was and I had a nasty feeling she was dead too.

146

9

The heavy showers continued and overnight the rain became continuous and torrential causing the old gravel pit to flood. According to the estate manager of Wrotherly Hall the water would take two to three days to drain away even if it did not rain again so work was transferred to the studio to film other scenes. Security would remain light and, on Carrick's advice, all administrative staff would be screened.

I had no idea if the change of venue would mean that Patrick would be involved in sequences involving clinches with Jaquie Lauderdale and suddenly did not care, finding myself now hugely indifferent to the whole project and yet at the same time worn down by being worried sick. Patrick, of course, was mentally conditioned to a job involving stress and a certain amount of tedium and, bound by a contract or not, I knew he would see it through. I hoped I was adult enough to realise that any man with red blood in his veins would relish the chance to mingle a little with La Lauderdale, never mind the quite ridiculous amount of money he was now being paid.

So, for the studio work at least, and with no real rôle now that Patrick was able to drive, I decided to stay away. I would go home and then pay another visit to Tredennis. I had pondered over this before but *had* Sonia Lockyer phoned her husband from there? And if so, why? Had she done so on the orders of someone else, perhaps the man – who may or may not have been Samuel Whitaker – with whom she had gone off? I was convinced she was dead: no evidence of course, just a feeling.

Another question mark concerned the likelihood of a man failing to recognise his own wife's voice over the phone if she made a good job of disguising it. On the grounds that I have known men not to recognise their own wives when they were standing not twenty yards from them in the street I decided to undertake a little experiment and dialled Patrick's mobile number.

'Gillard,' rapped out that well-remembered voice. He was a little out of breath.

'Darling,' I cooed breathily through my handkerchief. 'It's your little Snuggems. So *wonderful* last night. You were *fantastic*. Are you bringing some champers and your lovely big willy back here this evening?'

There was a silence and then Patrick, his voice higher than normal, if not slightly choked, said, 'Look, I think you've dialled the wrong number.'

I giggled in girlie fashion, shrieked 'Whoops!' and hung up.

Yes, so it was perfectly possible for a man not to recognise his own wife's voice. And did I have sex on the brain, or what?

The deluge had moved through the West Country where it was cool and blustery with the odd dark curtain of rain over the moors. One of these manifested at Lydtor just as I arrived at home and I got quite wet in the few yards from the taxi to the front door. No one was in, the three older children at school and Carrie out somewhere with Victoria. I took the opportunity to empty my suitcase, loaded the washing machine, repacked with fresh clothing and then sorted through the post. There was nothing that demanded instant attention.

With a mug of coffee I went into the new conservatory and sat in one of the wicker chairs. It was my pride and joy: not for me carpets and silk foliage and flowers but a tile-floored real plant heaven of ferns, palms, weeping figs and orchids. No, I did not want to move house.

Again, I thought about Sonia Lockyer and the way she had left home. It seemed that Samuel Whitaker might have got to know Vladimir Romanov before killing him and there was a chance he had befriended, or seduced, Sonia and persuaded her to go away with him. Was this how he worked and he got some kind of kick out of the deception? Had Melvin Lockyer written about 'Jack' without being aware that he already knew him? Despite the neighbour's statement that the house was often wide open it would explain why there had only been a disturbance in one room when Lockyer had been murdered, the study where presumably he had been working. I could picture the killer calling up the stairs and then being invited to go up.

Patrick though, had been fired at without any befriending preamble. There had hardly been time. Had panic set in due to the arrival of someone new on the scene who might just see through the pretext? The killer had missed, unless it had been intended only as a warning. As far as Sonia herself went, it was conceivable that such a vulnerable woman would respond to any sympathetic overtures especially if that person was known to her already. But all this must have been going on for some time. How long, for Heaven's sake, had the making of this film been on the cards? From my own experience I knew that the selling of film rights could occur a long time before anything started to happen, even if it ever did. And the first professional involved was usually the scriptwriter, in this case Lockyer.

'Everything points to this person working inside the film industry these days and not gallivanting around the globe killing people for money,' I said out loud. 'He's only gone back to his old ways now because someone's making a film about *him*.'

Why not though, target Rik Harrison himself, or Martin Longton or even David Goodheim?

The question was easy to answer if one took into consideration the fact that those people were not so accessible to him so that he could play the befriending game, which could even provide a bigger thrill than the act of murder. So he had to target smaller fry. It seemed to me that we were talking about someone seriously off his head.

Sonia might have been useful if she knew, through Melvin, of other people connected with the proposed movie. But weren't folk like stand-ins and so forth not engaged until there was a definite date for the start of filming?

'He's right in the middle of things,' I said to my variegated *Ficus benjamina*. 'Right in the centre, right from the beginning. And as he'd been pretending to Romanov that he wanted to get into films he had to kill him first, just before work started.'

All this would have been terribly risky as Romanov knew all kinds of people connected with the film industry whom the pair of them could have bumped into when they went to the Irish pub, Fanny O'Reilly's, but perhaps that was where the real kick came in, playing close to danger.

Or I might be completely on the wrong track.

As I would return before nightfall I planned to borrow back my own car, which Carrie uses when I am away or not actually needing it. She soon returned from her shopping trip to Tavistock and it soothed my guilty conscience to be told that Vicky's bothersome tooth had emerged and Matthew's torn ligament was on the mend although he was not yet able to participate in sport or PT. Katie was apparently still dreaming about ponies, literally, and I asked Carrie to tell her that there was no reason why she could not have one. We would talk about it soon. Patrick already has a horse that he rescued from being shot called Polar Bear, far too big for Katie yet, kept at livery. This gentle grey of sixteen and a half hands is aged but still quite capable of taking his saviour for sedate hacks around country lanes and on the Moor. Okay, I schemed, we could buy or rent a stable and field locally and look after him and the new pony ourselves, Patrick and Katie could go riding together and with a bit of luck everyone would be too happy, and exhausted, to want to move house.

I was not sure of my reasons for going back to the area of John Taylor's murder: it could even be the dishonourable one of the need to escape, distancing myself from *Blood and Anger* while kidding myself that I was doing something useful. I told myself that someone had to try to find out what had happened to the unfortunate Sonia and as James Carrick was heavily involved with trying to prevent anyone else being killed as well as catching his man it had better be me.

All I really wanted to do, of course, was stay at home and write.

Tredennis appeared to have suffered from minor flooding, gravel and earth washed into the road that wound through it. Ditches brimmed over with run-off from the surrounding fields, sending water in ripples down the hill into the centre of the village where a couple of cottages beside a stream had sandbags by their front doors. Otherwise nothing was different, not a living soul was in sight, nothing moved but a cat that had caught a small rodent of some kind and dashed away, belly close to the ground. This was, indeed, the classic dormant village.

Primrose Cottage slumbered on in its muddle of weeds, slipped slates and flaking paint but I drove straight on past both house and the shop next door: I had no intention of re-acquainting myself with either Teddy or his mother if I could help it. At the far end of the village street where the buildings petered out was an overgrown patch of land with the remains of brick walling that had once been the foundations of old-fashioned commercial greenhouses showing above the tall grass and thistles. I left the car there in order to explore this end of the village, mindful of glistening areas of small pieces of broken glass.

I went for a short walk and soon had seen it all; the adjacent pub, three cottages, two of which were protected from the wind and the outside world by high hedges, a gate that led into a large field, and a stone barn with sheets of plywood over the door and windows that had a For Sale sign on it. I headed for the pub in a quest for a late lunch and local gossip.

In complete and surprising contrast to most of the rest of Tredennis the whole place sparkled with cleanliness, the entrance hallway a treasure trove of antiques; furniture, brass and copperware, a table almost hidden by a superb arrangement of flowers. Another resided on the counter in the cosy lounge bar and it was the first hostelry I had been in for a very long time where you could not smell chips frying.

'Madam!' said an imposing figure behind the bar.

'Sir,' I responded. 'I congratulate you. What a wonderful surprise.'

He laughed and gave me a little bow. 'I do know what you mean – the village is a bit tatty now. But hopefully things will soon start to change. We were voted the best dining pub in Cornwall three weeks ago and these things do have a knock-on effect. Speaking personally, my feet haven't touched the ground since.'

I congratulated him, ordered a lemonade and orange juice with ice and then, speaking more quietly as I am not a trumpeting kind of person and we were not alone, said, 'Didn't having a sudden death in the village spoil things a bit?'

'Not at all! It gave folk two reasons for coming, didn't it? And now it seems it's a murder inquiry instead . . . ' He laughed again and rubbed a thumb and fingers together in an unmistakable and age-old gesture.

I found this hard-headedness gruesome and somewhat off-putting but asked if there was a chance of a sandwich.

'Naturally. Fresh crab from Padstow? Roast beef from Devon Rubies at Brentor? Eveything's locally sourced here. Or there's free-range cold roast chicken. All with salad grown in the Tamar valley.'

I settled for the crab and went to find myself a corner seat. There were two couples having lunch and a man on his own, probably a company rep, reading some kind of brochure over half a pint of beer.

My sandwiches arrived; proper bread, farm butter, the crab generously thick and luscious. When I had finished it seemed a good idea to ask a few more questions while ordering coffee.

'I'm not a ghoul,' I said when I had added a piece of chocolate gateau to my order. 'But was that poor chap who was killed a customer of yours?'

'No, I don't think so,' the man replied. 'He may well have been in with a crowd sometimes but I didn't recognise him from the picture that was in the paper. People say he was a quiet sort during the week but had a load of cronies from London at the weekends and they brought their own booze. . . and dope,' he finished by whispering.

'But where did all these people eat and sleep? The cottage is only small.' Quickly, I added, 'or looks to be from the outside.'

'They ate instant meals and slept on the floor, I expect,' said the man with a chuckle. 'They certainly didn't stay here. And you may depend the police would like to know who they were but according to those who live close to Primrose Cottage there was no one staying there the weekend he died. Or, as as we now know, was murdered. Someone went there though, didn't they?'

'You do accommodation here then.' At his words a ghostly tingle had crept up my spine.

'Indeed. And very nice the rooms are too. I'll show you when you've had your lunch, if you like.'

'Thank you. Did anyone stay here that particular weekend?'

He leaned across the bar with a twinkle in his faded blue eyes. 'Are you from the press?'

'No, I'm just trying to trace a woman's whereabouts.'

'That's all right then.' A slim green visitors' book that lay on one end of the bar was taken up and flipped through to the correct page. 'Yes, here we are. June 24th, wasn't it? Just three, a single lady, a Miss Jancis Wells – could she be the one you're looking for? – and a couple, a Mr and Mrs Lockyer.'

'Please tell me about the couple,' I requested.

'They arrived at around lunchtime on the Friday, the 23rd. Yes, I remember now – she went home before breakfast on the Sunday morning: a business appointment early the next day that she had to get ready for, or something. He stayed and had lunch here.'

'Can you remember what they looked like?'

'Now you *are* asking me. The wife'll know, she remembers faces better than I do. I'll get her to come through in a minute.'

The proprietors were, I quickly discovered, Bob and Joan Frappell and they had bought the little freehouse some ten years previously for a song when Frank had taken early retirement, sunk all their savings into it and concentrated on serving high quality food. Results had been slow to start with and any profits had been swallowed by the cost of improvements but now they were having to take on extra staff and had plans to expand.

'I remember those people quite well,' said Joan, who was blonde and homely. 'Probably because he, Mr Lockyer, asked if they could settle up on the Saturday morning, after breakfast, as they weren't quite sure whether they could stay another night. It sort of stuck in my mind. We usually get a bit cross when people do that as they'd originally booked for the two nights but we weren't that busy so it didn't really matter. But she paid with her credit card and I thought that a little odd too at the time. But perhaps it was his birthday and she was treating him. They did end up staying on the Saturday night, although she had to go off early on the Sunday morning to get ready for a meeting.'

'She went after breakfast?' I asked.

'No, before. There was just him for breakfast. He said he'd called a taxi for her for six-thirty. We didn't hear it but we're both quite heavy sleepers so could well not have done.'

'But she was here for dinner the night before?'

'No, they said they would eat out. They were out all day.'

'Were you up when they got back?'

'We'd only just gone to bed when I heard them come up the stairs. It was quite late – must have been after midnight. They had a key, you see.'

'Did you actually clap eyes on this lady after she paid you on the Saturday morning?'

Joan looked a little shocked. 'No, now you mention it – I didn't.' She turned to her husband. 'Did you, Bob?'

He had not either.

I asked for their descriptions. The woman had looked about forty-five, but seemed unwell so might have been younger, of medium height but a little overweight with mouse-brown hair and brown eyes. She had been very softly spoken with a slight Welsh accent. This fitted the description that Sonia Lockyer's one-time friend, Isobel, had given Sergeant Outhwaite and was the name that had been on the credit card. The man had been big and burly, his head shaven, and he had had a small black beard. He had apologised for wearing dark glasses all the time, explaining that it was not an affectation but an infection, making a joke of it. Both Frappells had found

155

him quite pleasant and Joan went so far as to describe him as 'a gentleman'. On an afterthought I asked if they could remember anything about the car they had arrived in and all they could tell me was that it was blue and had been hired.

I already knew from James that Melvin Lockyer had been thin, with bushy grey hair and five feet eight inches tall. There was no possibility therefore that Sonia had been with him. Whoever it had been could well have re-grown his hair now and shaved off the beard. The rest, other than his height and build, was still a mystery.

I asked them about the derelict nursery next door and they became very enthusiastic as they were soon hoping to buy the site, build holiday cottages on some of it together with a conservatory-type extension to the pub that would be a restaurant, and have plenty of space left for landscaped gardens.

After thanking them and duly inspecting the guest rooms, which, predictably, were charming and immaculate, I wished them well and left.

The wilderness of weeds and ruined glasshouses drew me. As with empty houses there is something about ruins, no matter how humble: they do not have to have been a castle or great church. Even a broken-down garden shed seems still to possess a lingering echo of the old man who put away his lovingly oiled but worn-out garden tools for the last time. This place I was carefully picking my way through now had almost certainly been worked by a previous generation of Cornish flower and vegetable growers. As with what happened at Heligan, earlier gardeners than they may well have gone away to fight in the Great War and never returned.

Behind what appeared to have been a small boiler house, the chimney still standing, I came upon signs of more recent activity; a polytunnel had collapsed on to hundreds of plastic plant pots with the rotting remains of plants still in them.

Next to it a corrugated iron shed had gone down like a pack of cards. The weather then, perhaps, had finally put an end to all this.

The nettles were getting bothersome, forcing me, stung around the ankles, to retrace my steps for a short distance and try a different route. I found traces of what had been a brick path that led directly to the ruined greenhouses, daggers of glass lying on and sticking out of the ground everywhere, young trees growing through the splintered and rotting timber, the path then swinging around to the rear on a slightly convoluted route to the boiler house that I had been heading for originally. I passed the remains of two wooden sheds, tripped over an iron bar hidden in the grass when I stepped off the path to examine them and nearly tumbled into yet more broken glass.

I could not believe that Sonia Lockyer had been obliged to leave early in order to prepare for a work-related meeting. To my mind her departure by taxi the following morning was a myth, for even people who admit to not being light sleepers are usually woken by engines running and car doors slamming right outside their own homes during what in rural areas is otherwise a quiet time of the day. Anyway, Sonia had already resigned from her job by then and, according to Isobel, was not working and drinking heavily. I thought there was every chance that her male companion had returned to the weekend accommodation alone on the Saturday night and had made enough noise, albeit quietly, for two. Whatever the truth, June 24th, being near the Summer Solstice, would not have provided many hours of darkness during which someone could dispose of a body without being seen so if she was dead, if indeed her grave was right here, he would have had to move quickly.

By the boiler house I stopped and perched for a moment on a low wall to think. Towards the end of June the growth would have been practically as extensive as it was now but much more green and lush. Now, at the end of September, the grass had been flattened in places by the heavy rain and fluffy seeds were being blown about by the light wind but from a practical, *grave-digging*, point of view conditions were practically the same as they would have been then. Nettles or not, I began a search for disturbed ground.

Twenty minutes later, stung to hell and back, I had to admit defeat. Either nobody had done any digging or the rampant weeds; docks, bindweed and dandelions, had colonised any freshly turned ground and concealed it. I had given special attention to places that were out of sight of the road but could see nothing suspicious. Almost everywhere in fact, despite the recent rain, was bone-hard from decades of weather and neglect.

It was only when I went close to the boiler house that I realised that some of it was below ground, a stunted ash tree concealing broken stone steps littered with rubbish and dead leaves. I pushed my way through the foliage and peered down into the dinginess. There were eight or nine steps, it was difficult to tell exactly how many, and at the bottom, its lower edge in foul water that had collected there, was a wooden door. It was ajar. A dank sort of smell wafted up.

I went down, holding on to a metal handrail but not trusting it as it was actually quite loose in the wall. I had broken off a piece from a thin fallen branch as I wanted to use it to test the depth of the water. True enough, it was at least five inches deep, a layer of rotting matter at the bottom and concealed another step. It was black, fetid and utterly revolting. My boots were in Patrick's car.

Using the stick I succeeded in pushing the door open a little more and then it snapped. I went right down until I was almost in the water, managed to lean across the gap to

158

support myself on the wall at the side of the door and shone the light from my torch inside.

The boiler itself was at right angles to the basement within, sodden cinders and ashes on the floor in front of it. A shovel with a broken handle lay in the far corner. In the other corner were pieces of wood and old sacks that looked as though they might be mounded over something. The stench was ghastly.

I can face some things but nothing would have persuaded me to wade through that nameless liquid in just my shoes to ascertain what it was.

Bob listened gravely to my request and then disappeared with alacrity to look for his Wellingtons. A couple of minutes later we were walking back towards the boiler house.

'It could be that a stray dog's died in there,' he had said in response to my statement that I was convinced the basement contained a body. 'Went to ground like, under the pile of rubbish to try to keep warm.'

I agreed that this could be the case, really hoping that it was even though it would mean I had achieved nothing and asked, 'Don't children play on the site?'

'There aren't any really. Tredennis is a place where most of the folk are either career-focussed or retired. Except for poor Teddy, of course. The school closed donkey's ages ago. Yes, come to think of it there are two kiddies but they live right up the hill in a big house and their mum and dad aren't the sort to let them run wild around the village. Dear me, no. Young Susie's got her pony and the boy's at boarding school. Besides which, they've got umpteen acres of their own to play in.'

We arrived and Bob expressed amazement when I showed him the steps leading down.

'You know, I've walked around here planning this and that and never dreamed for a moment that this old building had a cellar. But when you think about it boiler houses were nearly always constructed like this so the coal could be delivered at ground level and then shovelled down a chute.'

'Do take care,' I urged him as he descended. I had given him my torch.

'Something's dead down here all right,' I heard him mutter as he waded unhesitatingly into the disgusting water.

A couple of minutes dragged by during which I could hear him sloshing around as he shifted the pieces of wood. Then he exclaimed hoarsely and almost immediately appeared in the doorway. Grabbing hold of the doorframe he took a couple of deep breaths and said, 'You're right, Miss Langley. But God alone knows whether it was a man or woman – all that's left of the poor soul is just rags and bones.'

Sonia then, another person I had never met, was dead. I discovered that I was shivering violently and could not stop. Bob insisted on taking me tenderly back to the pub, where he sat me down and gave me a cup of tea. He then dialled 999 while I phoned James Carrick on my mobile.

I knew that secretly, in his staunch Scottish heart, James was not pleased with me. Friendship apart and polite remarks to the contrary, he was annoyed. It was not the first time that this amateur sleuth had sallied forth and gone straight to the truth of some matter, rubbishing hours of exhaustive police-work. Even if he had voiced his resentment, which was unlikely unless he carried on drinking whisky at the rate he was right now, it would have been a waste of breath to point out to him that no one from his own particular patch had been involved with investigations in Cornwall: his attitude would have been that he was in overall charge and the buck stopped with him.

On the following morning, and subsequent to making an official statement to Devon and Cornwall Police at Tavistock, I had returned to the South East. The Surrey fire brigade had been persuaded to pump out the quarry, the sun had shone and hopefully, shooting would resume early the following morning. This much I had learned from Patrick when I had called him with the news.

The three of us, as usual, met up in the hotel bar before dinner. I thought Patrick still looked tired – lots more rushing around or simulated bonking? – James under strain and, as just indicated, drinking rather too much whisky.

'James, old man,' said Patrick gently, reading the other man's mind like a book. 'All that has to appear in your records is that a member of the public happened upon a dead body. Ingrid isn't trying to prove anything here.'

No, I was just trying to hurry things along a little so we could relax and, or, bloody well go home.

'But if she'd got herself killed it would appear in my records, would it?' Carrick retorted, his Scots accent more pronounced than usual. 'Who's to say this maniac didn't follow her down there?'

'I appreciate it that you want to keep me all of apiece,' I said. 'But he didn't. He's working right here on the film.'

'You don't *know* that,' James said.

Which particular member of Cornwall CID was going to be nailed to the signpost at the crossroads near Tredennis? I wondered and merely smiled and murmured, 'No, of course not. Has it been confirmed that the body *is* that of Sonia Lockyer?'

Carrick emptied his glass and placed it on the table. 'The remains are those of a woman in the right sort of age group and she was probably strangled. That's all that's been ascertained so far as the body, as you know, was badly decomposed. The PM's being done at Derriford Hospital in Plymouth some time today so I should get the initial findings any time now. They sent for Mrs Lockyer's dental records but whether they've arrived or not . . . ' He shrugged, picked up the glass and said to Patrick, 'Will you have another?'

'No, thanks. I shall spoil my appetite.'

'No, I'm fine,' I said in response to the query.

'I might have a wee dram more.' James went across to the bar.

'It's all right,' Patrick whispered when I gave him a worried look. 'He's been on the go for at least sixteen hours and is stressed up to the eyeballs. If we talk him into having a large main course and then a stodgy pudding it'll probably as good as knock him out and then we can take him upstairs, forcibly if necessary, put him to bed and remove any alcohol that's in his room. No bloody good coppers are going down that road while *I'm* around.'

'So what have you been doing all day?' I asked him, loving him to bits for his concern.

'Walking down a corridor with Jaquie and getting into what looks like a lift but isn't. Going up the same two flights of stairs with Jaquie but shot from different angles and at different paces so that when the film's all strung together it'll look as though we're going up a whole load of floors. Oh, and taking out various baddies at the same time in various ways. It wasn't supposed to be funny but I think it will be. Back views of course, Rik's down for the rest.'

I had to know. 'What's she like?'

'She's what Elspeth would call a right madam. But as her main concern today was that she'd fall over in the quite ridiculous high-heeled shoes she had to wear it made her forget for a while to keep reminding people that she's the best, most beautiful actress in the world. I had to promise I'd catch her if she tripped. She didn't but I'm bushed.'

Was jealously really green or was it black? I asked myself.

Carrick had got into conversation with someone at the bar and when the man turned round I recognised the sound recordist who had been at the warehouse and Wrotherly, Len someone or other. When James returned he told us that he had dropped by to ask about the police presence at the estate the following day as he was concerned for everyone's safety.

'He's the union rep,' said James. 'Responsible for his members and all that.'

'What did you tell him?' Patrick said.

'Not a lot. Just that we would be there, some personnel would be in plain clothes, backing up the resident security staff. I assured him that public safety was my prime responsibility. But I'm not giving away details to anyone. He got a bit shirty when I wasn't more forthcoming – said we ought to have caught the murderer by now.'

'A big, burly sort of man,' I said.

'Yes. I'll watch him myself,' James vowed.

'At last,' I murmured in Patrick's ear when he came to bed.

'God, yes. I'm worn out.'

'I didn't mean it like that,' I told him, snuggling up close and running a hand across his chest and flat belly.

He seemed to drag himself back from somewhere else. 'Ingrid, I'm *really* tired. And when I'm tired I sometimes make a real Horlicks of it.'

I caressed a little lower. 'Sometimes when you're really randy and I'm tired I make an effort and end up enjoying it. Besides . . . ' My efforts had been rewarded.

'On auto,' he explained faintly.

Sheer pride prevented me from saying that women could get desperate too. But, for heaven's sake, he should know that already.

But he had drifted off again and I just caught a slurred, 'Why don't you go and give Carrick a nudge?'

I stared at him in amazement and then realised that he had been as good as asleep the moment his head hit the pillow, just like James, whom we had 'escorted' unresistingly to bed, not ten minutes previously.

10

The first thing that happened at Wrotherly the next morning was that Rik Harrison took a tumble and badly sprained his ankle. Bob Wayne, Rik's personal trainer, got the flak for this as he had seized the opportunity to take his charge on a fitness run when the commencement of filming was delayed by a vehicle bringing equipment getting stuck in the mud and blocking the road. The criticism was unfair as he had already been getting it in the neck on account of the actor's apparent inability to lose weight quickly. On one occasion recently an exchange of views about this had developed into a row with Wayne yelling at Martin Longton, accusing him of being unrealistic and callous in expecting Harrison, in effect, to thin himself down overnight. This time, restraint prevailed and Longton, seething like a witch's cauldron, retired to his caravan along with several others to try to re-work the schedule around the two difficulties. I was told that in most respects they failed in this and it was decided that with careful camera work, plus a pitilessly strapped and dosed-up main lead, everything they wanted to do could be achieved in two days, including the sequences that would be married up with the helicopter chases in post-production work. Oh, and because of the way he had successfully got himself into the rôle, Harrison's stand-in could do almost all the work.

'But if the character you're playing wasn't one of those captured what are you going to have to do?' I asked him.

Patrick had just been made up and was back in combat dress, his face streaked with camouflage cream. He said, 'The film's different from the book insofar as he *is* captured. But it's still left up in the air at this stage as to whether this was an arrangement between him and the IRA to make it look as

164

though he isn't to blame for the treachery. We start off with a short scene that in the finished film actually takes place before the crawling through the reeds, up the hill and into the bothy stuff that was filmed the other day. The guys are dropped off from a military Land Rover, ostensibly to make their way to the lake. That's going to be filmed on the lane itself,' he pointed, drank from the mug of coffee he was holding and went on, 'up there through the trees. We all have to roll into a ditch. Mike Cranley asked me if I wanted the stuntman to do it for me and I said it was hardly worth him getting togged up for before lunch. Then there's a few shots of us climbing out of the ditch and making our way uphill through the trees. Then this afternoon it's Rik's turn and while I have a rest he has to watch torture scenes in a fake farm building. That's still on the pick-up that got stuck in the mud, by the way. He can't stand seeing his three oppos being treated like this, even the the one who was supposed to have raped his sister, and attempts to rescue them and escape. He gets away but the others are shot so enter yours truly again for a little light being pursued around the quarry, run to ground, half kicked to death, escaping again, shot at but the slugs missing and finally getting away altogether. Ingrid, I'm really beginning to think I'm getting too old for this kind of thing.'

'It's only because it's a long time since you did any active soldiering.' That had been during the Falklands War when he had been one of the youngest Majors in the British Army.

He gazed at me in an unsettling way. 'I had a really weird dream last night that you slept with James and then told me that you wanted a divorce.'

'No,' I said. 'I *almost* did.'

I went to find myself some coffee.

It was a fine morning, early mist that wreathed through the trees and hung over the wet ground rapidly dispersing, already very warm down on the quarry floor, one corner of which I had crossed to reach where I was now standing. After the rain the polluted-looking pools were full and one was flowing into another, the water then running down a grassy slope into a brook. From a slight promontory crowned by a large oak tree, upon which I leaned cradling my coffee mug in both hands, I could see the way the miniature cascade glinted as it caught the light of the sun.

The vehicles were parked up on the lane or on sandy verges out of sight so, other than the offending pick-up that had now been unloaded and the riggers working near it, the space before me was comparatively empty. It amazed me how even with so many people in the vicinity a brooding silence could pervade all. As with Tredennis, something terrible seemed to have once happened here. I had needed to get away and be on my own for a little while: I was still haunted by what I had found.

The oak though was warm and friendly at my back and I was unashamedly using it, effectively or not, as protection from any sniper fire. Even a quick venturing out of the ring of stunted birches a few minutes earlier to avoid a boggy area on my way here had left me feeling very unsafe. Security was tighter than ever and everyone working on *Blood and Anger* had been issued with a new pass that had their photograph on it. Wrotherly's own security people patrolled on foot and in the estate's Land Rovers. The police had their own four-wheel-drive vehicles, the two members of the Mounted Branch and, although not officially confirmed, people up trees, this last information from Patrick, who had been trained to notice such things.

I had glimpsed James Carrick, wearing jeans and a sweat shirt, seated in an RRV, a Rapid Response Vehicle, talking into a radio while writing something down. Then he had got out and it had been driven away. He had not noticed me and had not appeared to be remotely hungover. I had wanted to ask him if he had heard any more about the PM on the woman's body but decided against it: he had quite enough on his mind already.

The cameras and other gear were already set up at the spot that Patrick had mentioned. From conversation overheard at the catering caravan I now knew there would be one or two close-up shots of Harrison actually getting out of the military vehicle and then Patrick would take over. This necessitated other technical alterations that I did not understand and there had been some grumbling.

I made my way back and then along the road to where they were going to film. Mike Cranley was chivvying everyone who was to feature in it with a mixture of Cockney rhyming slang and pure exasperation. By this time, I gathered, work was well behind schedule. The Land Rover arrived, and the six got in it, including Rik, who despite dosing and strapping was limping noticeably. I found myself a place to watch what was going on out of everyone's way: all I could do was be another pair of eyes and ears.

Martin Longton arrived from consulting with the lighting cameraman and the gaffer and took charge with the panache of a conductor at the Last Night of the Proms. There were a couple of rehearsals, adjustments and then three takes. They then moved on to the next scene of the men rolling into the ditch and one of them accidentally got a boot in his face. Patrick shouted at the culprit to get his act together and leave more space and after the wounded one had had his nosebleed staunched, they got that scene in the can as well. Things were rattling along nicely with a rehearsal underway for the crawling out of the ditch sequence and away up into the trees when there was a sudden gust of wind that whipped up fine sand from the road into everyone's faces.

'This isn't the Scottish play for God's sake!' Longton

bawled into the heavens, as people rubbed their eyes, spat and inspected lenses. He cast around. 'Where Rik?'

'Putting his ankle up,' said someone, probably one of the runners.

'We need him now.' Longton said, still looking. 'And Mike?'

The same voice said, 'You took over so he went for a pee.'

'Please go and get them back here.' His attention back on the rehearsal, Longton called to the camera crew, 'Was that all right?'

There was a thumbs-up sign.

'Well, it wasn't all right for me. A bit more grimness from the soldiers please. I want to see that you expect you might die tonight. Every tree trunk conceals an enemy. Okay, let's do it again.'

At the third effort he pronounced himself satisfied and they got the shot in the can on the second take, a policeman having inadvertently strayed into camera-range during the first. Rik turned up and there were a couple of close-up shots of him crawling through the bracken. Then, incredibly, it was twelve forty-five. The main protagonists then went away to snatch a bite of lunch while the riggers and technicians toiled to move everything into the quarry.

I turned to see James emerging from the cover of some hazels close by, a pair of binoculars slung around his neck.

'Anything?' he enquired laconically.

'No,' I said.

'That Len character seems on the line, this morning anyway,' he said. 'I've been sort of lurking but I've seen no one behaving suspiciously.'

'I don't see how anyone could dare do anything with so much surveillance all around them.'

'The body you found was that of Sonia Lockyer,' James said. 'I meant to mention it earlier. They identified her from her dental records. As originally thought, she had been strangled.'

'Does her mother live near where the Lockyers did?'

'No, Enfield, so that's another Force for me to add to my collection. They'd lost touch apparently before Sonia left home but had not been close for years. Mama hadn't approved of her marrying Melvin. Having said that, she's very upset, even more so as it appears that Sonia's killer might have made off with a bracelet that was this lady's mother's that Sonia never took off. Every inch of the boiler house has been searched, needless to say, but there's no sign of it.'

'An icon might be missing from Romanov's house.'

'I saw that in Foster's notes. Do you know why there's the uncertainty about it?'

'There's one missing from a group depicting the four apostles – you can see where the other one was hung on the wall. '

'He could have given it away.'

'Do you give away one of a set?'

'I wonder if anything valuable was taken from the Lockyer's house?'

'Or from the cottage in Tredennis.'

He wrote down a couple of reminders to himself.

'James, I think that as far as today's concerned, if anything's going to happen it'll be this afternoon, in the quarry.'

'I'll get as many people in strategic positions as possible but it's a huge area, and as you well know, modern weapons have a very long range. I've arranged a direct radio link to Longton in case of trouble and everyone will be briefed on a quick evacuation strategy. I'm damned if I can think of anything else that can be done that, given the circumstances, is practical.'

Patrick was sitting on the grass eating a sandwich alongside Mike Cranley and Cathy, who seemed to have struck up a friendship. She seemed slightly overawed by him, as well she might, I suppose. I sat down on Patrick's other side.

'It *was* Sonia,' I said very quietly into his ear.

He passed over a couple of his sandwiches. 'I think we both

had a nasty feeling it would be. I just wish we had more evidence to go on to catch the killer.'

We ate in silence for a little while.

'This place was once the pad of a North Country ironmaster by the name of Belper,' said Mike all at once. 'The Industrial Revolution and all that. There's strong evidence that he was friendly with the bod who ran the local clink and got free labour for the gravel pits and other workings here. Seems he even dug up his own garden for the sake of a few extra pennies and without the drag of having to pay anyone to do it.'

I said, 'Perhaps that's why his name wasn't mentioned in the introductory leaflet.'

'No, they wouldn't actually want to advertise this guy. Not many saw out their prison terms.'

'You mean they were worked to death?' Patrick asked.

Mike nodded soberly. 'I read up about the place in the local reference library in a book called *Historic Country Houses of Old Surrey*, when I knew we were coming here. There are detailed maps, you know, and it helps plan the shooting. Yeah, well this bloke was kind of twisted, thought of himself as the vengeful arm of God and it was his duty to make these poor bastards suffer for their crimes. Literally. He took a turn in the floggings and stuff like that. Turned him on a treat apparently and then he went away and rogered the maids.'

'I hope he met a nasty end,' I said heatedly.

'Yeah, well, a couple of convicts drowned him in one of the pools. And when they found him the next morning and got him out all the skin fell off the corpse.'

Cathy, aghast, cried, 'You mean we're going to be working in such a horrible, dangerous, place?'

'No, no,' Mike assured her. 'They found out where the caustic stuff was coming from and it was sealed off. That was done ages ago and it was the first thing I checked up on,

170

believe you, me, or the health and safety wallahs would have been down on my neck. Nah, the ponds are just a funny colour these days because of mineral salts or some such thing.'

'I don't think we'll be using the water to clean our teeth though,' Patrick commented wryly.

I shuddered, my cursed writer's imagination already having conjured up the spectre of an evil, flayed man forever wandering in the place where he had met his death.

A little later I had to admit that with the quarry area alive with activity, the sounds of human voices, power tools and vehicles as the set was prepared any air of menace was exorcised. Finally, when everything was ready and in position and it became quiet there was merely an air of people getting down to business.

Then the screaming started, echoing.

I knew it was going to happen, of course, but as when you watch a stage play, you become emotionally caught up in what is taking place. Actor friends have told me that it can take a short while even for them to 'find themselves' afterwards, especially if the story is harrowing. Across the quarry then, not far from where I was standing, I could convince myself that men really were being tortured.

Another camera and sound crew, referred to as the Second Unit, was inside the fake farm building, Mike Cranley in charge, while Longton waited outside with his crew for the next take which would film Rik's 'escape'. Or, at least, in a series of short takes, the stunt man would dive through a window and hit the ground in a forward roll, Harrison would be filmed getting to his feet and then Patrick would head off and out of sight between the piles of rocks.

I had tried to memorise everyone and what they did and endlessly tried to make certain that they were where they were supposed to be. But the nature of making films is fluid: runners working for the various departments were frequently going backwards and forwards, and actors came and went. Inside – and I could not go inside this time as there was not enough space for onlookers – I knew continuity people would be taking photographs, and, between takes, costumes would be adjusted, make-up re-touched and equipment checked and double-checked. All these people were milling around.

The screaming went on.

Near the building, leaning against a slender tree and deliberately looking dishevelled, Patrick waited for his cue in the next sequence. Not idly waiting: he had borrowed a pair of binoculars from someone and was scanning along where the road ran high above the quarry floor, only visible here and there between the trees. As I gazed in that direction a mounted policeman appeared in a gap, the horse trotting on a loose rein, and then was gone.

I went on a quest for shade, the sun was beginning to burn my face, and walked down the slope to stand near Patrick.

Filming progressed to the next sequence for the screaming ceased and was replaced by small arms fire and shouting. Then it went quiet and people drifted out of the building, some lighting cigarettes, so obviously there was a delay of some kind. Cranley then came into view and called to Longton that there was a technical hitch. These were not his exact words and although I had heard the expletives before, the piece of equipment to which he referred could have been an automatic Yorkshire pudding maker for all I knew.

Patrick wandered across to me. 'That bloke Len you picked out the other day,' he said quietly. 'He is a strange cove.'

I followed his gaze to where the man stood, hands in pockets, staring into space, as still as though turned to stone.

172

'I've watched him working,' Patrick continued. 'Very obsessive, always checking, always fiddling with things and so forth. Very obsessive people have been known to have a screw loose.'

I said, 'Isn't he usually part of Martin's crew?'

'He's doing as much of the sound recording as possible apparently – commuting between the two units.'

'And yet now it's as though he's completely switched off – like one of his machines. As you say, a little strange. He's the union man, James said, worried about security and got annoyed when he wouldn't give him any details.'

'A good front, wouldn't you say – to publicly tell the senior copper in charge that you were concerned for everyone's safety?'

'Together with trying to find out about police movements at the same time. And, as we said last night, he's a tall, strong-looking sort of man. What's his surname?'

'No idea – I'll ask Longton. Not that it would probably help us much.'

'This very moment wouldn't be a good idea.'

'That's true – I can see the steam coming out of his ears from here – but I wouldn't have bothered him with it now. If there's one thing the army taught me it was when to keep my gob shut. Carrick must know. Do you know his whereabouts by the way?'

'No, just that he's prowling. Patrick, I can never remember you *ever* keeping your gob shut if something was bugging you.'

'Just because you know the rules it doesn't mean you have to stick by them.'

The whatsits on the thingummybob were soon fixed and everyone went back to work. The man Len seemed to return from his state of ossification and disappeared inside again. He had a strange shuffling gait for his height and build that I had not noticed before. Genuine or assumed?

The afternoon dragged on. The escape through the window, with its rather complicated use of three men taking the part of one, took a long time to achieve to Longton's satisfaction and then one camera was mounted on a crane, another at the top of a twenty foot high tower built of scaffolding and planks that had been assembled earlier. Patrick caught my eye, grimaced, and prepared for some fast action.

The 'terrorists', the evil-looking bunch that had sprung the ambush at the bothy, had probably forgiven him for the deft way he had dealt with them on that occasion. It was they, after all, who had first thrown the punches. I had found this quite amazing until being told that they had been hired from an agency specialising in supplying tough and ugly actors, some of them one-time real criminals who had now pledged they were on the straight and narrow, as villains for this kind of film. Just high spirits, one of them had apparently excused himself by saying afterwards, grinning.

It was to be hoped they were not going to get too frisky now.

I gathered, watching rehearsals, that three of this group had been killed or wounded inside the barn when Rik had grabbed a gun. Then it had jammed, hence the bid for escape through the window. As the rehearsals progressed, the moves designed and closely monitored by the fight director, I saw that with Rik and Patrick working the rôle together in the usual way, that is, the former appearing mostly in close-up, he would re-acquire a weapon by overpowering one of his pursuers in a game of cat and mouse among the rocks and then lose it again when the remaining two jumped him. Then, as Patrick had said, he would be kicked and beaten somewhat before finally escaping altogether, the shots missing that were fired at his fleeing figure. Needless to say, all this scene was not all going to be filmed in one go but broken down into various different shots.

If there was ever an opportunity to shoot somebody for real, this was it.

I had borrowed Patrick's borrowed binoculars and now went back up the slight slope to my original position to get an overview of the action. Even from up here the concentration of Longton and all the technical people was almost tangible. I knew that films could be completely altered during post-production work but the magic, if it was to succeed at the box office, had to happen on set, not in the cutting room. To their credit I had heard no one so much as whisper that, with all the publicity surrounding the murders already, the movie could hardly fail.

I realised that I was sweating from nerves. Why the hell didn't they get on with it or was there yet another glitch? I surveyed the whole area below me through the binoculars and everyone, even Len, seemed to be in the right places. This was not to say that I could see behind the rock piles and boulders, to achieve that one would have to go along the road round on the other side. I knew there were police observers up there.

There was mild chaos below as a rehearsal started, people shouting and running about, handguns firing blanks and there was the chatter of a sub-machine gun that was obviously going to put in an appearance. Longton bellowed, 'Cut!' and there was a re-run, only at walking pace.

At last, after several tries, a good framework emerged and they got some of it in the can. It looked very convincing to me and I suspected the men might be collecting a few bruises. Once, my heart leapt as I saw Patrick go sprawling. But he had merely tripped, unsurprising taking into consideration the ghastly injuries he had sustained during the Falklands campaign. How many watching him, I wondered, would guess that, below the knee, his right leg is of man-made construction? His latest model, as he refers to it, made for him only recently, enables him not only to dance properly but run again, something he had only been able to do for very short distances. For that reason alone he was able to be down there, being chased around and possibly, at the same time, in the sights of a sniper.

Still sweating, I did not know whether to laugh or cry at this beastly irony. Actually, I felt like screaming for all I could do was helplessly stand and watch.

The former black sheep did seem to have adopted a more professional attitude. I knew that James was aware of their provenance, for he had been present when Longton had spoken about them, and had not appeared to be too concerned. I wondered if he was making a point of watching them now.

The work went on and down on the quarry floor violence was carefully stage-managed and kicks and punches did not quite connect. All the sound effects; grunts, thuds, and so forth would be added later. I noticed that Rik still limped quite badly but without that, even from this distance it was easy to tell who was who: strange really that Harrison, the younger man by quite a few years looked so lumpen alongside someone who quite a few people would regard as disabled. The actor's career, I felt, hung on his getting himself fit.

It came to the final part of the scene, the sequence where the central character at last escaped, and rehearsals got underway. Unable to watch any more I made my way down the slope, surprised that I felt weak and shaky, willing that the day's work would end and we could leave this place. I met Cathy.

'Are you all right, Miss Langley?' she asked, surveying me sympathetically.

'I'm fine,' I said.

'You don't look very well.'

'Just a bit tired, that's all.'

'Sit down and I'll get you a cup of tea.'

I would give her a signed copy of my latest novel, I promised her silently as I gratefully obeyed the instruction by sinking down with my back against a tree. She came back very quickly with a mug of tea and some biscuits, reminding me that I had had very little to eat since breakfast.

'I'm sure you're worried,' she said. 'Mike said that no one was looking forward to today.' She sat down beside me. 'I hate this place, don't you? Especially after what he said about it.'

'Lots of even lovely places have a nasty history,' I said. 'And some stories are wildly exaggerated.'

'I don't think Mike was trying to wind us up though. He's not like that – quite a kind sort of person really. Although he does have a wacky sense of humour.'

In the distance there was the sound of gunfire, and then silence for a while before Martin Longton called for action over his loud-hailer and it began again. Over this and approaching quickly I heard running feet coming from the opposite direction and turned to see Carrick heading straight towards us. He did not slow down though.

'The radio's packed up and I've got to stop it!' he gasped as he tore past.

I jumped to my feet and ran to catch up with him. This proved to be impossible as he was going like the very good rugby player he is and left me pounding along in his wake. I was a good twenty-five yards behind him when we reached Longton and by the time I arrived, everything having ground to a halt, the director was absolutely livid.

'Another few minutes and we could have had that in the can!' he was shouting in the DCI's face. 'Light right, all going like a poem and then you come along and say you've got a funny feeling about something. Will you get bloody real!'

Carrick was bent over, blowing like a racehorse but now straightened. 'Who keeps an eye on those weapons?' he asked grimly. 'Or are they just left lying unattended between takes for anyone to mess around with?'

'Well, of *course* they're not left lying around,' Longton replied furiously. 'They're the responsibility of the armourer, closely monitored, and kept in special boxes that are locked between use. I thought you bloody well knew that!'

James caught my eye. 'Gut feelings,' he said. 'You know how I always used to pooh-pooh yours.' To Longton, he continued, 'I've been watching what's been going on through binoculars and am particularly interested in the Heckler and Koch sub-machine gun that was handed back to someone and not used during rehearsals but has been returned now. Did it develop a fault?'

'No, it had just run out of blanks as we were using it earlier,' Longton said in not-suffering-fools-gladly tones. 'Look, in another ten minutes when this is in the can you can go and look it over yourself.'

'No one has been killed today – yet,' Carrick said very quietly.

Longton threw up his arms in dispair. 'Oh, very well. But you've no idea how much money your little whim is costing.'

The participants in the scene were returning, probably to see what all the shouting was about.

'It's the only hole in the security net,' Carrick said to Patrick as he came within earshot. 'The weapons. This is my fault.'

'They are capable of firing live rounds,' Patrick said. 'I had thought of it myself and checked on the handling of them. Are you worried about anything in particular?'

'Yes, the Heckler and Koch that was taken away and then brought back again just now.'

The armourer arrived, a man I had not seen before. 'What's the problem?'

His tardiness meant that Patrick had already acquired the weapon from the man carrying it. He looked it over, said something under his breath, walked away for a short distance and then turned and pointed it in the direction of the largest pool. The gun roared, the water's surface whipped into flying spray as the rounds hit. When the echoes had died away leaving a stunned silence he came back and carefully handed it to Carrick, saying, 'I don't need to tell you it's been loaded with live rounds. I suggest an urgent inspection is undertaken of the rest of the weapons. Thank you James, you've almost certainly saved both Rik's and my life.'

Carrick asked Longton to suspend filming until the check had been done and then went off to ask a lot of questions. This culminated in the arrest of one of the armourer's assistants.

'Most definitely not our man and I've released him,' said James later that night. 'He put the weapon in a bag used for those to be checked over and cleaned before storage and just took another one that was ready. There are witnesses. He simply took the one on top of a pile of three and the weapon was a substitute, not one already in use that had been loaded, accidentally or otherwise, with live ammunition. The cases containing guns and so forth were in the back of an estate car and someone was always supposed to keep an eye on it. I've interviewed all of these someones. They're all adamant that no one who shouldn't have been in the area wandered by – and let's not forget, everyone on site has their pass inspected when they arrive – or was hanging around, but needless to say film personnel were to-ing and fro-ing, some of them carrying props of some kind. They didn't notice anyone else with a gun or standing near the vehicle. Frankly, I think a couple of these blokes dozed off in the sun and don't like to admit it.'

'But they saw the man you arrested bring back the weapon and take another?' Patrick said.

'They did – that was quite late on.'

'Wasn't he sufficiently knowledgable to know live ammunition from blanks?'

'No. He's a student in his early twenties earning some money before going to university. It's not something that's particularly obvious though, is it, even to professionals, especially at the end of a long, hot afternoon?'

'It should be and the lack of supervision was truly dire.' Patrick raised his whisky glass. 'Here's to damned fine coppers. Lang may your lum reek.'

'To James,' I said.

'I feel quite weak at the knees thinking about what would have happened if you hadn't intervened,' Patrick continued when we had drunk the toast. 'Where the hell do you reckon the gun came from?'

'That's the awkward bit. It actually belongs to the Met.'

'*What*?'

'There was a raid a couple of years ago on what had been regarded as a very secure warehouse in Loughton used to store all kinds of police equipment. The gang went mostly for the weapons, of course, and nearly all of them were recovered quite quickly afterwards. Several people responsible were sent down but some of the items they made off with have never been found and presumably are still sculling around somewhere in the underworld. That sub-machine gun was one of them, no one had even bothered to erase the serial number.'

Patrick shook his head in despair. 'We're really no further on with this, are we?'

11

A somewhat subdued, but dogged, Martin Longton oversaw the completion of the postponed scene the following morning. All that then remained to be done at the old quarry area, right over on the far side of it, were some 'infill' shots that would eventually form part of a longer sequence, some of which was being filmed in Lincolnshire. I already knew the reason for this was that it involved a helicopter doing extreme manoeuvres and permission for such aerobatics were not countenanced anywhere near Heathrow, airspace being crowded enough already.

No one was talking of giving up, there was too much at stake, mostly financial.

Overnight, Rik Harrison had undergone intensive treatment for his ankle and with more strapping, plus a painkilling injection, it was felt he could carry out the whole morning's work. Patrick would still be required as the minor injury could have had no effect on Rik's outline. The latter was loudly insisting he had lost three pounds in weight during the past few days and had cut down his food intake to eight hundred calories a day. I heard at least two people wondering aloud why he had not done it weeks ago.

Me, I was just blaming that red-haired bat, Deena O'Leary.

The session would involve Jaquie Lauderdale as, together, hero and heroine would evade the henchmen of the criminal mega-boss he had blown up in the scene filmed in the warehouse. Enter more villains hired from Crooks R Us, or whatever the hell the agency called itself. By this time, I reasoned, mentally bracing myself for a final few hours at Wrotherly, the late scriptwriter had obviously thrown the book right out of the window.

'That's it!' I shrieked.

Patrick, who was driving, normally has nerves of steel but jumped out of his skin and the car swerved momentarily.

'That's it!' I repeated before he could say anything. 'The motive. Not only did the author of *Blood and Anger* write mostly a bunch of lies, the film has gone on to trivialise – no, rubbish when you think about it – what happened to this man and turned an account of his life into a shallow, trashy, Hollywood-style poor cousin of a blockbuster even though they've changed the storyline to make it look as though he wasn't actually guilty of treachery to his chums. When he heard the film was being made he found out who the scriptwriter was and got to know him so he could discover the treatment the book was being given. Having discovered how cheaply his story was being handled someone already a bit off his head planned to wreck it.'

There was silence from my right for a few moments and then Patrick said, 'That actually has rather a lot going for it. I think we all know that revenge is the name of the game but the rationale was always a bit hazy and one assumed we were dealing with an all-round maniac. I wonder if we can use that theory in some way in order to identify him?'

'Well, as you know, I think he's chummed up with his victims so far before he killed them. Is there anyone who's been particularly friendly to us and others in general?'

'No one who really sticks out. Going back to the author's time in Tredennnis: whoever it is could well have been one of the weekend visitors.'

'Who were an anonymous, undesirable bunch whom no one in the village could, or would want to, describe or put a name to. Just like it's been all along with this character, who obviously has used various disguises anyway.'

'As you said yourself, that's where the fun is, where he gets the kicks from. I reckon yesterday was to have been the high point: to get Harrison, possibly his stand-in and a few others all at the same time in a few seconds' burst of real gunfire.'

'And now what? Think,' I urged him. 'You're a man who underwent the same kind of training and conditioning. What would you do now your *pièce de résistance* has been thwarted?'

'Ingrid, I may have been an undercover soldier but I'm not *like* this nutter,' he said with a hint of plaintiveness.

'Okay. Programme this in: you're working undercover for Queen and country on an assignment in a war situation and you're behind enemy lines. So far your deception has been perfect and you've succeeded in taking out several dangerous enemy agents without anyone suspecting you. But the most recent plan, to neutralize Alpha One plus a few of his minders – probably your final task – has come to nothing and you're forced to think of something else fairly quickly. What would you do?'

'Tough old trout, aren't you?' Patrick said amiably. He then did not speak again until we drew up in the main car park at Wrotherly Hall, thinking. 'Pride,' he said, yanking on the handbrake. 'It would have to be something better, more ambitious, to bolster the battered ego and get back the high and the feeling of invulnerability.'

'Go on,' I said.

'Oh, I don't know . . . Take out Longton, I suppose. We're returning to the studio tomorrow so that could be blown to Kingdom come along with everyone inside it. Or third time lucky with me as he might reckon me to be of the same breed, still more of a threat to him than the police and therefore a more satisfying target.'

'Isn't there *anyone* you get funny feelings about?'

'Nope.'

The previous evening Carrick had told us that he intended to work very late with all the known facts relating to every murder to try to find even the smallest clue that would lead to discovering the killer's identity, or rather his present identity. Having registered our worries about his intake of the land of his birth's most famous export, a bottle of which had been tucked beneath his arm as he went up to his room, he had laughingly said that it helped him to think but Joanna did not allow him to overindulge at home.

'You didn't actually say anything, did you?' I had said to Patrick when he had gone.

'Yes, I did. I felt I had a right to. Besides, we're both people who appreciate straight-talking and wouldn't have fallen out if he'd told me to mind my own effin' business. But he didn't, realising we were only concerned for his welfare. He's okay.'

James was not in evidence this morning but it did not mean that he was not on site. It was clear though that more police personnel had been drafted in, one of whom had been assigned as personal guard to Jaquie Lauderdale and another to Harrison, in addition to his minder. They could only be of use, of course, when the actors were not in front of the camera, a time when they were, in theory, at their safest.

Burly protector, dresser and hairdresser in tow, Jaquie made straight for and proceeded to stick like iron filings on a magnet to Patrick, something I could understand as he does tend to exude a certain steady competence. Her state of nerves was manifest. I thought it about time she and I exchanged a few words other than 'Hi!'

'Martin's going to give us a briefing in a minute,' she said after we had greeted one another with 'Hi!', she jiggling on the spot in her agitation. 'And apparently a Scotch cop's going to say something too. Gee, I have to admit I wish I was someplace else. Where's Rik? He should be here right now. And my stand-in, Martha, she's not arrived yet either and if they think I'm going to go right out there into the open . . . Oh

184

God, he might be training his rifle on us right now!' she finished by shrieking.

'Scottish,' Patrick corrected gravely. 'You drink Scotch. You'd probably benefit from a bracer of it yourself right now.'

Jaquie was exquisitely attired in the obligatory kind of garment that Hollywood heroines wear to be chased around barren wastelands by gangsters; a sage-green silk one-piece trouser-suit that accentuated all her voluptuous curves gathered into the waist by a fine suede belt of the same colour. The shoes, flat ones this time, thank goodness, were made from matching leather. Tied loosely around her neck was a flame-coloured floaty scarf, a perfect foil for the long, glossy black hair. She wore no jewellery except for tiny gold stud earrings and a heavy gold bangle encrusted with sparkling stones of some kind which she now wrenched from her right wrist and tossed at the dresser.

'I can't wear this, it catches in everything.'

'I think you'll have to, my dear,' said the dresser, a quietly-spoken, matronly woman. 'I have an idea it's written into the script as a gift from the character Rik's playing.'

'I'm not wearing it!' stormed Jaquie.

Everyone but the actress sighed and found something very interesting to look at on the horizon.

Carrick suddenly arrived, giving every appearance of having a responsibility overload. 'Good morning, everyone. Miss Lauderdale, I understand you drove straight through the security check on the gate a short while ago almost knocking over a constable and one of the estate's security guards. I'd like to remind you that we have had several serious crimes committed since the start of the making of this film and – '

'I'm an American citizen,' the woman butted in. 'I don't have to obey your stupid security guards.'

' – if you do it again I shall have no choice but to arrest you for dangerous driving and refusing to stop when requested to do so by a policeman,' Carrick went on, grittily. 'Is that understood?'

She glowered and pouted at him.

'Is that understood?' Carrick repeated.

'Okay,' she drawled in a little girl, bored voice.

'Good.' From then on he ignored her completely. 'Is Martin Longton around?'

His question was answered immediately for Longton turned up looking very crumpled and with his hair uncombed, as though he had slept, but not for very long, in his clothes. 'One crumb of good news,' he began by saying. 'Mike's succeeded in getting permission for a limited amount of low flying with a chopper which will arrive at any time now. It means we won't have to rely so much on special effects nor take a full production team and the guys playing the crooks up north. They're just going to do the aerobatic stuff up there with a more experienced pilot. God, and the weather's still holding! Is something going to go right for once? Sorry, Chief Inspector, were you in the middle of briefing people?'

'No, but I do have something to say,' Carrick said. He stood up on a large flat boulder and addressed the whole unit. 'As far as firearms are concerned, a police weapons instructor will be backing up the armourer from now on and will double-check each one as it is given out and handed in. I would like to emphasise that anyone not wearing their pass, unless working directly in front of the cameras and who acts in a suspicious manner while carrying a weapon, including a knife, will be challenged. If they fail to stop they will be shot.'

There were several gasps and someone laughed nervously.

'The situation *is* as serious as that,' Carrick continued. 'And if any of you see anything suspicious, even the most seemingly insignificant thing, then I would like you to come and report it quietly to the nearest policeman. I shall be right here, on the set, until the work's finished. Thank you, that's all I have to say.'

Longton then took Jaquie and Rik aside, the latter having just arrived, and gave them their instructions for the scene. The area was cleared and several close-up shots were done of the pair of them at different parts of the foreground of the quarry floor. They acted out short dashes from the cover of one rock to another, gasping for breath while hiding among the larger piles of boulders, ducking down, gazing at the sky and finally, kissing as though they wanted to devour one another.

'I can't remember pausing for a snog when we were being chased by undesirables,' I snorted to Patrick who had just returned, probably from a short stroll. Like Rik, he was dressed in black jeans and black silk shirt and as usual, his normally wavy hair was flattened down with gel. It made him look a trifle sinister.

There was a short break while the camera and its rails were moved to another position before the stand-ins would be called. I noticed a woman apparently arguing with Longton and when she saw her Jaquie ran over to them, the result of which was that the temperature of the proceedings reached boiling point.

'What d'you mean they won't goddamned-well cover you?' I heard the actress yell.

'I have an idea that's Martha,' Patrick said to me. 'Lauderdale's stand-in. Could it be that her insurance company's being difficult?'

This turned out to be precisely the problem and they were still arguing when the helicopter, a nifty little orange and white machine, put in an appearance, tree-hopped over the high ground to one side of the quarry and landed neatly in a clear space much too close for comfort. There was a big blast of exhaust-reeking air, laden with dead leaves and pine needles, followed by vivid swearing by the technicians as they frantically dusted off their equipment.

'We might be here for quite a while,' Patrick said, sitting down with his back to a rock and closing his eyes.

'Look!' came Longton voice's on the breeze. 'That bloody thing's costing around a hundred pounds for every five minutes you females stand there arguing with me.'

Whereupon Martha walked off saying she could not work without insurance and Jaquie flounced off back to her caravan. I saw that Longton's fevered gaze had come to rest on me. He hurried over.

'Ingrid.' There were real tears in the man's eyes. 'You look even more like Jackie than Martha does. Please help me out and do this work with your husband. I think you'll find it quite good fun and you're a fit sort of girl.'

I suppose I gawped at him. 'What, me? But I'm a good ten to fifteen years older! And my hair's not anywhere near so nice, nor as long.'

'You're perfect,' Longton wheedled. 'And you can wear a wig. And Len will fix you up with an Equity card.'

'More to the point, I would have thought,' said Patrick, getting to his feet, 'is that should both the parents of our children be at risk? I have to point out also that neither of our life insurance policies covers us for working in the film industry.'

'Wait,' said Longton, fishing for his mobile in a pocket and walking uphill away from us to get a better signal. He soon came back. 'I rang David Goodheim. He will pay half a million dollars for any injury and two million if either of you is killed. If you're both killed the children get five. He gives you his word and would keep it – David is a good man.'

'But he could offer that to Martha!' I exclaimed.

Longton lowered his voice. 'He might but I doubt it. For one thing I told him that I don't actually believe her. Like Jaquie, who it must be said is worth a lot more than that, I think she's just chicken and therefore would be pretty useless on the job.'

Patrick and I looked at one another.

Ten minutes later I was adjusting the soft green suede belt around the waist of the outfit that Martha was to have worn. Fortunately we were roughly the same size. The floaty orange scarf was in place, as were the tiny gold stud earrings and then the dresser, with a wink, handed me the gold bangle and I put it on, only to immediately discover that it did indeed, catch in everything. I slipped on the shoes, which were a little tight but that was better than them falling off my feet and then looked at myself in the mirror. Five minutes after that I looked again and yes, I would grow my hair, the wig was rather flattering. Another five minutes went by after some fairly frantic work as Longton was getting impatient and another woman gazed at herself, make-up completed; a Jaquie Lauderdale lookalike.

I had not expected to be made up for distance shots but it was explained to me that, on film as well as stage, my face would look just like a white blob without it. All this was more than worth it just to see Patrick's astounded double-take.

'Is that wig well-anchored?' Longton asked the hairdresser. 'She'll get really blown about by the chopper.'

A few more grips went in.

We were then briefed in some detail. I was also told to wiggle my hips as I walked, run as though I was not in the habit of doing so and drape myself around Patrick as much as possible for protection during pauses in the hazardous bits as the woman I was playing, Ritz, was a clingy type. Silly to even think about it after all this time but no one had been called Ritz in the book: 'Jack's' woman had been a one-time hooker by the name of Karlie.

It was strange, surreal even, walking out into the large open space of the set, me practising my wiggle, Patrick already adopting Rik's macho gait, and then, when he paused, standing uncharacteristically with hips thrust forward, legs apart while we listened to a postscript to the instructions from the director over his loud-hailer. First, as usual, would be rehearsals which would be done without the helicopter, travelling in which would be another cameraman in radio contact with the director, until everything came right.

This part of the quarry, although quite close to 'Northern Ireland', where the filming of the soldiers being tortured had been carried out, looked quite different. It was more open but the piles of rocks were larger, one long one resembling a miniature curving ridge of hills. There were pools here too but they were clear and looked deep, with rushes and sedges growing around them. There were even a couple of small trees and a patch of grass.

We held hands as we walked to our positions, getting into our rôles perhaps or, then again, just holding hands.

'This has to be the bloody daftest thing we've ever done,' Patrick said.

'Oh, I don't know,' I said. 'What about the time in Canada when you were pretending to be a horrible gnome-like gardener and to enhance your cover you pretended to rape me? It got a bit out of hand as I was pregnant without knowing it and my hormones were right off the scale so I got really upset, screamed the place down and someone rushed in and thrashed you with his riding crop.'

He glanced at me sideways. 'Sometimes you *can* over-egg the pudding,' he observed, mouth twitching with suppressed laughter. 'And when we were pretending to be Hell's Angels and you had to wash your hair with washing up liquid until it looked like an unravelled Brillo pad and put on lots of black eye stuff to make yourself look like a biker's trollop.' He uttered a hoot of laughter, multiplied by echoes.

'That wasn't funny,' I pointed out tartly. 'D12's resident

medic put needle marks in my arms so I could pass muster as a junkie. They took ages to fade and I got some really strange looks from people afterwards.'

'Get ready for a rehearsal,' Longton called.

'God, I really, really want to send this up,' Patrick said fervently.

We scampered into place, tittering like naughty children. Why? I asked myself – always somehow able to stand back mentally and assess my own behaviour – we could be shot dead at any moment. No doubt we were just plain stupid but whatever the truth we had to concentrate on what we were supposed to be doing and trust Carrick's tight security arrangements. My own private opinion was that given the heavy police presence any attack would be something unexpected, like the previous day, where any weaknesses in the security net would be sought out.

'Why did Longton say we were here?' Patrick said. 'I wasn't really listening.'

No, he had been eyeing up everywhere from a staying alive point of view.

'You've rescued me from the clutches of the henchmen just after you blew up the boss-man who had grabbed me to be his very own. We got away in a car that just happened to be handy but it broke down so we're walking across bare country to a safe place you know of, somewhere remote where you were taken on holiday as a child.'

'Do we know each other already?'

'Er – I think so. Yes, that's right, I was the spotty kid with plaits next door.'

'So if we've only just met up again why are you supposed to drape yourself all over me?'

'Because this is a film, silly, plus I'm a complete wimp and, as it's really Jaquie, sex, sex and more sex. Which reminds me . . . '

'What?'

'It doesn't matter. No, to hell with it.' And I grabbed him for a kiss, cameras, focus-pullers, grips, clapperboard and all. Initially unresponsive, as he is not the kind of man to do this sort of thing in public, he soon warmed to the idea.

'Just keep telling yourself, later, later,' I tore myself away to breathe in his ear.

There was a burst of applause and a couple of sardonic cheers from the production team.

'You knew these jeans were too tight, you baggage,' Patrick complained and walked away for a few paces to cool down.

The fight director had produced a map, or rather a diagram, with the moves that we should make marked on it with numbered lines that we had had to memorise. There was one rehearsal, which Longton liked, but we suggested a few changes which we thought would look more realistic and these were adopted. It was not a bad idea to change manoeuvres that someone hostile might have committed to memory or informed others about.

Another two rehearsals followed and we remembered to keep our faces turned away from the camera as much as possible. Then we went for a take and the helicopter whirred into life and 'chased' us as we went through the same routine; ducking and diving among the rocks while at the run and, half blown away by the gale from the rotors, I was reciting, 'wiggle, drape, wiggle, drape', out loud all the way through knowing full well that because of the racket the sound track would have to be dubbed in afterwards. There was another take when the helicopter was required to fly a little closer, mostly to enable the cameraman we could now see in the cockpit to get extra footage. It was not really close to us at all, although Martin had explained that in the finished scene special effects plus shots from later filming would ensure that it looked dangerously close. Add sound effects, digital editing, a musical score and the whole fantasy would be complete.

By lunchtime the second sequence was in the can; more manoeuvres and the disembarking of several heavies from the helicopter who would proceed, during the afternoon, to try to finish us off. One would be tossed spectacularly into a pool – this was the uneviable lot of the stuntman – the others would gradually be disposed of in similar dramatic fashion and I thought I heard someone say that the final henchman would get his head lopped off by the rotor blades.

'Aye, that's right, lassie,' said one of the special effects men, Hamish, when I queried this. 'And the pair of ye get a bucket of fake blood tossed all over ye. That's why it's bein' done last as it'll ruin the clothes.'

I gazed sadly down at my sage-green silk. It was glorious to wear and I was getting very fond of it.

'D'you want to see the head?' Hamish asked gleefully and before I could reply he had dived into the box of tricks at the back of his van and hauled forth his masterpiece.

'Ye gods,' I heard myself say. 'That's ghastly.'

It was. But perfectly faked just lopped-off human heads usually are. He had somehow achieved a quite sickening expression in the eyes.

'Yon mannie's going to chuck it into one of the ponds,' Hamish continued, pointing to Patrick. 'That's why I've made it about half as heavy as a real one – to make sure it goes in with a good splash.'

'Surely that shot'll be down to Rik.'

'They'll both do it, I reckon. I think Longton'll use the stand-in's actual throw as he's got a better way of movin'.'

'Patrick will enjoy that,' I said. 'But how are you going to retrieve it after the first throw?'

'By tying fishing line with a high breaking strain to a metal ring I'll screw into it.'

'You're a genius,' I told him and he gave me a wide, gap-toothed grin.

Almost inevitably, in the finished film the helicopter, after decapitating the final henchman, would take off and fly straight into one of the cliff sides to explode in a huge ball of flame, something that Hamish was looking forward to helping to create. He had a ready audience in Patrick and the pilot who joined us over a short lunch break, as he explained how this would be achieved with special effects and during post-production work. But my attention soon wandered and I was getting to the stage where I would never believe anything I saw in the cinema again. Naïve of me? No, not really, he was just destroying the magic.

Not a lot of magic was in evidence during the afternoon session, due partly to the weather threatening to break. Longton drove everyone relentlessly, dashing between his monitor, viewing things with his own eyes, all the while scanning the sky for approaching rain clouds. Problems started; I got grit blown into my eyes that necessitated attention from the first aider and the offending particles were flushed out with drops, still leaving them reddened and sore. The contingent from Crooks R Us had already been proving very slow to learn what they had to do and a whole half hour was virtually wasted while the fight director cum stunt man drilled them, having borrowed Longton's loud-hailer. I knew that Patrick was itching to bring his parade ground voice and choice of adjectives to bear in order to hasten things along a bit he but had to kick his heels like everyone else.

Finally, after yet more rehearsals, only involving us as well, filming started. It was hard and dirty work.

It amazed me how much action could be packed into a six-minute-long sequence. The men, who had already been filmed disembarking from the helicopter, fanned out and would effectively surround us with a view to take us back to HQ for horrible retribution, as we began the scene standing with our backs to a large rock. As in the best Westerns, some would come around the sides, others would try to climb down to us from above and the last one would be chased back towards the helicopter whereupon his head would eventually appear to be neatly sliced from his shoulders by one of the rotor blades. Several experiments had been conducted by Hamish's boss while everyone else was having lunch, weighted lumps of the resin used to make the head thrown into the pool to see what kind of splash they made. Not good enough, had been the verdict so an electronically triggered charge had been dropped into the water to ensure a satisfying fountain.

Even though the violence was faked there were still five of them against us. Timing had to be perfect in this rough ballet and, when it was still not right on the third take and Longton was pouring scorn on the ungodly, their tempers began to fray, culminating in a situation similar to that which had occurred on the bothy set. A muddled 'villain' seemed to be suddenly taking everything personally and not only refusing to go down after Patrick had 'hit' him but still advancing.

'Fall down, you stupid bastard!' my husband roared and when the man, who looked like, and appeared to have the cerebral acuity of an Ork from *The Lord of the Rings*, took a swipe at him, Patrick ducked and then clipped him on the chin for real, thus ensuring that he went over like a tripped bullock.

I burst out laughing and it took us a couple of seconds to realise that the cameras were still rolling and that one or two of the felled one's companions had seen what had happened. Invigorated by fresh enthusiasm and abandoning the painstakingly learned instructions they closed in with every indication that they intended to get even.

Mindful of my instructions, I ran to Patrick and hid behind

him for protection, slipping in a kiss and a sexy moan in his ear.

'Later,' he said with a chuckle.

'Later,' I purred.

Then a kind of inspired madness came over him and I found myself being waltzed around, *Singing Butler* style, the heavies gawping at us. Not for long, one of them grabbed me in a bear hug, actually as planned, and hefted me off my feet to carry me away. He should have released me and crumpled when he felt the edge of Patrick's hand touch the back of his neck but did not.

'What the hell are you *doing*?' I yelled, twisting round to slap him on the ear with my one free hand.

The fool started to run with me and I had a grandstand view of what happened next; a perfect *coup de grâce* from the rear across his size eighteen collar neck. I almost went down with him but was caught, spun round, dumped back on my feet and Patrick's momentum and one flying fist caught the next opportunist full on the nose. He reeled away to trip backwards over a small boulder.

We did a little more waltzing and then there were two.

They rushed him together, one of them punching him in the body, the other swinging his foot for a vicious kick, which had it landed would have caused serious injury. It did not, for Patrick, somehow recovering from the body-blow, jinked, caught the foot, cranked it up to impossible heights and the kicker toppled backwards, cannoning into his friend. They crashed to the ground together in a flood of obscenities. The one who had been forced to act as fender then picked himself up and ran away, quite coincidentally in the direction of the helicopter.

'I can do that too,' Patrick said joyously and set off after him.

'Cut!' Martin Longton shouted.

Cinema audiences never saw Rik Harrison land a well-judged uppercut on the last henchman who was then horizontal instead of vertical in order to be decapitated, that piece of film ending up on the cutting room floor.

'Bloody marvellous!' Longton enthused, having rushed over, wrung Patrick's hand and then given me a hug. 'I'm really grateful to you for having a confab with the guys and sorting out something that worked better. And the pair of you dancing around in between – that was cool.' His gaze took in the wounded ones and comprehension dawned. 'Did it get a bit hectic, chaps?' he called. 'Not to worry. You'll get danger money for that take – bump up the old salary quite a lot, eh?'

There were then the short scenes. An out of camera shot Hamish sprayed phoney blood over us as someone else tossed the head so it flew by, and then it was filmed again, in close-up, with Rik and Jaquie. Afterwards the head was sent into a watery grave, Rik, dripping with gore, throwing first and deciding on a two-handed baseball shot quite near the water. He got quite wet as the charge went off. But he carried it off brilliantly, turning and giving Jaquie a sardonic smile.

'That's good,' Longton said. 'I'll use it. There's no need for the stand-in to do any more.' And then, louder, 'It's a wrap, folks.'

No one had been killed, the scenes were in the can and, although I had been told I could throw away my costume as it was ruined, I soaked it in the handbasin back at the hotel while we showered and all the water-based red colouring came out.

'Women!' Patrick said scornfully. 'Anyone would think that was the best result of your day judging by the soppy look on your face.'

'It's beautifully made from very expensive material and I hate wanton waste,' I said. 'No, the best part of my day is going to happen right now.'

'But I've just got ready for dinner,' he protested as I removed his jacket.

'If you'd been wearing armour I'd have found a tin-opener,' I told him.

12

Everyone was later than usual for dinner, Carrick having phoned to tell us he had a debriefing with Martin Longton.

'There I was,' he said by way of a greeting, 'sweating for your safety and there *you* were, dancing!' He was smiling as he spoke but obviously still feeling the strain.

'Only a little artistic licence,' I said.

'Seriously though, it's all very well our meeting up for dinner like this every night but murderers do work a twenty-four hour day, you know. Aren't we getting careless? Suppose this character came in right now and started shooting?'

'Sit down and I'll get you a drink,' Patrick said. 'Then we'll talk about it.'

James slumped into a chair. 'God, what a day!'

'I agree with you in a way,' Patrick said when he came back from the bar. 'But from the point of view of someone who presumably doesn't want to get caught or unmasked, as they say in corny detective stories, it would be very unwise to go for that kind of attack. Our man would expect you, James, to be armed and, not only that, a good shot. He might also assume me to be carrying a firearm, legally or not, because of my provenance, so to speak. Any attack in a place like this, which for all he knows is protected by armed plainclothes police, would therefore carry extreme personal risk on several counts.'

'Are you armed?' Carrick asked him. 'Strictly in confidence, of course.'

'Only with my knife. Most times it would suffice,' Patrick replied simply.

James did not ask me.

'We spotted absolutely nothing suspicious all day,' he went

on to say. 'I suppose I could congratulate myself and call it a success but there's this nasty feeling that someone's just waiting for me to blink.'

I said, 'At least that's the end of outdoor filming as far as we're concerned.'

'There's just the helicopter stuff and some car chases,' Patrick said. 'But as you say, not us but stuntmen and women. No, I think we can safely say that all remaining work will be done in various indoor venues.'

'Longton told me about it just now,' James said. 'You're not quite right insofar as there's some filming at an airport, probably Heathrow, and also some street scenes work to do at the end but it doesn't involve the main leads. Interior-wise there's one real hotel lobby, a big room in a country house and a lot more studio work and special effects sets. The rest will be stock film; aircraft taking off, city views and so forth. There will have to be a significant police presence at the hotel and the country house and I intend to take a few blokes along with me to the studio complex.'

My ears had pricked up at the mention of the country house. 'Not Wrotherly again.'

'Wrotherly,' Carrick confirmed. 'You don't like that place, do you?'

'The house is probably all right.'

'Yes, it's the quarry where Longton said there's supposed to be a ghost – a previous owner who drowned in an acid pool and walks with his skin all hanging off. Heard about it?'

'Mike Cranley told us the story but not about any ghosts,' I said.

'There *are* some people who believe that kind of codswallop,' Patrick said. 'Can we go and eat now before I starve to death?'

My imagination had conjured up a ghost but I had to admit that changed nothing as far as codswallop ratings went.

***

'There's one small lead,' Carrick said over coffee. 'You remember when Isobel Kent said she saw Sonia Lockyer drive off with a man when she was looking out of an upstairs window to see if the fishman was on his way? Well, my new sergeant, Lynn, has found the fishman. It turns out he remembers a car, a small red one, outside the Lockyer's house one morning and, from a distance, seeing her getting into it. The same car had clipped his van at a nearby road junction. It had been driven off before he could do anything but he wrote down the registration number in his diary and reported the incident to the police. The problem was there were no other witnesses, which as you know, makes a prosecution difficult.'

'Had it been stolen?' Patrick asked.

'No, it had been bought from a secondhand car dealer in Bristol, the sort that operates in railway bridge arches, the day before. The man, whom the dealer remembered as he had felt intimidated by him, had given the name Jennings and paid in cash, and no proof of identity had been asked for.'

'Intimidated?' I said.

'Yes, I was just coming to that,' Carrick said. 'He was described as shaven-headed, a tallish, thickset man with a small, pointed black beard. He wore dark glasses. The dealer was glad to see the back of him and had accepted an offer for the car that was lower than he had wanted. The interesting bit is that a vehicle with that registration was later found abandoned on wasteland in Plymouth. Someone boobed and no check was made to see if it was connected with any crime outside the area. Enquiries have now been made at car hire establishments in the city and it's been discovered that a couple calling themselves Mr and Mrs Lockyer hired a dark blue Ford on the morning of the day when Sonia Lockyer and the

201

man we have to suspect of killing her arrived in Tredennis in a blue hired car.'

'What was the name on his driving licence?' Patrick wanted to know.

'No one saw it: the woman was the designated driver. Perhaps they swapped over when well out of sight.'

'But the woman's credit card must have been imprinted. Did he pay cash when he returned the car?'

'Yes, he did.'

'What happened to the red car?' I asked.

'By the time someone reported its presence it had been heavily vandalised and an attempt made to set it alight. Crunched, I'm afraid, after it was established it wasn't stolen.'

Patrick swore quietly. 'And the hired car will have been thoroughly cleaned a hundred times so no DNA there either.'

'Sold off, actually.' Carrick poured himself some more coffee. 'The other thing I have to tell you is that no trace of the bracelet Sonia Lockyer's mother mentioned was found in the house so it could have been stolen at the time of her daughter's murder.'

'What about the rope that was used to hang Lockyer?' Patrick enquired.

'From the point of DNA again, you mean? Talk about from one extreme to the other. As you must realise the place was like a slaughterhouse.' James glanced at me worriedly but carried on. 'There was blood everywhere and it's going to take a while to analyse everything. I have to say I'm not terribly hopeful. This man is organised, has a good set-up, and, at a guess, a well-organised base. He obviously has access to weapons from criminal sources but it doesn't appear that he has a criminal record in this country although according to Taylor's book he's done all kinds of hatchet jobs abroad. Why don't we know what this man really looks like?'

'He has several personas,' Patrick said. 'And several – I

nearly said faces but it's true. He has a different identity to several, possibly up to a dozen, different people.'

'The base has to be mobile,' I said.

'Mobile?' Carrick echoed.

'Yes, like a caravan. I mean, if you're carrying real firearms around in order to either use them yourself or leave them for other people to pick up, and you're working on the film you can't just pop home and get one. Several of the film crew have caravans that they live in while away from home. The leading actors and actresses use caravans provided by the film company to give them privacy.'

James shook his head. 'I'm still not at all sure that whoever he is has any major function with regard to the film but he could well be somehow remaining undetected on the peripherals. Sorry, Ingrid but we've screened everyone working for the film unit until the pips squeaked.'

'Suppose he's working here under his *real* or a new, permanent identity?' I persevered. 'Everything would be fine – bank details, driving licence, you name it.'

'All the names were changed in the book,' Patrick ventured. 'Not only that, you can change your name to anything you like.'

'I'd never get warrants to search people's caravans without some hard evidence,' James said.

It might just have to be done sneakily then.

Martin's Longton's troubles were not over. The following morning we walked into the studio and also into a crisis meeting, Patrick discovering at the same time that he would have been bounced into involvement with a love scene. The 'would have been' was due to Jaquie Lauderdale having woken up with a rash that could easily be chickenpox.

'Where?' Rik asked baldly.

'On her – er – chest,' Longton answered. 'She's seen a doc

but you know how it is with these things, you have to wait for a little while to see if it gets worse.'

'Has she been feeling off-colour?' I asked.

'Said she had a headache yesterday.'

'Didn't we all?' Patrick groaned under his breath.

'I suppose we could do the soft focus through the net curtain really randy-looking stuff,' Longton said brightly. 'And then Rik and Jaquie could get their kit off for the mostly heads and shoulders shots later when we know she's got nothing catching.'

'I shall want it in writing that it's not catching,' Rik said heavily. 'Some of these spots, mumps and rashes kind of ailments aren't too good when you're grown up and a bloke.'

'What about you?' Martin asked Patrick.

'*What* about me?' Patrick said blankly.

'Have you had chickenpox?'

'God knows. I'd have to phone and ask my mother.'

'You have,' I told him. 'When you were seven. I asked Elspeth when Justin caught it.'

'That's all right then,' Longton carried on happily. 'This morning we'll get footage of Patrick and Martha and hope to hear from Jaquie meanwhile. The set's built so I'm damned if I'm getting behind schedule. Carrick's cops are all organised for when we film at the hotel starting at six tomorrow morning and Wrotherly Hall is booked for the day after that. There's no leeway at all.'

'Martha's gone,' Mike Cranley said. 'You told her, if you remember, that she'd invalidated her contract yesterday by refusing to work so she upped sticks and went. I think she'd heard about another job, mind.'

Longton suddenly looked old and dog-eared.

'You already have your lady,' Mike said to him. 'Ingrid. And they're married so it'll be more natural for people who aren't pros.'

'I am not making love to anyone, not even my husband, in public,' I stated emphatically, appalled.

Mike talked me into it. We would not have to strip right off and a sheet would cover potentially naughty bits, as well as Patrick's leg as they now knew about it, only a minimum film crew would be present, we would be filmed through moving hazy gauze as though through a net curtain at an open window, and, finally, no one was asking us to do the real thing.

'I'm completely knackered after last night anyway,' Patrick said into the pillow when he had flopped down beside me in a vast, totally over-the-top ornate bed. 'Just as well you seduced me again after dinner.'

It had not been quite like that. I said, 'This is getting stupider and stupider but did you check under the bed for explosives?'

'Carrick's mob searched everywhere and everything. Sniffer dogs, the lot.'

'He's not here now, is he?' I said, mortified at the very thought of his presence. I had been given a dressing gown to slip off at the last minute as, back to everyone, I had got into bed and, like Patrick, was only wearing my pants.

'I don't know.'

'Patrick - '

'Can we have a rehearsal for lighting purposes, please?' Longton called. 'Just remember that you're supposed to be stealing a quick one in somebody else's house. So urgently, please folks and really use the space on that bed.'

By three that afternoon Jaquie's spots were deemed to be a rash caused by some kind of allergy. A doctor was persuaded to provide what was light-heartedly referred to by the film crew as a 'vet's certificate' and she returned to work, not remotely amused by the joke. By six-thirty all filming for the day was satisfactorily completed and a start made on dismantling the set with a view to commencing work on some extensive and complicated ones that would take a couple of days to erect. Mike Cranley carted the director away for a celebratory drink to settle his nerves. This we learned much later that day from James as we had not been present having been given the afternoon off.

'I hear you two were doing the X-rated stuff today,' he began by saying.

After chickening out of an invitation to watch the 'rushes' of our morning's efforts, Patrick and I had decided to get right away and go for a walk in the hills somewhere. But, succumbing to a doze after lunch back at the hotel, we had slept soundly until four. All there had been time for was a breath of fresh air in a local park which I had enjoyed once I had succeeded in pushing the prospect of a possible sniper to the back of my mind.

Patrick said, 'I think we both quickly discovered that simulated sex is much more tiring than the real thing but with none of the wow-factor. Good aerobics though.' He laughed.

'I couldn't do it.'

'Old son, if you were out of work, had four young mouths to feed back at home and someone dangled a thousand dollar bill under your nose you'd caper around for a while mostly under a sheet with Joanna.'

'You're getting paid that much?' Carrick exclaimed.

'That's for both of us, per day as stand-ins. There's a little danger money included in there too for work like yesterday's.'

'As far as I'm concerned it was another quiet day: we found and saw nothing, though I'm still not happy about that sound recordist, Len. He's a really strange bloke. Seems to go into a trance between takes – got a screw loose if you ask me. But all the checks we've done on him haven't shown up anything interesting.'

'I think we ought to set some kind of trap,' I said, having been deep in thought and only vaguely hearing them waffling on.

'Trap,' James repeated, switching his attention immediately.

'Yes, a sort of lure – something this man we're after simply won't be able to resist.'

'It would be helpful to have an idea who it was first.'

'If only so we can then blow his bloody head off,' Patrick declared, having drained his whisky glass. He usually drinks beer in pubs at home but hotels rarely serve real ale. 'My round.'

'This *has* to be achieved within the law,' Carrick said to him grimly.

'Just testing,' Patrick murmured, gathered the empty glasses and went away.

'It worries me when he's like that,' James said to me. 'Sometimes he sort of *fizzes*. I hope he's not planning any independent action.'

'I would be the first to tell you if I knew he was,' I said, meaning it but not adding that he himself would avoid any possibility of that happening by simply not involving me in whatever it was.

'I do appreciate that he takes it a bit personally – someone playing cat and mouse with him like this when of all people he should be able to find out who it is.'

I then had the most bizarre thought. No, Patrick wasn't doing anything, not the tiniest amount of sleuthing around, prowling the sets looking for clues, asking questions or openly doing any kind of research. The biggest insult to a mentally unbalanced man who had tried to kill or seriously injure him twice already? For a Lieutenant-Colonel with Patrick's reputation, even a retired one, to appear to shrug his shoulders and walk away, not even acknowledging that his enemy was worth engaging . . .

It seemed to me that the trap might be already set.

'Would you do something for me?' I asked James.

'Of course, if it's within my power.'

'Would you assign one of your men to watch over him in particular for the next few days without him knowing? I've got one of my funny feelings.'

'It might be difficult to do it without him noticing. But, yes, of course.'

I had been asked if I would carry on as stand-in for Jaquie Lauderdale and saw no reason why I should not. As was the case with Patrick, a professional performed the stunts so my task was actually of a mundane nature – if the making of *Blood and Anger* can be described in those terms – lighting rehearsals and so forth, as, unlike Harrison, the actress did not require anyone to do more of the work for her. I was glad that I now had a really good reason for hanging around.

The hotel used for interior shots, King's Court, on a corner site just off Park Lane, had undergone a complete refurbishment but was not yet open for normal business. The vast lobby, where we would be doing most of the work and that appeared to house the national collection of cream-coloured leather sofas, had a midnight-blue ceiling complete with a full moon and stars that was, to my eyes, indistinguishable from the real thing and, eerily, moved. Observing Jaquie the next morning I felt that she was at home in such surroundings, easily described as select and opulent.

'This is better,' she said when she found me at her side. 'I'm not an outdoors person. Where's Rik?'

I had noticed this trait before; constantly wanting to know people's whereabouts. Everyone, it seemed, was required to report to her personally rather than her go to them.

'He's over there,' I said.

'Your husband should be here too.'

'He's standing not three yards behind you,' I told her.

She gave me an old-fashioned look. 'You haven't been a stand-in for very long, have you? Haven't quite gotten to know how to speak to the artistes.' Shrugging dismissively she added, 'You can do all the lighting rehearsals – it's too hot in here for me.'

Longton called her away to rehearse her lines with him and I counted up to fifty: she had been present when David Goodheim and I had discussed resurrecting my novel, *A Man Called Celeste.*

The morning progressed slowly as several sequences which took place in different parts of the film were completed. Rehearsals were lengthly and complex as in one of them all the lights were supposed to go out and then just a few come on for exactly fifteen seconds, go out again, after which there was just 'moonlight'. While this was going on actors had to find new positions in comparative darkness. As might be expected, people bumped into the furniture and fell over one another and the sound recordist, Len, ended up with an inundation of bad language, got quite upset about everyone's lack of professional behaviour – in other words he ranted and raved as well – and Longton had to calm him down. During the third take, which I did not see as I had escaped the heat of the lights for a couple of minutes to get a drink of water, someone trod heavily on Rik's bad ankle. Such was the commotion when I returned that I thought for a moment there had been another attack.

'I am never, ever, going to do this again,' Patrick said to me, having to raise his voice over the hubbub, dropping on to one of the aforesaid squashy cream-coloured sofas. 'As you know, all the guy had to do in the reduced lighting was walk across the room, find Jaquie, take her out through that door over there, come back in pursued by heavies and make for the lifts. The extras were told to keep out of their way but he managed to set a collision course for just about everyone. Hell, I've done the rest of his morning's work for him, even signing the bloody hotel register and now we'll be back to where we were the other day with him just appearing in close-up. I think I'll go and join the army.'

'The men playing the heavies – are they from that same agency?'

'So I understand. Mike Cranley read the Riot Act over them, reminded them there was a problem and told them to behave themselves or they might get shot by the police by mistake. I thought that was rather good and, let's face it, he's the right kind of bloke to sort them out.'

'It seems such a risk employing people like that in the circumstances.'

Patrick yawned. 'Carrick seems perfectly happy about it. Apparently all their CVs are in order and not one has ever been in the armed services so our man can't be among them. I gather that quite a few of them have spent their lives first in care, gone on to young offenders' institutions and finally to prison. If they can forego crime and make something useful of themselves doing this kind of thing then good luck to them.'

Longton was beckoning to him and he went off again, leaving me feeling somewhat lectured at.

'Thanks to you there have been developments,' James Carrick's voice said suddenly in my ear, startling me slightly. 'See you at lunch.'

The sequence had to be rejigged slightly, using different doors, to enable Patrick to undertake the mobile sequences with Jaquie without his face being seen, and there were various other shots of Rik and Jaquie that would eventually be interspersed with the other footage, the former heroically trying not to limp or wince, until it was all finally in the can. The rest of the day would be devoted to face-to-face work with the two stars and sequences when they would be filmed mostly sitting on the sofas talking with others and at the lobby bar. I would not be required.

'Longton was a bit short with Jaquie,' Patrick reported. 'I think you can thank him and Cranley for having the rest of the day off. He told her she could do her own rehearsals this afternoon as you'd been cooking under the lights all morning and, anyway, you were doing everyone, including her, a favour. Mike had told him she'd been overheard making some kind of remarks to you. Did she?'

'She bitched,' I replied.

No doubt in return for a staggering amount of money from the film company, the hotel was using the unit's presence as a rehearsal of their own; for The Verandah restaurant staff. A sumptuous buffet-style lunch was available at no charge.

'I've been to worse wedding receptions than this,' Carrick said, arriving with a loaded plate and seating himself. 'You know, this situation is bloody unreal. One moment I'm half off my head with worry and the next sitting down to a free feast. I've never had a case like it.'

'Like film making,' Patrick said. 'Completely unreal. The important thing is not to drop one's guard.'

'And your good news?' I asked James, after having allowed him to take the edge off his appetite.

'Ah, yes. You mentioned the things missing; possibly an icon and definitely a bracelet. Although Bristol CID are doing the local legwork for the Melvin Lockyer case I asked Lynn Outhwaite to contact Sonia Lockyer's mother to ask her if there were any other items of sentimental or monetary value, family pieces and so forth, that might have been in her son-in-law's house at the time of his death. This enquiry is prior, you understand, to requesting her to come down and have a look round the place herself. She mentioned several things that had been given to the couple, either as wedding presents or

211

afterwards, three in particular; a silver Georgian coffee pot that came from Melvin's side of the family, some Bristol glassware and a very small, almost a miniature, oil painting of chickens that *might* have been done by one of the Glasgow Boys but has never been shown to an art expert. Lynn went to the house, located the coffee pot and glassware in a display cabinet and then found a hole the size that would be made by a picture pin in a small square of unfaded wallpaper in the hall. I've arranged a search of the whole house in case the painting's packed away and something else was in the hall – also contacted his bank as it might be in a vault somewhere.'

'It's another small item easily slipped into a pocket,' I observed. 'Who cleared John Taylor's house?'

'I'd already thought of that. No one seems to know. We know nothing about Taylor at all really.'

'Except that his real name was Rundle,' Patrick said.

'I suppose I could run it through the CRO computer,' Carrick muttered.

Patrick gave him a look that suggested he should have done so already but James was concentrating on his lunch and did not notice.

Martin Longton arrived like an untidy whirlwind. 'More bad news,' he announced. 'Rik's gone off to A and E to have his ankle X-rayed. I'm convinced it's only had a bang but that agent of his has turned up and put the idea in his head that he's chipped a bone. Have you met Deena O'Leary? Yes, I thought you would have done. The woman's a real pain in the backside. If they keep him in or decide that he ought to – '

'Do sit down,' Patrick interrupted, drawing up another chair.

'Sorry, I really mustn't – '

'Sit down, man! We'll fetch you something to eat. Otherwise you'll end up at A and E too.'

Longton subsided, gratefully, I saw with surprise, so

perhaps it was a nice change to be told what to do for once. After consulting with him I went to get him some lunch.

'I'll go to the hospital,' Patrick was saying to him when I got back. 'At least then you'll get no-crap, no-frills feedback.'

'I'm most grateful,' the director said earnestly. 'Mike offered to go too but I could do with him here, just in case we get some work done this afternoon. Have you noticed that Rik's lost weight? He told me he's definitely thinner around the middle.'

Patrick had lost almost half a stone.

It obviously paid to put ideas into a policeman's head for Carrick undertook further checking and, that evening, showed me a list he had made of those working for the film unit who were living in, not just using, either caravans or some other kind of mobile home for the duration of the shooting. There were eight and one of them was the sound recordist, Len Greening.

'They're all out at Wrotherly ready for tomorrow,' James told me. 'You can't easily park things like that in central London, anyway. A minibus was organised to bring their owners in.'

'Can I have this?' I asked.

He gently removed the piece of paper from my fingers. 'No. I don't want you, or that man of yours, breaking and entering. Where is he, by the way?'

'They were still shooting half an hour or so ago,' I said.

I went on to tell him that after he had fired a broadside at Deena O'Leary – who had then presumably limped into port – Patrick had remained with Harrison and his minder until it had been established that the ankle had only suffered minor bruising in the area of the original injury. It had been restrapped and the actor given more painkillers whereupon the trio had returned to King's Court. Patrick had discovered that he was required for close-ups of his hand holding a drink and, later, slipping a gun inside his jacket.

'It wasn't all a waste of time,' Patrick said when he turned up fifteen minutes later. 'I found out quite a bit about that sound man, Len. For some reason he started talking to me while we were waiting for the lighting to be sorted out. He told me he used to work for the BBC and has travelled all over the world. After being badly injured in an ambush in the Middle East that left him with only one lung and other physical problems he decided to work on feature films, but only in the UK. Being shot-up badly affected his nerves and he gets really het-up sometimes when things go wrong. Perhaps he was trying to explain his behaviour this morning – didn't want me to think he was a nutter. It might explain why he goes off and is a bit quiet between takes. You could always check with the BBC, James.'

'That's useful,' said Carrick. 'Thanks. I will.'

Patrick said, 'Going back to Melvin Lockyer telling Ingrid about the woman who made the phone call to him . . . We don't know whether she phoned from John Taylor's or not, or even if it was on June 24th but if it *was* Sonia Lockyer then had she been present when Taylor was murdered? Had her killer forced her to make the phone-call? And then, did he kill her shortly afterwards in the cottage as well? We haven't begun to make any guesses as to where the woman was murdered.'

'I can't believe he'd have risked openly carrying a body to the boot of his car, even after dark,' I said. 'Suppose he made her use his or her own mobile phone somewhere else, somewhere remote perhaps, then killed her and put the body in the boot of the car?'

'Why force her to make the phone call at all?' James said. 'It was a hell of a risk as she was phoning her own husband. He might have recognised her voice. She might even have blurted out in her terror what had happened.'

As the conversation was absolutely no laughing matter I kept quiet about the little experiment I had conducted as 'Snuggems'.

'So do we rule her out?' Patrick asked. 'If so, it means there's another woman involved.'

'Which complicates matters,' James sighed. 'Why do I have a ghastly premonition that this investigation is going to go incredibly tits-up?'

'Then work on the theory that he made the phone-call himself,' I suggested. 'For if this man's so clever at using different personas he can probably disguise his voice to sound like a woman as well.'

'Ingrid,' said James. 'Sometimes you're a real inspiration.'

Only sometimes though.

13

The banqueting hall at Wrotherly was to be used for the scene of one of the movie's grand set-pieces; the assassination of an African Head of State, together with his aides, by the man Rik Harrison was playing, Jack. It amused me that while just about everything else in the novel had been abandoned, the first name of the central character, even though a pseudonym, had been retained.

The Head of State was definitely fictitious but very recognisable in today's world; an obese, corrupt, surrounded-by-armed-thugs-when-at-home character who was channelling all aid intended for his country's starving millions to his relations and cronies while rounding up political opposition and torturing them to death for his own private amusement. This individual was being played with enormous relish by a genial Namibian actor, Josh Rainstall, who had the loudest and deepest voice I had ever heard. Even when he whispered, which was not very often, the whole room, fifty feet long and twenty-five wide, overheard everything he said.

Why this despot was being wined and dined by Her Majesty's Government was, predictably, being glossed over but the hall, which had originally given Wrotherly its name and had very early origins, the long oaken banqueting table arrayed with fruit, flowers, glass and silverware, was a matchless backdrop for murder on a grand scale. On each side of a fireplace, in which you could have parked a medium-sized car, and opposite the three ceiling-to-floor windows on the opposite wall were two ornate tables. In the centre of each was a vase that replicated Wedgwood black basalt and two silver-gilt candelabra, one on each side of it, all made of polystyrene painted to look like the antiques they were supposed to be, the latter matching those on the central table.

Except for a few adminstrative offices and kitchens for the use of outside caterers when there were functions, the entire ground floor of the building had been given over to the film unit. This was necessary as there were a lot of extras required, nearly everyone would be in evening dress so the possibility of having bad weather and people standing in the rain, waiting to be called, was out of the question.

Jaquie Lauderdale, and therefore her stand-in, was not required at this location but having got this far I was determined to see everything through right to the end. I made myself useful to the florist and his assistant, who had been late having been held up in traffic, by helping to carry in potted palms and then shoving greenery into faux lead urns prior to their adding the flowers. I had not seen Patrick at all since we had arrived but as Rik Harrison's rôle demanded that he be one of the guests at the dinner he was presumably getting dressed up.

James Carrick had been working late every night either with his laptop in his room or with DI Foster and his colleagues at the nick, brainstorming the case from all angles. Information was coming in from the various police forces involved, most of it, as James put it, 'routine and useless', but he had added that nobody could be condemned for lack of effort. He had told us that he was as aware as anyone of the bad publicity that had resulted after the police had made mistakes in several recent high profile cases and that this time, if someone else was killed, the buck would definitely stop with him.

As the script called for security men (minders), Longton had solved the problem of having too many such people underfoot, real and otherwise, by coming to our hotel the previous evening to ask Carrick if his contingent could be attired in lounge suits and thus appear in the film. They would be paid as extras. James had answered that as long as whatever they had to do did not conflict with their duties it was all right by him. Would the DCI, the director had gone on to cajole, really like to be in the thick of things as one of the guests and wear a kilt?

'What on earth for?' Carrick had asked.

'Visual balance,' he had been told. 'The set designer's getting on to me about it as there will be a lot of black people in the room and folk with dark clothing. We need to lighten up the colours a little. You're very fair and if you'd like to be in your national dress that's even better. I'll put you on the payroll as the Scottish Ambassador.'

'I don't think Scotland's had ambassadors since the early eighteenth century,' James had said with a laugh.

With his boyish grin Longton had replied, 'The Yanks are paying – they won't know.'

After a reluctant pause Carrick had slowly said, 'I'll do it, but only if you find me a Kennedy tartan kilt with a proper evening sporran, a velvet coatee, preferably dark green, black shoes with silver buckles and a white frilly shirt. Oh, and not forgetting a skean-dhu.' By so stipulating he probably reckoned himself safe.

Not so. The wardrobe department, it transpired, could lay their hands on anything this side of a twenty-four carat gold fig leaf.

'So what is it to be? A bomb?' I asked Patrick, actually not all that interested, when he found me tucking in the last of the foliage.

'Nothing so clumsy and indiscriminate,' he said, done up like a dog's dinner and, this time, actually made up to look more like Rik Harrison as there would be a shot of him dashing up Wrotherly's grand staircase quite close to the camera.

The result was so effective as to be spooky and I had to keep reminding myself that, yes, this really was my husband to whom I was speaking.

'No, they're all going to be picked off, one by one, and with great rapidity with a Glock 17 semi-automatic pistol starting from a position up on the gallery.'

'While the minders of all these people are taking tea with the Queen?'

'The minders are being depicted as slow and stoopid, some of whom, ironically, are now real cops, and only wake up to what's happening after the third shot by which time Jack is well on the move, still firing while ducking and diving behind the furniture and flowers. All the guests are milling around in a state of total panic and the minders daren't fire back in case of hitting the wrong person. Meanwhile the assassin is bringing down chandeliers on their heads – only that bit's being filmed later in the studio – and splattering them with the contents of fruit bowls. Without the bodies it has the potential to be dead funny – if you'll excuse the pun.'

'Are you the one doing most of this, by any chance?'

'The stuntman's going to do the jumping over the gallery rail, onto that grand piano – it's not a real one by the way – in order to get down here but, basically, yes.' I must have looked a bit dubious about this for he went on, reading me wrong for once, 'Carrick has this place ring-fenced and there are four of his team in here. You're not the only one getting a bit twitched. And the story's violent – guns and explosions and so forth so nervousness on anyone's part is to be understood.'

'It's also bloody corny!' I burst out. 'You're risking your life for a can of worms.'

'It's rubbish but it's harmless,' he countered. 'The end product, I mean. People might even enjoy it. Was it all right for me to get paid risking my life really killing people just because they were enemies of the Crown?'

I stared at him, unable to answer the question. Then he had to go and smiled, shrugged, gave me a yummy kiss on one cheek and disappeared into the throng.

All unnecessary personnel were then asked to leave as rehearsals were due to start and I realised with a pang that I had no excuse to be present as, although plenty large enough, this was no vast warehouse or outdoor site where one could tuck oneself out of the way. As it was, for the first sequence the camera was already perched high up on the gallery Patrick had mentioned that ran the length of the room. There was another small, minstrels', gallery situated on the end wall at right-angles to it but there were no musicians, just a couple of the large flower arrangements.

To begin with, it appeared, there would be general shots of the crowded area below. Catering staff were bringing cheese, fruit and wine and laying out napkins and cutlery while the florists scurried to complete decorating the table with small silver-coloured baskets containing roses and carnations.

'Quiet, please!' Mike Cranley called over his loud-hailer as I was making my way out. And then, 'Don't go, Ingrid! Martin would like you up here, please.'

'Just thought you'd like to see what was going on,' Longton said when I arrived. 'Okay, Mike, let's get those seated who are supposed to be and make some sense of it all down there.'

Gradually everyone was sorted out.

'Right folks,' the director said. 'The meal is almost at an end. You know the ropes, you don't need me to tell you: toy with the food, pretend to talk animatedly to the people sitting near you, just behave normally and let the main characters do their thing. Let's have a little practice of careless laughter and chat while we get ready for the first rehearsal.'

It was a very colourful setting, men and women in full evening dress, the candles on the tables now lit. Each had had a piece cut from its length to give the impression that it had been burning for some time. I noticed that Josh Rainstall, well-padded in deliberately over-tight clothing to make him appear even fatter, looked hot and uncomfortable. James, resplendent in his kilt, was not seated but standing close to an empty chair towards one end of the table, his gaze constantly sweeping the room as he absent-mindedly nibbled a piece of cheese. I recognised one or two of his team who, needless to say, looked exactly like minders without even trying.

Rehearsals and the initial overview shots were soon completed and then the unit had to be moved for various scenes, close-ups and otherwise, down in the hall itself. This took a long time and the decision was made to have an early lunch-break to leave the afternoon free for the assassination sequence.

Patrick was talking to Mike Cranley so I left him to find his own nourishment and went outside for some fresh air. It was a strange surprise to walk out into bright sunshine as indoors the curtains had been drawn because it was supposed to be night time.

'God, it's hot under those lights,' James said, coming up for air from a pint of orange juice when I came upon him standing not far from the front entrance in the shade of a tree.

'You look good enough to eat,' I said liltingly and he laughed.

'I kept my pants on though,' he rejoined crisply. 'Some of those women in there look wild enough for anything – not to mention a few of the blokes.'

Not for the first time, and feeling a little ashamed of myself, I wondered what he was like in bed.

Longton was coming to the end of his instructions. 'Remember, for this next scene you're still having fun until the shooting starts. Novice extras please note the bangs will be loud and it's okay for the ladies to jump out of their skins and scream a bit but don't overdo it. Otherwise just act as people would in such a situation and cower down.'

The unit was back up on the gallery and so was I, right on the end of it tucked into an alcove behind the camera and sound teams. I shared the space with Longton's video monitor to which he constantly referred during rehearsals and takes.

Martin had been right; Rik had lost a little weight. Despite everyone's best efforts though, he still limped. Careful camera-work could conceal this up to a point but it appeared that the fight director had had to rethink much of the choreography that he had created before filming started. I had heard someone say that he had been working on it in this room for most of the night.

James had told me that, in view of his experience in what he loosely described as warfare, early suspicion had fallen on this ex-Chief Petty Officer – whose name was Chris – but his credentials were copper-bottomed, including proof, photographs, of time served on the Royal Yacht just prior to his leaving the Navy. Chris was now coaching Rik and Patrick in what they had to do. To one side, Carrick's weapons instructor was holding the semi-automatic pistol ready to hand it over.

The special effects team had a few stratagems concealed in the hall, devices that would cause a few of the fruit bowls to fountain their contents, not widely, as 'bullets' hit them. The crowning glory was a gismo that would mimic a direct hit on Josh Rainstall's immaculate, albeit straining, shirt-front, 'blood' spurting forth. As might be expected, timing was vital.

There was a rehearsal of the first shot, Rik sauntering along the gallery, his back half to the camera but looking down into the hall, and then his hand going beneath his jacket to grab the gun. He still limped – did I imagine one of the sound crew whispering the suggestion that his other ankle be kicked so he walked evenly? – so a different routine was perfected that involved almost a few dance steps suggesting coolness and insouciance, thereby disguising the problem. The time ticked by as then there were close-ups of Patrick's hand holding the gun and then of both he and Rik firing it at several angles, plenty of material for the editorial stages. Then it was time for the camera to be transferred downstairs to film them doing exactly the same thing from below. I went as well to park myself to one side of a window, again behind the sound crew, and no one stopped me.

By three-thirty the shot involving Chris jumping over the gallery rail on to the piano was in the can and cold drinks had been handed out to the parboiled cast. It was decided, after a couple of runs-through for the next sequence that Rik's kind of hop-skip-and-jump routine worked well, forcing the long-suffering man in my life to learn to do it as well. He only tripped over the edge of the carpet once but was driven to complain to an obviously impatient Mike Cranley, 'You try doing this with no feeling in your right foot!'

'Okay, the Head of State and his minions are dead,' the director shouted. 'We'll do their actual death bits last as they, plus a few other people, will get splattered with gore. Let's have the minders at last getting their act together and trying to apprehend the killer.'

There were four rehearsals and then three takes, the pauses between the latter more protracted as the mess from the 'exploded' fruit bowls had to be cleared up each time and renewed. The bodyguards, including one member of Carrick's team, all had to be 'shot' and tumble over on to hidden cushioned pads in a welter of arms and legs and felled guests. This was entered into with great gusto and I began to see what Patrick had meant when he said that, without the bodies, it had the potential to be dead funny. Not that this was permitted: Longton now intimated that there would be close-up shots of them later after the make-up people had graphically depicted their mortal wounds.

'One more time, please,' Longton called. 'Patrick, a slight change to give it a bit more oomph. This time when you fire the last shot at that black fella over there and make for the door, would you duck, turn, fire once more as someone will have taken a pot shot at you and it will have ricochetted off the doorframe. Don't worry, that'll happen in post-production work. Sorry, we'll do the shot of you belting up the main staircase in the entrance hall tomorrow morning as there'll be some final work to do there and just outside.' He turned to the assemblage. 'Bear with us, folks. There'll be another short break for you and then we'll get on with the finale.'

Patrick, his forehead shiny with sweat, had a drink of water and then his make-up was repaired. The clapperboard banged down. Slightly deafened by all the explosions I watched him go through it again, jinking around the urns of flowers and potted palms, using the armchairs by the fireplace as cover and all the while carefully, almost surgically, 'picking off' the opposition. There was no doubt at all in my mind that had the ammunition been live the men would be as dead as they were supposed to be.

When he reached the door and just before he ducked, another shot rang out and splinters smashed off the doorpost. I registered that it was at Patrick's head height, vaguely remembering him being in a slightly different position to last time, and then he had automatically, or perhaps still sticking to the story, fired back. The sound seemed amplified, no, two shots at once.

'Cut!' Longton roared. 'What the hell's going on?'

There was consternation towards the far end of the table.

'The bloke in the kilt's been hit!' a man's voice shouted. 'Call an ambulance!'

In the stunned silence that followed this announcement the stuntman, Chris, jumped onto the table and made his way along it, deftly avoiding everything, shouting that he was trained in first aid. I think I was praying as I stepped up from a chair and followed in his wake. There was always a first aid person on duty, the kind soul who had flushed the grit from my eyes. Perhaps between them they could . . .

People had drawn back to leave space and I had no choice but to remain on the table to give the first aiders room. Etched into my mind always was the sight not only of the large and obscenely spreading redness on James Carrick's beautiful evening shirt but the blood oozing from his mouth. Well out of camera shot, he must have been standing either to watch the filming or keep surveillance for he had fallen by the wall. His eyes were closed and his face had the pallid sheen of death.

The next twenty-four hours were a waking nightmare. Most of them I spent at the hospital, sitting, waiting. Joanna, James's wife, arrived and we sat holding hands, waiting. Patrick came and went, having absolutely no choice but to continue working and when he was with us we sat, holding hands, waiting. I got to know every detail of the dreary pictures on the walls of the room in which we sat and waited, right down to the exact number of whiskers on a very badly painted kitten.

James had been in the operating theatre for four and a half hours while the surgeons fought to save his life. The bullet had entered his chest on his right side, smashing the third and fourth ribs, somehow missed his heart, damaged his left lung and come to rest jammed in his ribs on his left side just above the waist. Despite the efforts of the first aiders he had lost a lot of blood before the ambulance arrived and had had to have twelve units during the operation. Now on a life-support machine he had been given a fifty-fifty chance of survival.

Almost beside himself with anger and the feeling of helplessness Patrick had called upon his father to come and sit with James, a priest being the only person at present permitted. Joanna was dreading that, any time now, she would be asked to go and be with her husband for no other reason than there was no hope and he was dying.

'If only they'd let me *see* him,' was her agonised whisper to me.

'It would make it worse for you if you did,' I told her. 'I once saw Patrick in similar circumstances and didn't recognise him. When you've had a lot of anaesthetic you simply aren't the same person for a while.'

'Will John pray for him?'

'Well of course he'll pray for him! Why else do you think Patrick asked him to come?'

'I just thought he might have done it so we'd know how James was firsthand. I've never really gone in for – well – praying. And Patrick . . . he's so worldly and pragmatic. I can't imagine him believing that would – achieve . . .' She floundered to a halt.

At one time I had not been able to understand it either and had finally come to the startling conclusion that God has very little to do with flower rotas, bring and buy stalls and the wearing of dog collars but is highly involved in watching over pragmatic souls who honestly believe that good should triumph over evil and communicate with Him by prayer. I shared these views with Joanna and she looked startled too.

'John and Patrick are very much alike,' I ventured quietly. 'John won't let James give up.'

A ballistics expert was convinced that the weapon used,

another Glock 17, had been fired from the minstrels' gallery, the first shot chipping the doorframe at the far end of the room instead of blowing out Patrick's brains, the second hitting Carrick. The hewn-from-granite Metropolitan Police Detective Superintendent, no less, who had been drafted in to oversee the case and told me this was sure the hitman had shot the DCI in a fit of pique having failed with his chosen target for the third time. I could not fail to realise, having met him fleetingly at the hospital, that his anger matched Patrick's, in a word, incandescent.

Superintendent Aston had immediately, and to Martin Longton's utter horror, requisitioned all the film that had been exposed that day without giving any guarantees if, or when, it would be returned. Before his arrival at Wrotherly statements had been taken from everyone present, a lengthy process I unwittingly escaped by lying through my teeth saying that, after his wife, I was James's next of kin in order to get myself in the ambulance taking him to hospital.

'But you are in a way,' Joanna said, when I now related this lapse to her. 'Neither of us has any relatives. Besides, we're Victoria's godparents, aren't we? – that's good enough for me. You're family.' And, at last, she burst into tears.

One of those who had bobbed nervously in Aston's wake, a DC who just introduced himself as Will, had been commanded to sit down with us and take my statement. He had had to give his hand a rest part way through because like most professional writers I have a very good memory for places and events but, in my case, not always for names. I had related everything that I could remember of the day that I thought relevant and probably included things that were of no importance at all. He had become particularly interested when I told him about that final, fatal take and Longton's suggestion of the shot to the doorframe that would be faked in afterwards.

'Was it the director's idea then?' he had asked.

'Yes, but that's what directors do,' I had replied. 'He said it would make it more exciting – or words to that effect.'

'But it hadn't been rehearsed up until then – it was just a last-minute idea?'

'Yes, but again that's how filming is. Surely you can't suspect Martin Longton. Anyway, he was right there in the room all the time.'

'I understand though that he moved around, watching monitor screens and so forth.'

'Yes, he did.'

'Where were the monitors?'

'Just in front of a window alcove directly behind me.'

'Ah, so you wouldn't necessarily have noticed if he'd left the room altogether?'

'It would be unthinkable. Other people would have seen him leave.'

'But if all attention was on the take?'

'I still don't think it would have been possible for the director to have left without it being noticed.'

Will clearly still had reservations about this but had said, 'He might have mentioned the idea of the shot hitting the doorframe to someone else first then.'

'That's perfectly possible. To his assistant Mike Cranley, or to the special effects people. Or to Chris, the fight director cum stuntman. Any number of people.'

'Can you remember if any of those you've just mentioned were not in your view when the two shots were fired?'

'No. People like me standing anywhere behind the camera and also those at the back of the gallery wouldn't necessarily have been in my line of vision unless I'd turned round. Remember, altogether there were at least a hundred people in the hall. Come to think of it, I can't remember seeing any of those people.'

'Have you any idea who suggested to DCI Carrick that he be down on the set?'

'That was Martin Longton too,' I had been forced to admit.

I had seen that he made a special note of that, underlining it.

'I've spoken to your husband – er – ' he had consulted his notebook, 'Patrick Gillard. He said he had probably not exactly mirrored his movements for each take out of sheer force of habit from his service days.'

How could I have voiced my relief with Joanna present?

Patrick returned, the three of us were in the room, drinking our umpteenth cup of plastic-tasting coffee and he was trying to cheer us up by recounting how he had fallen flat on his face while running up the grand staircase. He did not tell us then about the episode of Joss Rainstall's shirt-front stubbornly refusing to explode: to mention things like that in the circumstances would have been crass and I found out about it much later.

John Gillard came into the room.

'I've been asked to fetch Joanna,' he said simply.

The colour drained from her face. 'You mean . . . ?'

He shook his head. 'I don't know. All they're saying is that there have been – changes.'

She jerked to her feet.

John said, 'My dear, I've nodded off a couple of times but I must go and have a short rest and something to eat. Perhaps, though, it would be better if you and he were alone for a while. I shall continue to pray for both of you.'

Joanna held out her hand, not to me, but to Patrick. 'Please come with me.'

'Will they let – ?' I began to say but stopped when I saw the expression on Patrick's face.

Yes, they would, they would have no choice in the matter.

'Shouldn't you go back to your hotel and try to sleep?' John said to me when they had gone and he had slumped into a chair. In his seventieth year, his hair was now almost white, his face lined and I had noticed with a pang as he entered the room that he had developed a slight stoop since I had last seen him.

'I can't,' I said.

'At least keep an old man company while he has a bite to eat,' he said in a quavery voice.

This was not John's style at all and I smiled.

'That's better,' he said robustly.

'But you don't really want me along. I shall be a distraction.'

He rose and tugged me to my feet. 'Praying isn't like those folk who chant like zombies for weeks on end, you know. And being familiar with Patrick's methods I have an idea the Almighty's getting a real earful right now anyway.'

It was a shock to realise that it was not only just before midnight, but midnight on the day following the one James had been shot. After I had managed to eat a little John persuaded me to allow him to drive me back to Wrotherly to fetch the car. There, he then virtually ordered me go to the hotel, where he was also booked in, for some rest. I urged him to do the same but he told me he would return to the hospital, in case he could be of any use, and would have a doze on the bench-seating of the waiting room. He was used to long bedside vigils, was his parting remark.

I showered, suddenly feeling remarkably grubby, and then must have simply fallen asleep on my feet and somehow made it back into the room on auto for I had no recollection of towelling myself dry and had not switched off the light, waking with a start at seven when the phone rang.

It was Martin Longton. He apologised for disturbing me so

early but thought he would try to catch either of us to ask how Carrick was before we went to the hospital. His concern was tangible. The damned film was responsible, he told me in his impetuous way. Films that unleashed maniacs from the murky past should not be made, he raved. Was there anything he could do?

I answered his questions as well as I could and made other suitable noises, including politely refusing his offer to drive me to the hospital as our car was now at the hotel. He finished by saying that he regretted it but Patrick would be needed at the studio, eight-thirty at the absolute latest. Was he there with me?

For some reason I lied and said that he was in the shower.

For some reason I no longer felt safe on my own.

Whoever it was got a kick out of befriending people before he killed them.

The clandestine caravan search had, for various reasons, fallen by the wayside and I could not envisage any likelihood of my being able to carry it out. Especially now with the work continuing at the studio, the crew's vehicles and any mobile homes now parked in an area covered by CCTV cameras and patrolled by security guards.

Over a scanty breakfast, mostly coffee, I was forcing myself to think about this, trying to be positive and carry on with the investigation but it was pretty hopeless as I simply could not concentrate. All I could think of was James, connected to machines that helped keep him alive. It took a lot of willpower to ring Patrick to give him Longton's message as I had a terrible feeling that I would hear the worst possible news.

But it had to be done as it was now seven-thirty.

It rang for a while and I could imagine him leaving the ward in order to answer it.

'Gillard.'

231

'It's me,' I said.

'Sorry I took such a long time to answer. I programmed the ringtone on my phone to play *Scotland the Brave* as I thought he might hear it but – ' His voice broke and he was unable to speak for a few moments. Then he went on huskily, 'It should have been me. James was only shot because the filthy bastard got in a temper after he'd failed to hit me again.'

'But your body would be in the mortuary right now,' I pointed out. 'While James has a chance. Please tell me how he is.'

'He's holding his own. The changes Dad heard the medics talking about were half-expected and have been dealt with. He's being monitored all the time and everything possible's being done.'

I told him about Longton's phone-call and he swore.

'It'll help if you keep busy,' I told him. 'I'll come over, pick you up and take you to work. Then I'll go back to be with Joanna.'

'Oh, I forgot. Aston's lot have found the weapon that was used. It had been hidden in one of the flower arrangements on the minstrels' gallery. There were no fingerprints on it but it was another of the guns stolen during that robbery at the Met's warehouse. We'll have to wait to find out what forensic make of the samples that the scenes-of-crime people took; fluff, hair – the usual bits and bobs.'

'I'm really surprised Aston let you know about it.'

'So am I. But I had told him that, after Joanna, we were James's next of kin.'

14

When I went to collect Patrick from the studio that evening –
he had rung me at midday to ask if there was any improvement in James's condition, there wasn't – I discovered to my
surprise that filming had finished for the day. Martin Longton
was not around but Len, the sound man, and a few others
were still tidying away. He had been left with a message for
me, should I turn up, asking if I would be available for some
light duties the next morning.

'I like it when it goes quiet,' Len said when he had checked
that I had Longton's mobile phone number. 'The pressure gets
to me. Plus the problems we've had with this project. It's like
being back in a war zone.' He took a breath between each
short sentence or every few words and I recollected what
Patrick had said about him having been wounded in the
Middle East.

'I meditate, you know,' he went on quietly, his dark eyes
seeming to stare right through me. 'Between takes. And in my
caravan, morning and evening. It really helps. You ought to
try it. I could give you a few pointers, if you like.'

'You're very kind,' I murmured, resisting an urge to run like
blazes despite Patrick's statement that he was probably all
right. 'I'll think about it. Do you know where Patrick is?'

He slapped his forehead. 'Here's me a forgetful fool! I was
to tell you he's gone to the pub – with Mike Cranley. They
reckoned they needed a pint. The Brown Bear. D'you know
it?'

I shook my head 'No.'

'It's just a couple of hundred yards from the gates – turn
right in the direction of the big RAC place.'

I thanked him and turned to go.

'How's the cop?'

'Very ill, but still holding on.'

'He's a tough cove. Scots are. It's all that bloody porridge they eat.' Len then uttered a bark of laughter and shuffled back to his task.

The two were tête-à-tête in the public bar of the Brown Bear, engaged in what I am forced to describe as sniggering, all the body language pointing to the aftermath of the punchline of a dirty joke. I also saw that Patrick was smoking a small cigar, something he does but rarely, usually when the occasion can be defined as 'being out with the lads'. He turned as I approached.

'Ah, you found us. What will you have?'

I replied, tartly, that as I was obviously the designated driver I had better stick to orange juice.

'Go on, you can have one without being over the limit,' Mike said. 'Let me get you a G 'n' T.'

I was about to refuse but did not when Patrick's toe nudged my ankle in a silent request.

I made it last though and somehow survived the tedium of watching them have another two pints while they set the world to rights. At last Patrick said that he ought to go and they called it a day.

'See you tomorrow,' Mike called to us as we left, having said he would stay on for a while.

'Sorry about that,' Patrick said as we walked back to the car.

'Checking out the chummy ones?' I queried.

'Umm.'

'But he doesn't really fit the description. Although he's broad-shouldered he's not particularly tall – not as tall as you by at least a couple of inches.'

'No, but that still makes him a six-footer. And if all the descriptions we've had so far of the man we're after have been given by people who are short and he's been seen with people of comparatively small stature it could give the impression of a man taller than he really is. Don't forget he's also been seen behind the wheel of a small car. Cranley's quite strong enough to have lifted a man of Melvin Lockyer's stature. I shall keep an open mind.'

'We didn't actually learn anything useful about him from what he said, did we?'

'No, you're right, not much.'

'It's Len who really gives me the creeps.'

'Ingrid, we're not *looking* for a man who gives people the creeps. This guy will be ordinary-seeming and pleasant to just about everyone.'

'Did Mike ask after James?'

'Yes, he did. But then again, everyone is.'

'Len did,' I persevered stubbornly, and then laughed.'

'Perhaps he thinks the attack on Carrick is peanuts compared with what happened to him and everyone's making a hellava fuss.'

'He told me he meditates as he gets stressed-out and sort of offered to instruct me on how to go about it.'

'Why don't you take him up on it? He might even show you his etchings.'

'There's no need to be so sarky!'

Patrick took my hand and gave it a squeeze. 'Sorry. I'm stressed-out as well.'

'I take it you want to go to the hospital before we do anything else.'

'I must. Any developments?'

'I've been there all afternoon. Your father and Joanna said he's just the same.'

James was not the same. Half an hour before we arrived he had been taken back to the operating theatre for further surgery when it was realised that something was preventing his heart from functioning properly.

'This really is crunch time,' Joanna told us. 'The surgeon's been lovely about it and talked me through what they're going to do – not that I understood all the medical terms. He said that James has a very strong constitution or they wouldn't have risked doing it yet. But if they'd left it much longer he might have died anyway. I thought he looked a terrible colour,' she finished by saying wretchedly.

'Please go back to the hotel with Ingrid and get some rest now,' Patrick begged her. 'I'll stay here and let you know the minute there's something to report. You can't do anything while he's in theatre.'

'I can't leave him.'

'Look, he's going to be recuperating for weeks. You'll need all your energy to look after him.'

For some reason this worked and, like a lamb, Joanna came with me. At the hotel she seemed to gain strength from being in James's room surrounded by his clothes and other possessions, the reverse of what I had expected. We arranged to meet in half an hour to have something light to eat.

'You know, I can hardly believe I used to be James's sergeant,' was her opening remark as we went down in the lift.

'What was he like to work for?' I asked.

'Very precise and professional. Very much under control – to begin with anyway. His wife was dying from a rare form of bone cancer but he tried not to let it interfere with the job.' There was a catch in her voice but she went on, 'He was a brilliant boss – shouldered the blame when things went wrong and took us all down the pub when we got a good result. That's very rare. And then after a while it became obvious that he couldn't handle the situation any longer. He'd given me a lift home one night after a raid when everyone got a bit

236

battered and just followed me in. We – we made mad passion-
ate love on the hall carpet.'

'When we've checked with Patrick how he is,' I said carefully, 'how do you fancy a little unofficial police work?'

'What, tonight?'

'Yes. Someone's offered to teach me how to meditate and as
Patrick and I have a theory that the man we're after has a policy of befriending people before he kills them I thought I'd use
the opportunity to give this particular individual a surprise
and a grilling instead. I could do with some back-up.'

'Suppose he turns nasty.'

'He could do anything but professes to be a nervous wreck
so it will be interesting to see if that's genuine. Anyway, I've
got a gun.'

Not batting one neatly plucked eyebrow Joanna said, 'So
you're going to threaten to fill him full of lead and if he completely freaks out it'll prove he's on the line?'

'Perhaps not *quite* as brutal as that.'

'You really suspect him of being the killer?'

'To use the time-honoured expression, I want to eliminate
him from my enquiries.'

We reached the restaurant and as we were shown to a table
my mobile rang. I apologised to the people nearby and
answered it. It was Patrick.

'James has just been taken back to the High Dependancy
Ward,' he said, his voice clipped with tension. 'They're not
saying much and I intend to find the surgeon, who might be
more forthcoming. Would you please ask Joanna his name?'

This I did.

'Try to keep her with you for as long as you can,' Patrick
continued when in receipt of the information. 'Dad and I'll
stay here and take it in turns to sit with him. Perhaps you'd
give me a ring later.'

When I had relayed the news to Joanna she said, 'I wonder

if James saw the man who took a shot at Patrick and that's why the weapon was turned on him?'

I immediately rang Patrick back with this, suggesting that he ask Superintendent Aston to provide a police guard. He promised to do so immediately, probably annoyed that no one else had thought of it earlier.

It was almost dark when Joanna and I reached the film studio. I had to stop at the gate and show my credentials, explain we were going to see someone and Joanna was given a visitor's pass. Parking close to where the group of caravans and mobile homes were all clustered together on the side of the car park farthest away from the main road we got out of the car into the smell of cooking and the muted heavy thump of rock music. A train clattered by.

'Which one does he live in?' Joanna asked.

'I don't know,' I admitted. 'Shall we light a small fire under all of them to find out?'

She placed a hand lightly on my shoulder. 'Hey, hey, you *are* angry.'

My tears took me completely by surprise.

'I'm really sorry,' I gulped after a while.

Joanna had had her arms around me but now rummaged in her bag and gave me a wad of paper tissues. 'Have a blow. Why on earth should you apologise? You've been going through hell just lately.' She then went over to batter on the door of the nearest caravan.

The door opened and bright light flooded out around a woman's silhouette.

'Yes?'

'We're looking for – ' Joanna glanced across to me.

'Len Greening,' I said.

'Len Greening,' she said.

The woman pointed. 'That one.'

'Thank you,' Joanna said. 'Sorry to have bothered you.'

'I thought you were the police,' the woman said and slammed the door.

'I am the police,' Joanna announced to me, marching off very straight-backed to the large camper van on the end of the row. 'This is for James,' she said over her shoulder. 'I'll do the talking and you won't need your pop gun.'

How Bath must have trembled when the pair of them were on the loose.

The vehicle indicated was not the one from which the rock music emanated. In fact, hot on Joanna's heels, I could distinctly hear Mozart as we approached.

'Wait!' I hissed.

'What?' Her knuckles had paused seemingly half an inch from the door.

'Look, I know this sounds pathetic,' I whispered. 'But if he *is* okay and telling the truth about himself we might do him real harm if we – well – fly off the handle.'

'I have no intention of going berserk,' Joanna answered stiffly and knocked, though with restraint compared to last time.

The horn concerto was silenced and after a short pause there was the sound of shuffling footsteps within. Several locks and bolts were undone and the door was opened a few inches on a security chain.

'Yes?' said Len's voice from the dimness within.

Joanna said, 'My name's Joanna Carrick and I'm here with Ingrid, Patrick's wife. We'd like to talk to you about the shooting.'

'So it is,' he said. 'Just a minute.'

The door closed, there was a clatter as the chain came off and then he opened it again.

'Can't be too careful these days, can you? Just a minute and I'll put another light on for you.'

I hoped I refrained from gaping as we went in and I saw Joanna's eyes widen.

The interior was utterly sumptuous with oriental carpets not only on the floor but hanging like tapestries on the walls. Rich silk curtains screened the tiny kitchen area and a doorway into what must be the bathroom. Along one wall was a padded bench that probably opened out to serve as a bed with lockers beneath and there was no other seating, just several large, jewel-bright velvet floor-cushions. A music system and books filled the shelving above the bench.

'Take a pew,' Len said, folding up awkwardly but ultimately neatly on to one of the cushions. 'Sit on what I call my sofa if you like but I prefer the floor.'

We sat on the cushions.

'Do you like soft lights?' Len continued. 'Shall we just have the lamp?'

This was an ornate metal, rather beautiful affair hanging from the ceiling that I had almost hit my head on. The sides were like miniature stained-glass windows. When Len took our hesitation in replying as agreement to his suggestion he leaned over and turned off the single tablelamp on a lower shelf. The patterns in the lamp immediately revealed themselves to be that of flowers and flying birds. Its light, subdued but not gloomy, imbued our surroundings with a serenity hard to explain.

'Like it? I got it in Kashmir. The old man who made it said he got the idea from a magazine article he'd read about Tiffany's. Now, what did you want to ask me?'

I pipped Joanna to the post with, 'Why did you laugh when I told you that Joanna's husband was still very ill?'

He gave her a surprised stare. '*That* Carrick?'

'That Carrick,' Joanna echoed grimly and I was glad I had not mentioned it to her before.

'I forget what was said exactly,' Len murmured. 'But I

assure you I found nothing amusing in the fact that he'd been shot. There, and you've come all this way to sort it out, no doubt suspecting I had a hand in it.'

He still took a sharp breath between each sentence but appeared much more relaxed in his own environment. Not only that, he gave every impression of enjoying our visit, not what I had planned at all.

'Together with several other people you could well have done,' Joanna said. 'It has to be someone closely involved with the making of this film.'

'It's not me. For one thing I can never leave my sound equipment during takes or even during rehearsals.'

'Do you have an assistant?'

'Yes, I do, Jock. And there's Nev the boom operator.' He added, hopefully, 'You could talk to them, they're both strange coves.'

'In what way?'

'It's – er – nothing you could put a finger on. But they laugh at me, behind my back.'

They probably thought he was a very strange cove. You are Len, you are. I asked, 'Were you in the army as a young man, before you joined the BBC?'

'*Me*?' A bony forefinger jabbed into his own chest. 'No! I couldn't even kill a rat.'

This was an example of a common public perception that because a man is highly trained in what I shall call war games, he is happy to exterminate everything on the planet that moves, preferably from a helicopter with a machine gun. This was how Patrick had acquired his horse. He was once asked, bizarrely, by a senior officer who of all people should have known better, to shoot his old and neglected grey hunter. Patrick, raging, had borrowed a Land Rover and trailer without asking and brought the horse home instead.

Unfortunately this little mental digression had not proved

241

whether Len was telling the truth about his past or lying. All the wind appearing to have gone out of Joanna's sails after her initial enthusiasm I said, 'And yet despite people understandably getting very jittery after all these attacks you wander off between takes and meditate thereby offering yourself as an easy target.'

'If you're going to get shot you're going to get shot,' Len muttered.

'This vehicle is bolted and barred like a fortress though and you displayed some nervousness before you let us in.'

'It's the young buggers you have to watch who'll kill you for the price of a fix.'

'Oh, so you know you're not next on the list then.'

I thought for a moment that he was about to flare up but he merely said, 'No, of course not. Would you like a cup of tea? I've got some nice chocolate biscuits.'

Joanna caught my eye with a 'we're getting nowhere' look.

'Yes, please,' I said, getting up. 'I'll make it.'

'Thinking I might poison you?' Len enquired with a sly grin. Then, slapping his forehead with a hand, he exclaimed, 'That was it! Porridge!'

'Porridge?' I said.

'You asked me why I laughed. I'd said something about the Scots being tough because they ate a lot of porridge.' He gazed expectantly from one of us to the other and saw that we were not exactly rolling in the aisles. 'No, it's not really funny, is it? Still, it's not as though the man's going to die.'

'Yes, James might die,' Joanna said, fighting tears. She jumped up. 'Ingrid, I suggest we go home. We're completely wasting our time here.'

I gave her the car keys. 'I'll catch you up in a minute.'

'You sure?' she said dubiously, giving Len a dirty look.

'Sure.'

I let her out and sat down again, pulling my cushion up a

bit closer to Len's. 'Well now,' I said. 'You've got rid of one of us but this one's going nowhere until you drop your silly old gaffer front even if it takes all night.'

'Oh, aye?' said Len.

'Shall we get down to business?'

'I can't help you with this.'

'Someone in this film unit is a serial killer. Quite a few years ago he was in one of the British armed services undercover units and after he was blamed for betraying his comrades on a mission he became very bitter, went abroad and hired himself out as an assassin. If you've read the book that this stupid film's based on you know all that. But I don't think he went away for very long. He could well have been badly injured on an assignment, as you say you were. Then, and this was probably after he returned home under a false passport and made a whole new life and career for himself, he discovered that a film was going to be made about him. A man calling himself John Taylor had written a book about the operation in Northern Ireland that had resulted in the deaths of the three soldiers. Taylor's real name was Rundle and he was probably a relation of the real betrayer. Taylor's story not only blamed the one he called Jack but the entire work was third-rate, full of purely gratuitous sex and violence and very badly written.

'Worse,' I continued, 'Jack, or whoever he really is, then found out that the film bore very little relation even to the novel and his whole story had been completely trivialised. No one had ever tried to clear his name or investigate what really happened and now he's getting his revenge, picking off those involved with the making of *Blood and Anger* one by one. But DCI Carrick is different, for although he's trying to solve the case, he's an outsider. It's quite likely he saw the killer fire from the minstrels' gallery and that's the only reason he was shot.'

I went on, 'I'm coming round to the idea that you know

who it is. You might even be quite friendly with him and he's promised you you're not on his list. Because you were horribly shot up in the Middle East and sympathise with this man you approve of what he's doing in a sick kind of way. Here are a lot of people suffering in the same way you and presumably some of your colleagues did. *That's* why you laughed – it had nothing to do with porridge.'

'Ever been in a burning car full of burning screaming people?' he asked me in a deadly whisper.

'No. But then again the scriptwriter was hanged and disembowelled and his wife was strangled. Taylor had his brains beaten out with an iron doorstop. Romanov was shot between the eyes. A whole lot of people, extras included, were nearly gunned down in the quarry. Patrick's jugular vein and windpipe could have been severed by those shards of brick. And now Joanna's husband is fighting for his life. When's it going to stop, eh? When you feel all nice and cosy inside, like you try to be in here, say enough's enough and tell the police?'

'I'm not behind all this!'

'No, Len, you're just an accessory to murder.'

He sat, shaking his head, eyes tightly closed, rocking backwards and forwards. After half a minute or so he muttered, 'Please give me those pills up there on the shelf.'

'Balls,' I said.

His eyes flew wide open. 'God, you're a hard bitch.'

'No doubt,' I said wryly. 'And James Carrick is a friend of mine.'

He went in for a little more rocking. 'Eighteen months in agony in hospital counts for nothing then.'

'Not in the sense that it has to be cancelled out by visiting the same on other people. You know that. Deep down you may well be disappointed as you were hoping Carrick was soon going to solve the case and you'd be left alone in your

244

sad little world hating the rest of humanity for what life's done to you.'

'No one talks to me like this,' Len groaned, rocking more quickly.

I got to my feet and at the slight sound he opened his eyes again, alarmed.

'You *are* nervous,' I commented. 'Perhaps he's not a friend after all and you're scared stiff of him. The police would give you protection, you know.' When he said nothing, I continued, 'Working out whether it's better to be thought bananas or a coward?'

'Go away.'

Someone thundered on the door, making us both jump. 'Ingrid, are you all right in there?' said Joanna's voice.

Len lunged to his feet and opened it. 'She's just coming,' he reported eagerly. Then his gaze went beyond her. 'Mike!' he exclaimed. 'I seem to be very popular tonight.' He turned to me and said in quite a loud voice, 'Mike's interested in learning to meditate as well.'

Fuming, I left, stepping down just as the assistant director arrived. I introduced Joanna. 'I actually came over to find out if you'd like a quick pint before the Brown Bear closes,' he said to Len. 'And you girls as well, if you like. That's my pad,' he went on, gesturing towards a state-of-the-art twin-axle caravan hitched to a Shogun. 'I'd ask you over for a nightcap there but the place is a real mess.'

'We'd love to go for a quick drink,' I said, not even looking in Joanna's direction.

'Len?' Mike said.

'Well – er – yes, perhaps I will. I'll just lock up.'

'The man's security mad,' Mike said under his breath as we went on ahead. 'Still, after what happened to him I suppose it's to be expected. Having said that, I suppose I'd better lock up too.'

We changed course slightly. I was absolutely furious with Joanna for interrupting just when it seemed I had a good chance of making Len tell me something important.

'Are you really interested in meditation, Ingrid?'

'No,' I said, also speaking in an undertone. 'But like everyone else I'm feeling helpless and thought I'd try to be useful by asking people the kind of questions that the police might not get around to.'

'No, me neither, I just say I am and take the guy out for a drink sometimes. I understand you and Patrick were with MI5 – it must be hard to stop investigating.'

'Yes, but of course we no longer have the same freedom of conduct.'

'What did you make of old Len, then?'

I decided that this was not a good moment to reveal my real thoughts. 'He's completely away with the birds – harmless though.'

'The man's brilliant at his job.'

'I'm sure he is.'

Joanna's mobile phone rang and for a moment she froze to the spot, unable to answer it. Moving like a robot she then did so. After listening for a short while she whispered, 'I see. Thank you very much, Patrick.' Then she fainted.

'Oh, my God!' Mike exclaimed. He had moved quickly, not quite succeeding in catching her but had at least prevented her head from hitting the ground. He lifted her and bore her to his caravan. I opened the door for him and he carefully negotiated the narrow entrance door with his burden, went within – I was right on his heels – and laid her down on a black leather sofa.

'I'll get some water,' I said, opening doors at random in a search for the bathroom but not really thinking what I was doing, aware only that James was dead.

'Second on the left,' Mike called.

246

'This is dreadful,' he said when I returned with a towel, one end of which I had soaked with cold water. 'You know what it means, don't you? He's gone.' He got up and went over to stand with his back to me, head slightly bowed, perhaps not wishing me to see his emotion.

I turned to place the wetted towel on Joanna's forehead and saw that she was looking up at me.

'I want to go and see him,' she said softly.

'Are you sure?' I asked.

For an answer she sat up, took the towel from me and patted it over her face. 'Yes,' she said. 'Please take me now.'

I found that I did not feel too good myself but took the towel from her, buried my own face in its coldness for a few moments and then helped her stand. I think I thanked Mike for his kindness and when we met Len on the doorstep I seemed to remember afterwards that I mumbled something about having to leave and then we were in the car and I was wondering if I was in any fit state to drive.

Joanna was in tears by now.

'I'm so terribly, terribly sorry,' I said, ready tears of my own springing to my eyes.

'No, no, no,' she sobbed. 'He's all right. They really think he's going to be all right. He woke up a bit while Patrick and John were there. Isn't it bloody wonderful?' she wailed.

I gave her a hug and then started the car, praying to the patron saint of Land Rovers to help me drive it, her words hardly believable. Later I would tell her that, by her actions, wittingly or not, I thought she had been instrumental in solving the case for James. But first of all it was vital to get away from this car park.

'I'm sorry, but I can't arrest someone on the strength of his caravan being tidy when he'd said it was a mess,' Superintendent Aston said when he rang me the next morning in response to my call to the nick just before midnight. 'He obviously made the excuse as he didn't really want all you lot in his place. It's the kind of excuse you and I make every day. And you said that because there were several mirrors in the living area and you could see that he was really grinning all over his face instead of looking sad when he thought DCI Carrick was dead then he's as guilty as hell. I agree it's odd but perhaps he has a secret hate thing about cops. Quite a lot of people do. The icon you *think* you saw in his bedroom that *could* be one that *might* have been stolen from Vladimir Romanov's house is a fairytale, not evidence.'

I had been to see James, kissed him and felt him squeeze my hand in response so was still on too much of a high to be utterly crushed by this judgement.

It would have to be Plan B, whatever that was.

15

Aston's call had woken Patrick. He squinted at his watch, groaned and buried himself beneath the quilt again.

'Don't you have to go to work today?' I asked.

'Not until later this morning,' he replied, surfacing. 'Who was on the phone?'

'Aston. Basically rubbishing everything I told the police last night.'

'I really didn't expect him to do anything else. And it was a stupid thing to do – you and Joanna wandering around right where we think the killer might hang out.'

'I seem to remember that it was me who thought that. *You* suggested that I went to see Len and the rest just happened. If Joanna hadn't become worried about me and banged on the door I might have found out something.'

'Did you mention that to the cops too?'

'No, there was really nothing to tell.' In the cold light of dawn I supposed Aston had a point; too many 'ifs', 'mights' and 'maybe's'.

'Why d'you reckon Mike turned up when he did? Was it really to ask Len to go down the pub with him?'

'If he's a suspect then he might have wanted to find out why we'd gone to see Len. I think Len knows who the killer is. He appeared to be a bit nervous of Mike but then again he's a nervous kind of man. Mike was quick to tell me he wasn't really interested in meditation and was only being friendly. Which is a word I don't like right now.'

'And *was* he trying to hide a big smile on his face or were his features distorted because you were seeing them courtesy of any number of mirrors, some of which could have been fairly rubbishy?'

'Two good-quality mirrors,' I responded urbanely. I had got used to this in our MI5 days; the clinical dissection of any potentially significant findings of mine where he himself had not been present. 'I know my seeing an icon's iffy as far as evidence is concerned but they're hardly common. In fact I don't think I've ever seen one before outside a museum, a really upmarket art dealer's or Romanov's living room.'

'But it was similar to Romanov's?'

'Yes, it was. And the frame was the same colour.'

'I'll think about when I've had some coffee,' Patrick muttered, heading for the bathroom. 'God, I'm tired. I don't think I've felt as tired as this since yesterday.'

'It's good about James though.'

'Which more than makes it all worthwhile. Before he had that second op though we thought we'd lost him twice.' Through the open doorway, after I had assumed he was including himself with the medical staff, he added, 'He owes Dad and me a pint, if not several.'

'It's infuriating but Aston was right; he simply wouldn't be able to get a search warrant on the strength of what you saw,' Patrick said later. 'Personally, I'd like to break into that caravan and not only purloin the icon but have a damned good look for Sonia Lockyer's bracelet and the picture that seems to have gone missing from their house. But it's the same old story, isn't it? Back in the D12 days we had *carte blanche*.'

'Back in the D12 days you weren't nearly so law-abiding,' I said crossly.

'That's what I've just said, haven't I?'

'I'll put it another way. Back in the D12 days you exceeded our *carte blanche* status, the purpose of which wasn't intended to ensure that, more often than not, we left behind us a trail of destruction and dead bodies.'

'Eh?' he said blankly.

'Patrick, you have a very short memory!' I blared at him. 'And now you're tiptoeing around the very concept of a fifteen-minute job that might result in catching a serial killer.'

He gave me a crooked smile. 'I agree that not so long ago I would have grabbed my skeleton keys and gone in there, come hell or high water and whatever policemen say. One of the problems with it is that the caravan is parked in a high-security area: CCTV cameras, patrols, the lot. If Mike Cranley is our man he would be highly amused if I was nabbed for breaking and entering. Another point to take into consideration is that if he has any sense he will have moved these things by now.'

I had just recollected my own comments about our post-MI5 days to Cranley the night before. 'We do nothing then?'

'Nothing too obvious – just for a little longer. Very soon, he'll make a mistake. And Ingrid – take care. I think he may target a woman again next time. It's easier and offers the chance of sex, whether she's willing or not. So please don't go off on your own or just with Joanna again.' He must have detected a hint of mutiny in my demeanour for he continued, 'Yes, I know you're a big strong girl and in the past managed to fend off a would-be rapist but this one would be like fighting *me*. What chance would you have then, honeybunch?'

Not a lot.

The two large sets had been completed. The first was a painstaking recreation of the hall at Wrotherly, necessary because the script called for – surprise, surprise – explosions and other highly damaging mayhem, including the chandelier crashing down in the scene in which the African leader was assassinated and which, for obvious reasons, could not have been done in the house. The second, to which the set-dressers were adding the final touches, was another copy and much more extensive; a section of the palatial lobby of the

King's Court Hotel together with a couple of connecting corridors and rooms off. It was the setting for the film's finale when someone whom 'Jack' knew from his army days would appear with evidence that would prove the real identity of the Northern Ireland betrayer. The news would have the effect of saving Jack's life as he had been tricked into an assignment that was actually a trap set by the harpy-like daughter of the mega-gangster he had blown up in revenge for Daddy's terrible demise. She had taken Ritz hostage as a back-up plan. Having paused for thought after being given the news that he had been cleared of the betrayal, Jack would perceive that he was about to be ambushed and there would then be the mother of all shoot-outs, chases and every pyrotechnic device the special effects team could think of before he released Ritz from where she was being held by other sundry undesirables. They would fall into one another's arms and, after eluding the rest of the heavies, live happily ever after.

I was part of this – it was scheduled to be filmed first – already made-up, be-wigged and wearing a kind of black boiler suit, again made of silk and belted with a gold chain. I was rather hoping the outfit would get soaked in fake blood like the first so I could make off with this one too. The shoes were another matter, vertiginous high heels having made a comeback. Jaquie was not happy with them either, darkly promising that she would break a leg with all the hotfooting she was required to do and had therefore decided that I could do as much of it as possible as well as all the lighting rehearsals.

Superintendent Aston was providing a police presence even for this studio filming – they were said to be in every nook and cranny – and had already conducted heavyweight interviews, trying to establish everyone's exact position when James was shot. The East-End humour of some of the riggers and electricians had resulted in a rumour going around that the director had asked him if he wanted to play the part of a door-pillar and Aston had refused on the grounds that he could not act. This light-heartedness did not come amiss for there was a general aura of nervous despondency. Several people had left, contracts notwithstanding, adding to a trickle of technicians and others who had gone in the name of personal safety since the first attack. Patrick and I had known nothing about this development until it was mentioned by Longton shortly after we had arrived for work. The director was really worried now that the trickle would turn into a torrent.

Rik Harrison's ankle was better but he still could not run and the conclusion had been reached that any kind of ruse to disguise his limp would not do for this scene. There could be only one answer to the problem and he was standing right by my side wearing a pearl-grey Italian suit, black shirt and tie, his hair as I am used to seeing it and, Heaven forfend, a single gold earring.

'It's stuck on somehow,' Patrick said, seeing my gaze on it. 'Jack's disguising himself as a Mafia man.'

'You did once have your ears pierced though – for the Hell's Angels job.'

'Yes, in a backstreet place. I forget exactly where but if I do ever remember I'll go down there with a hand grenade. It hurt like hell and the rings must have been brass because my earlobes went bright green and then got infected and I felt a right prat afterwards when I had to go to the doctor's.' He surveyed the rest of the set from our good position to do so, a small landing at the turn of a staircase that did not actually go anywhere but ended just past a false wall. 'Ah, there's Aston. I understand he went to visit James hoping to be able to ask him if he had seen the gunman but as the man's still on a respirator and can't really communicate yet he didn't get any joy.'

'I didn't disturb Joanna this morning in case she was asleep.'

'I haven't spoken to her today either. I got that little gem of information when I overheard a couple of Aston's blokes talking.'

'Mike Cranley appears to be behaving normally – no more and no less edgy than just before a shoot. '

'Martin Longton looks as though he could spontaneously combust at any moment. That's normal too.'

Chris, the fight director, was busy with a tape measure and, as we watched, he backed off, ran and performed a neat cartwheel that took in a sofa, a coffee table and an armchair. He shook his head and moved the armchair a few inches. I had an idea we would all be earning our money this afternoon.

Everyone was then called to order and work started. First of all Martin Longton made it clear that filming would continue until the scene was completed to his satisfaction, if necessary on into the night after an afternoon break. The reason for this was an almost impossibly tight schedule now that Detective Superintendent Aston had said he wanted to hold a reconstruction of the attempted murder of Detective Chief Inspector James Carrick first thing the next morning. Failing the availability of the room at Wrotherly Hall itself, which was booked for a conference, he was insisting it be held instead in the studio's replica.

Six hours later we were still hard at it. As had been normal procedure, close-up shots involving the main leads had been completed before they became too tired and dishevelled and then, after the lunch break, work had moved on to the action scenes. With regard to the plot I gathered that the phoney assignment organised by the gangster's daughter that she hoped would result in Jack's demise was the gunning-down of a Saudi prince on his arrival at his hotel prior to a UK

OPEC meeting. But the prince was merely one of her recently deceased father's bodyguards in disguise, his retinue other heavily armed minions who would turn the tables on the would-be executioner. So instead of behaving the way Jack had been led to believe they would come in by another entrance five minutes earlier and seek out Jack where they knew he would be concealing himself.

'I've been meaning to talk to you about Katie having a pony,' I said to Patrick. He was waiting to be called for what amounted to a gunfight at the OK corral, only indoors.

'She's been bending my ear about it too,' he said, scanning the area: not for the usual security reasons this time but trying to remember his rather complicated moves.

'Really? I only heard about it when I called in at home on the way to Tredennis. What did you say?'

'I told her I could see no real obstacles to her having one but I'd talk to you about it. Sorry, I'd forgotten. It might be a good idea to rent a field with a shelter and keep Polar Bear and the pony together. But horses are a lot of work and there would have to be real promises that you and I would not be left with all the muck shifting.'

'I'd been thinking of something along those lines myself.'

There was silence for a moment between us and then Patrick said, 'The first aid man must be expecting a few mishaps. I can see him over there with his bag. Please make sure it's not you with those ridiculous high heels.'

The rehearsals were chaos, brought about partly by a new tranche of heavies from Thickoes R Us who possessed the intelligence and lightness of foot of blindfolded walruses. After a particularly bad session when Rik had collided with one of them and the pair had gone down like ninepins Len blew his top because everyone had burst out laughing. Longton then thundered over his loud-hailer, work came to a standstill and there was a ten-minute breather while the

guilty were redrilled by Chris. The man who had been in collision with Rik had a small cut on his forehead attended to by
the foresighted first aider as he had crash-landed onto a small
table. I saw Mike Cranley with Len, a hand on his shoulder,
talking to him. Len appeared to be in tears.

Four and a half hours later again, after another break for
refreshment, the studio was full of smoke, quite a lot of the
floor space inhabited by 'bodies' and Patrick and I had
paused in full flight: the scene, a panned overview, abruptly
halted when a large spotlight failed. Thankfully, the following sequence would be done at some stage by the stunt team;
the driving of a getaway car through the supposed hotel's
security gates, just slammed shut in their faces by the ungodly. So all Patrick and I had to do was escape from the crazed
with blood-lust bodyguard, who was still disguised as an
Arab prince.

'We won't tell the children we did this,' Patrick was driven
to say. We had both flopped, out of breath, onto one of the
cream leather sofas. 'We won't tell them we were involved in
this crappy production, not for ever and ever.'

'I've come to the conclusion that Mike and Len are genuinely friendly,' I said. 'We ought to talk to them again, no,
you ought to talk to them.'

'I'll think about it.'

'I could always go on my own.'

'Ingrid . . . '

I felt impassioned enough to sit up and cradle his face
between both hands. 'The time has come to do something!'

'Okay, put me down. I promise, I'll think about it.'

So far I had managed to avoid having any disasters
brought about by the shoes but in the second take, after the
light had been fixed and when we were both heading at
speed for a corridor on the right hand side of the set, one of
the heels caught in the carpet, the world turned turtle and I

finished up, amazingly, caught. Patrick, who had stooped, went down on both knees but did not drop me.

'Cut!' Longton shouted. 'Print that.'

Rik and Jaquie were then called to shoot an extra scene of him getting to his feet, carrying her, and then setting her down, she smiling knowingly as he murmured sweetnothings in her ear.

'His little Snuggems,' I whispered to Patrick.

'I thought it was you,' he said, giving me one of his stock-in-trade hard stares

'No, you damned well didn't!'

Predictably, the Brown Bear was packed to the doors with studio personnel quenching their thirsts but, by a combination of charm and shoving, Patrick and I got in. Initially, we thought that the men we sought were not there but persistence paid off and we found them hunched over their beer and a plate of chips in an alcove in the saloon bar.

'Forgive the instrusion,' Patrick said, having disappeared for a moment or so through a door marked PRIVATE and returned with a couple of wooden beer crates that he plonked down on end for us to sit on. He seated himself, smiled into their unwelcoming faces and added, 'What will you have?'

These magic words lightened the atmosphere slightly and they both opted for whisky.

'So what's it to be, gentlemen?' Patrick said on his return with the drinks. 'A nice anonymous chat here or a much longer and bothersome one down at Aston's mega-nick?'

'You've nothing on us,' Len said.

'Ingrid reckons you're an accessory to murder.'

'You're not a cop,' Mike grated.

'No, but James Carrick is a chum of mine. What I'd like to know is why did you look so happy when you thought he was dead?'

'Who, me? When the hell did I look happy about it?'

'In your caravan. Ingrid saw you in the mirror. You appeared to be smiling.'

'I wasn't. I just get a terrible pain in the guts if I get a bit of a shock. Perhaps I pull faces.'

'And the icon she saw in your bedroom?'

'What's an icon?'

'A religious painting, often of Russian origin.'

'Oh, that. I cut it out of a magazine and stuck it in a frame. My mum had one almost the same, only a real one, and had promised it to me but it didn't come my way when she died.'

'Okay, we'll leave that for now. As far as Carrick goes he may well have made a mistake by not stationing one of his men near the little gallery in the Hall but it's not worth arguing about now and I should imagine it was a case of not having enough people for them to be placed absolutely everywhere. But he could have seen whoever took a shot at me and paid the price. The gun – you might not know this – was found in one of the flower arrangements up there. Like the other weapon found at the quarry it had been stolen from a warehouse used by the Metropolitan Police. It would appear then that the killer has links with London mobsters. Vladimir Romanov had links with one. How about you two?'

'I'll have you know,' Mike said furiously in a low voice, 'that neither I, nor Len, has *ever* been on the wrong side of the law. So I suggest you take your fancy arse right out of here before we get very angry.'

Patrick had bought one of the small cigars he sometimes smokes and now lit it pensively. 'You have that advantage over me then. Cops have been waving their fists at me for years. When I was working for MI5 you have no idea how many set-ups of mine the police walked into and buggered up.'

The two looked surprised.

'So you're not talking to us because Superintendent Coldfish asked you to?' Mike said.

'No, of course not.'

Mike passed over the dish to us. 'Have a chip.'

'Thanks, I'm starving,' Patrick said. 'How long have you known one another?'

'A long time,' Len answered shortly.

'So you, Mike, worked for the BBC too?'

'I did.'

'And were you in the Middle East as well when Len was injured?'

Mike stared into his drink for a second or two and then said, 'I don't suppose it matters if I tell you. I was the cameraman, Len did sound. We were the only two survivors. We've stuck together ever since.'

'Men in the services tend to do the same when they've been under fire together,' Patrick said. 'Who was it, terrorists?'

'Islamic extremists I think they're politely called these days although that isn't what Len and I refer to him and his followers as. He didn't want the British media on his patch, especially the BBC as we had a reputation for getting to the places that the other guys couldn't reach.' He emptied his beer tankard in one fierce swallow. 'A rocket-propelled grenade makes a real mess of a vehicle and whoever's unlucky enough to be inside, not that he risked any of his own bunch being seen anywhere near us. He hired a mercenary.'

'That's enough, Mike!' Len said urgently.

'What the hell!' Mike continued furiously. 'You might think I'm the iron man to be there to hold your hand when it all gets a bit too much for you. But what about me, eh? I've still got bits of metal embedded in my leg, insides that are about three feet shorter than they should be and, like you, skin grafts from the burns. And all because of that bloody bastard who's – '

'Shut up!' Len mouthed, gazing around anxiously. 'For God's sake think what you're saying!'

One of Mike's hands came down to grip Len's wrist like a manacle. 'Does it occur to you we might be talking to the right bloke?' Without waiting for an answer he turned to Patrick to say, 'Suppose we do you a deal, eh? I'll tell you what you want to know in exchange for you doing what I'm sure you used to – take him out. But on one condition; the police aren't involved.'

Patrick blew a smoke ring at the ceiling. 'Are you saying that it's one and the same person, the man the book was written about who we think has subsequently killed several people involved with this film and the mercenary who fired a rocket-propelled grenade at a car carrying BBC journalists?'

'Do we have a deal or not?'

'I presume you've had some contact with him and he's threatened to get even if you blow the whistle on him and that's why you don't want the police involved. If he's sentenced to life imprisonment you're fairly safe.'

'He told us he has friends – and who knows, the prosecution might screw up.'

'Mike, how do you know this for sure – I mean that he was the one who fired the grenade at you?'

'Because he tried to warn us off first. In friendly fashion of course, didn't mention that he'd be the one doing it.'

'And you've recognised him on this film set?'

'That's right. Never forget a face, I don't. He likely thought he'd killed the lot of us.'

'But it's been assumed that he uses various disguises.'

'I don't know anything about that. He had a little black beard when I first clapped eyes on him but that's gone now.'

'He had a small black beard not so long ago, when he killed John Taylor and his wife.'

'Her too?'

'So it would appear. But there's hardly a shred of evidence. We only know that his real name is probably Samuel Whitaker.'

'Doesn't mean a thing to me,' said Cranley, shaking his head.

'Come on man. *Who* is he?'

'Do we have a deal?'

'Look, I've never been a hitman in the sense that he has. I'm not a criminal either and I no longer have access to weapons.'

'That's not my problem.'

I said, 'If we knew who it was he could be grabbed when he's least expecting it without any need for –'

'He's got to be dead,' Mike interrupted. 'Then Len and I can sleep at night for the rest of our lives.'

'For all you know he might have primed his oppos anyway.'

'We'll take the risk.'

'Then no deal,' Patrick said, rising to his feet.

'Don't you want to get even on your own account?' Len asked, clearly astonished.

'I could say the same to you. Turn him in. Okay,' Patrick continued when the pair just stared stonily at him, 'you give me no choice but to inform Aston.'

He walked out.

'Grab one of them when they leave,' I urged, having had to run to catch up as he was walking very quickly. 'It would only take a few minutes to get the truth out of them.'

'I can't. You know I can't.'

'But it might save someone's life!'

'Ingrid, you must understand that I simply can't torture – and that's what it would amount to – innocent members of the public just because they won't tell me something that I want to know. Even when we were working for D12 the people whom I used the third degree on were either hardened

261

criminals or suspected of very serious crimes. And that was bad enough. For *me*.'

'Patrick . . . '

'I mean it, no.'

'You're misunderstanding me. I wasn't suggesting that you hurt them. But you only have to be in the same room as people and look really grim and they – '

He stopped walking. 'Perhaps I'm not a man of iron either. I can't do it. Not to those guys – not after what they've been through. I've seen soldiers who have been badly hurt like Len; his personality's half destroyed, he's a sick man. How long can he carry on working? Just as long as Mike continues to prop him up?'

'But the police will interrogate them and they might not be so patient as you!'

He continued walking, muttering, 'You're right. I won't tell them then.'

'That's hardly right either.'

'Should I agree to kill him and then, when I know who it is, tell Aston instead?'

'I can't answer that – it's up to you.'

'You can be too fussy, can't you, in matters of conscience? And there's no time for all this stupid farting around.' Abruptly, he turned and set off back the way we had come.

'What are you going to do?' I asked, staying where I was.

'Tell them I'll kill the bastard.'

'Patrick, you'll go to prison!'

'So be it. As you said yourself, it's time we did something.'

His mobile phone rang. He snatched it from his pocket and I thought for a moment that he would hurl it into the darkness without discovering who wanted to speak to him. But he did not and for several seemingly endless moments listened without speaking. Then he said something, I could not hear what as I was still standing several yards away, and put the phone away.

'Who was that?'

'Joanna.'

'Has James taken a turn for the worst? I asked, alarmed.

'Out of danger, awake and off the ventilator. He's obviously still very weak but able to say he didn't see who fired the shot.' Patrick sat down on a low wall. 'Nothing's changed then.'

'Please wait until the reconstruction tomorrow before you do anything.'

After an aching silence he said, 'Yes, I suppose it would be a slap in the face for our Jockanese hero, after all he's been through, if he ended up having to shove me in the slammer for murder.'

16

'It'll be interesting to find out if anyone doesn't turn up,' I said.

Patrick said, 'Folk have a job to do but apart from that I think you'll find that everyone will make a real effort to be present in case the finger of suspicion – if you'll forgive the corny expression – is pointed at them.'

'I presume the police can't impose a three-line-whip – only request that people attend.'

Patrick's eyed the detective superintendent as he strode on to the set with a small entourage. 'But he would if he could, wouldn't he? – with real whips.' Not actually required for the later filming he was just wearing jeans and T-shirt – probably envied by the rest of the cast in their evening clothes.

The reconstruction was being staged before filming of the scene started, while the set was all in one piece, and I knew that the director was hoping, nay praying, that it would be over in about an hour. I found myself admiring Longton enormously when he suddenly appeared on the gallery and called everyone to order, thus forestalling any move that Aston might make to take charge.

'There's no need for me to tell you why we're doing this,' Longton began. 'And it's vital that everyone here behaves and moves in exactly the same way they did when Detective Chief Inspector Carrick was shot. So we'll go back to that scene, ladies and gentlemen, and I want you to treat it as a rerun. We are not going to film but everything will be videoed as normal by both film unit staff and the police and I must tell you that this might be shown in a court of law. To remind you then, the African leader and his aides are just about to be picked off by the assassin from the gallery and he then jumps over the gallery rail and lands on the piano. After a little more firing around the furniture and so forth, during which more minders are taken care of, he makes for the door. At that point, a real shot was fired at Rik Harrison's stand-in and another at Carrick.' Longton turned to Aston. 'Do you want someone to take Carrick's part?'

'Yes, I think so,' Aston replied.

'That's me,' said Joanna, who was standing next to me at Longton's invitation.

'If you're sure you . . . ' Aston began dubiously but, to Mike Cranley directions, Joanna was already making her way down the room.

'Who is she, by the way?' asked someone at my elbow and I turned to see that it was Hayley, the continuity girl. I told her and it was then her job to position the cast exactly where they had been just before the time of the attack.

'One thing before we start, Mr Longton,' Aston said. 'I understand that it was your idea that a change be made to the shooting script. The shot hitting the doorframe was not part of the original plan.'

In the intervening period Longton had come down from the gallery and taken up his position by the camera. 'No,' he replied. 'It wasn't.'

'Don't you think it odd that something that you personally thought of, seemingly at the last minute, should instantly result in a real attack?'

'Yes, it would have been if I had just thought of it,' Longton replied.

'So you'd mulled it over earlier?'

'Yes, with the assistant director and a couple of other people.'

'Who? Can you remember?'

'Hamish from special effects and Jeff, the cameraman,' Mike put in.

'But *whose* idea was it?'

Both men looked at one another and shook their heads.

'Dunno,' Mike said. 'It sort of happened.'

'Ideas don't just happen,' Aston growled.

'Perhaps you'd be good enough to leave that one with us for a while so we can get on with this,' Longton said smoothly.

'Martin's great with people, isn't he?' Patrick said in my ear and Aston swung round and glared like a schoolteacher who suspected that someone was talking in class.

'Okay, let's run it through first folks,' Longton called. To Aston he said, 'I suggest that if you want to see the whole sequence in one go roughly the way cinema-goers will, we play it so Rik Harrison starts the action up here, the stuntman does the jump off the gallery on to the piano and then Patrick Gillard carries on as stand-in to Rik and acts the moves that he did the other day. We'll do all that without a break: three men taking the part of one. Is that all right?'

Aston was not sure. To be fair he probably found the whole concept as confusing as I had to start with.

'You're really only interested in the last few seconds,' Longton observed.

'No, I'm interested in everything,' Aston countered. 'But carry on – have your rehearsal and then we'll talk about it.'

'As usual, we're using real weapons that fire blanks,' said, or rather drawled, Mike. 'Don't want any of you guys to think you're being shot at.'

'Is that really necessary for a reconstruction?' Aston enquired sharply.

'Yes,' Patrick said, 'Because I for one am *not* running around pointing my fingers shouting "Bang!" '

From up on the gallery both Chris and Rik gave him enthusiastic thumbs-up signs.

'As you wish,' Aston said loftily.

'Quiet – standby for a rehearsal!' Mike sang out.

'Action!'

The first thing that happened was that the policemen rapidly got out of the way, obviously taken unawares by the mayhem that broke out when Rik started firing. The African contingent 'died' dramatically, diners screamed, threw themselves under tables and generally gave the officers of the law their money's worth. Then Chris leapt over the ballustrade, like Patrick attired in jeans and T-shirt, landed on the piano, took a few more shots at the advancing minders and then ducked to one side to allow Patrick to carry on. When he reached the door he mimed getting shot at, turned to fire again and Longton called 'Cut!'

'Is everyone sure that was how it went before Carrick was shot?' Aston asked, emerging from a window recess.

A couple of people pointed out minor differences and they were rectified.

'You fired back,' Aston said to Patrick. 'Were you asked to do so by the director?'

'No, I did it automatically,' Patrick replied.

'I noted that, this time, you fired up towards the minstrels' gallery. Did you do that the first time?'

'I might not have fired so high but my reaction at the time was that the shot had come from that end of the room.'

'I find it strange that, so far, this person has missed you every time. Have you any theories on that?'

'What's that supposed to mean?' Patrick retorted.

'Kindly answer the question.'

'Any theories I might have on that subject are irrelevant as I am not in league with whoever it is.'

Realising he had found someone he could not bully Aston made 'let's keep our hair on' movements with both hands. 'Your professional opinion then.'

'It's a combination of pure luck plus an average expertise

267

on my part, but possibly also because he's over the hill and drinks too much.'

'What was James doing while all this was going on?' Joanna wanted to know in the short silence that followed this remark.

'Looking around watching for anything suspicious,' Longton answered. 'At least, that's what he'd been doing previously.'

'No one knows for sure then,' she persisted. 'Surely everyone else was concentrating on the action. I was told that some of his team were in the film to prevent having too many people cluttering up the set so were they acting or carrying out surveillance?'

'Is that right?' Aston asked and I saw Patrick wince as the same idea crossed his mind as it had mine; that she might have unintentionally dropped her husband right in it.

A man stepped forward. 'Sergeant Dean, sir. The real actors do the stuff, sir. We were told to stay in the background to make up the numbers but stay on our guard. I think Constable Miller cleared it with the boss to get shot and fall over but that was all.'

'Does Constable Miller fancy himself as a film star?' Aston asked coldly.

'I don't know, sir.'

'And *none* of you saw anything suspicious? I'm flabbergasted, sergeant. Not one of you saw who shot the DCI?'

'Most of us had our backs to the little gallery, sir. There were no vantage points to watch from the other end of the room without getting in the production crew's way or being right in camera-shot and getting shouted at by Mr Cranley.'

Who, still burning with resentment at having been recently caught speeding in his four-wheel-drive vehicle, had bellowed at them to get their blankety-blank butts out of it.

'No one was actually stationed on the minstrels' gallery itself?'

'No, sir, not actually on it. That was a no-go area in case we were visible on film.'

'But all the exposed film has been closely examined and the gallery was *out* of camera range. Otherwise we might have seen who fired the shot.'

'We had to follow the wishes of the director, sir.'

'You're completely and utterly inept!' Aston yelled.

Justifiably angry he might be but he seemed to have a regrettable penchant for public humiliation. I thought the remark grossly unfair. Aston had not witnessed the way they had sweated, sunburnt and bitten by insects, for days in the area in and around the quarry.

Longton said, 'It was a deliberate decision of mine not to have any security people, actors or otherwise, on that gallery during actual takes. That was why the floral displays were up there. For one thing it is a very good vantage point from which our assassin could easily have been picked off so from the story point of view we portrayed the minders as some-what slow and inefficient. As far as today's concerned I hope you realise that there's only a ladder and a platform behind that gallery and not the passageway from a narrow staircase with rooms off as there was at Wrotherly that the cast were using for getting into costume.'

Aston asked Dean, 'Were any of you in the vicinity to the entrance of the gallery between takes?'

'Yes, sir. I was.'

'And you saw no one hanging around rather than going about their business?'

'No.'

'Before we do anything else I'd like to move on to the pro-duction side,' the senior policeman went on, turning his back on Dean to face Longton and his team who were grouped around the camera and sound equipment like soldiers defending the last remnants of a fort. 'Are you all sure in your minds that you followed your exact moves when you were originally filming that scene?'

'We stayed in the same place, if that's what you mean,' said Len.

'Except for me,' Longton said. 'I commuted between here, where I'm now standing, and the video monitor and can't be expected to remember exactly where I was at any given moment.'

'Where is the monitor?'

'Over there by Miss Langley.'

'Very well. Did any of you notice your colleagues doing anything different from on the first occasion?'

There was a general shaking of heads.

'I should like to go for a recorded rerun now, ' the superintendent said, 'But this time, when the director shouts "cut" I want you all to carry on and react the way you did after Carrick was shot. Can we keep the video cameras rolling for that please.'

Patrick said, 'I suggest that one of your men is given a blank-firing Glock pistol and fires it twice, but not in rapid succession, when I reach the door. That will jog people's memories and also they'll know when to act.'

'I agree,' Aston said.

When this had been organised and at a signal from Aston there was the usual call for 'Quiet – and standby for a take,' and Rik took his place again.

'Action!' Longton shouted.

Again, it was re-enacted. To me it seemed as though I was watching a ballet, a kind of dance of death. I am not usually superstitious but by our actions were we willing it to happen all over again?

Rik shot the delegation from Africa, Chris landed on the piano and Patrick wove and ducked before making for the doorway. The first extra shot rang out. Patrick had already jinked as he reached the door, again moving at a slightly different angle to last time, I could not help but notice, and turned and fired back at the same time as the second shot from the policeman's pistol cracked out.

'Cut!' Longton roared. 'What the hell's going on?'

'The bloke in the kilt's been hit,' a man shouted. 'Call an ambulance!'

Chris jumped up on the table and ran along it, still managing to avoid everything, shouting that he was trained in first-aid. As I had done before I followed suit and almost tripped over a flower arrangement but got there right behind him. Joanna was sitting on the floor with her back to the wall looking flushed and a bit bemused.

The video operators had arrived too and were recording everything that took place.

'Well, where is he?' Chris said, looking around, after some twenty seconds or so had elapsed.

'Who?' Aston asked.

'The bloody first-aid guy!'

'Oh God, I've just remembered!' Hayley cried. 'I saw him. Up on the gallery. Not here. At Wrotherly. He was looking out over the room and then disappeared. I think he had his first aid bag with him.'

I suddenly realised that Patrick was standing right beside me, only down on the floor, and put my hand on his shoulder.

'I should have thought of him,' was all Patrick said.

DS Aston marched up to Hayley. 'When exactly was it you saw this man? How long before the shooting?'

'I – I'm not sure. During one of the rehearsals, I think.'

'Did you see him do anything else? Take anything from the bag?'

'I'm not sure,' Hayley said again.

I thought for a moment that Aston would grab her by the

271

shoulders and shake her but he found Sergeant Dean a more worthy target. 'Did you see him?' he demanded to know.

'There were dozens of people going backwards and forwards, sir,' Dean almost whimpered. Then the twin barrels of Aston's eyes must have activated his memory for he said, 'Yes, come to think of it I did see him. He said to me something like, "Let's hope they don't all want indigestion tablets after eating that cheese – it looks as though it's been around for quite a while." Then he laughed, he's a cheery, quiet sort of bloke.'

'Did he go on to the gallery?'

'I didn't notice, sir. I was trying to look everywhere all the time.'

'Watching out for armed men in combat dress and balaclavas?' Aston said sarcastically. 'Well, it looks as though we have a suspect.' Then to his group, 'Shall we go and find him?' In the studio doorway he paused, pointed at Hayley and said, 'I shall want a statement from that woman later. Meanwhile you may all carry on.'

'I still love ya, babe,' Martin Longton said to Hayley, who was fuming at the rudeness, when they had departed. 'I suggest we have a short break, fifteen minutes, no more, and then get on with the work. Where's Rik? I need to talk to him about it.'

But Rik Harrison could not be found and real alarm only set in a little later when his minder was discovered in a cleaning store, unconscious.

'The man was lucky,' Patrick said. 'He'd been shoved in there with such haste that his feet prevented the door from being closed properly. Otherwise he might not have been found for hours.'

'There's no sign of Harrison?' James Carrick whispered hoarsely. By some miracle of persuasion he had convinced

272

the nursing staff that he would recover much more quickly if he could apply himself to unfinished business. Wanly propped up on pillows, still connected to drips and with blond stubble on his chin he still gave every impression of being capable of leaving the ward under his own steam should the place catch fire.

'Not a trace,' Patrick told him. 'Aston raided the address that was on record with the film company for the first aid man and, naturally, it turned out to be a false one. But they took a chance that he lived in another of the flats in the same block as it's the one that's near the car park where Romanov was killed. So they did a house-to-house on every flat on the side of the building that overlooks that area – working on the theory that he potted the poor guy from one of his windows – and finally found someone who recognised the description as his next-door neighbour. They barged into that place – probably without a warrant but no one's complaining as they found a whole arsenal of weapons hidden in wardrobes and suitcases. No Samuel Whitaker though. It looks as though he has Rik so we're praying there'll be a ransom demand soon rather than a corpse later.'

'You're being very pragmatic about this,' I accused him.

'Well of course I'm *worried*,' Patrick said. 'And as soon as there's any news I shall go and look for him myself, with or without Aston's blessing.' It went without saying that he was the instigator of the conspiracy to get information as he had told Aston that James would recover far more quickly if he was kept abreast of what was going on.

'Was the bodyguard badly hurt?' James asked.

'Slightly concussed. He doesn't know who, or what, hit him. The man's useless.'

'I hate to be pessimistic,' James said, 'But I think we'll end up with a body. He's killed everyone he's got hold of so far.'

'But he's been rumbled now so money and getting away might be the name of the game.'

'I hope you're right.'

He looked very tired even after only a few minutes and I gave Patrick a nudge.

'He may well have gone to ground in Wrotherly,' James said as we were leaving, having promised him that we would let him know as soon as there were any developments. 'He was there for a few days, remember, and learned the lie of the land. There are acres and acres of the place that we never even set foot in.'

Patrick put a hand on his shoulder. 'That's a good theory. Rest though, don't lie there fretting or you won't be well enough to come to our place over Christmas.'

'That would be great,' James said, his voice now trailing away. 'I think Joanna had been planning on going skiing in Austria but that's out of the question now.'

Outside, I said, 'Would a man like Whitaker go back to Wrotherly?'

'I think it's quite possible – unless he has already organised bolt holes. I have actually set foot in most of the estate, between takes and when I wasn't needed.'

'I wondered where you kept disappearing to.'

At six that evening a phone-call was made to the news desk of the *Evening Standard* by a man who refused to give his name claiming that he had taken Rik Harrison hostage. He wanted five million dollars ransom and safe passage out of the country. He made the usual demands; no police involvement, nothing published in the media, any infringement would result in Harrison's death. Asked for proof that the call was genuine he had hung up. Then twenty minutes later he rang again, before the police had had time time to arrange a tap on the line, and gave details of Harrison's family and other personal information that the man in the street could not possibly know. The money and plane ticket to Chile were to be left in a phone box on the corner of named streets in Reigate.

Aston arranged that a bag be left with scrap paper inside it in the phone box and positioned a couple of dozen undercover personnel in the immediate area. No one came near, except a woman to make a call who exited rapidly when she saw the bag, probably thinking it was a bomb. An hour and a half later a small weighted package was tossed into the lobby of Kingston police station which was immediately evacuated as that too was suspected of being an explosive device. Members of an army disposal team decided it was too small to warrant carrying out any kind of controlled explosion on, which was just as well as it contained the tip of one of Rik Harrison's little fingers. A bloodstained note with it promised that the next parcel would contain the actor's head if further instructions, to be advised, were not followed to the letter.

Patrick's language when he learned of this dismal failure on Aston's part might have made the superintendent wish he had not made the call to tell him the news, especially when it was pointed out to him that his priority was to keep the kidnap victim alive and not just nab someone who happened to have shot a policeman. I was surprised that such a senior officer was keeping him informed at all, a friend of Carrick's notwithstanding, and could only think it was due to the 'MI5 factor'; Patrick's name somehow still bouncing around favourably in the rarefied air of the upper regions of the Metropolitan Police.

'That's it,' Patrick said after the call. 'I shall go into Wrotherly. When it's dark. If they're not there nothing will have been lost, if they are we have a better chance of success than Aston who would go in with choppers, several hundred cops, three brass bands and the police show jumping team.

No, and in case you weren't listening I didn't tell him or he'd have rung the estate to clear it with them first. Policemen do things like that. God, I hope they've got that bit of finger on ice so it can be sewn back on. Well, are you coming?'

Yes, I would go with Patrick who was obviously as worried as hell about his protégé. I had a sudden memory of the man I must now remember to call Samuel Whitaker bending over James, just looking at him as he lay on the floor bleeding and Chris shouting at him to get a move on and do something.

17

'We already know you can get away with firing shotguns in this place without anyone bothering too much,' Patrick said, nevertheless speaking in a whisper. 'And I checked when we were here and there aren't any security cameras on the boundaries, only on the official entrances and outside the house itself so getting in here should be easy.'

As we had also discovered previously, the estate had originally possessed several gated entrances in the high brick boundary wall which were connected by carriage drives. Closing off a couple of these that had exited onto a minor country road, presumably for security reasons, had involved no more than locking and padlocking the gates, putting strands of barbed wire across the tops and cementing iron bollards that resembled cannon across the driveway outside. This much was clear in the light from a crescent moon.

We had not parked in the immediate vicinity but some fifty yards away among the trees on the twenty foot-wide verge below the boundary wall. There were no street lamps and the dark blue Range Rover was invisible from the road, something we had guaranteed by draping over it a broken-off branch we had found together with some fern fronds. Before parking the car we had conducted a careful, but of necessity not too protracted, search of the stretch of road that bounded the estate on this side, about three-quarters of a mile in length, including the other closed entrance, and had seen no other parked cars.

Patrick gazed up at the ten foot high wooden gates, using his tiny burglars' torch, the beam travelling slowly along the barbed wire. 'I can't see any other wires that might be connected to alarms,' he said. 'We will have to go over the gate as the broken glass and spikes on top of the wall would tear us to ribbons. Are you going to cut the wire while I support you?'

I told him that was preferable to the other way round and found myself going skywards up the right-hand side gate.

'For goodness sake watch it doesn't whip into your face when you cut it,' came the instruction from below.

The wire was not particularly taut though and I was able to drop the longer cut ends out of the way on the far side of the other gate. Having cut the strands I then grasped the top of the gate and transfered my feet – one onto a hinge, the other to the doorknob – and pulled myself up. Then came the diffi-cult bit of swinging a leg over the top but the massive gate pillar came in handy as a support and I was able to perch on the top of the gate. Everything on the other side was in deep-est darkness.

'You'll probably have to jump,' Patrick said.

'I can't see what I'm jumping into. There might be more wire strung across.'

'Then you'll have to climb down and hope for the best.'

Muttering, I succeeded in rolling over onto my front, found a toe-hold and somehow, let myself down. Then there was nothing for it, dangling by both hands, but to let go.

'Are you all right?' The question was somewhat gruntingly uttered as Patrick had obviously taken a run at the gate and was now wriggling himself over the top.

I had landed on one side of what must have been quite a high pile of rubble, slithered and then turned my ankle on a rock and crashed into the space between the heap and the gate. It stank of everything putrid and shitty and both hands, which I had automatically braced before me, were up to the wrists in something unspeakable.

'Ingrid!'

'Take care,' I managed to say, before retching.

There were scrambling noises and a foot landed on my back.

'Where are you?'

'You're standing on me.'

A few expletives later we were both upright on flat ground.

'For God's sake shine your torch on my hands,' I begged in a muffled squeal.

'Mud,' was the instant male diagnosis. 'Wipe them on the grass.'

'It *stinks!*'

For some reason he remained patient. 'Cow manure,' he amended after a brief examination of our immediate environs with the torch. 'Just over there. A big heap. They must leave it here to rot before putting it on the gardens and gunge from it's run this way.'

I wiped off the filthy muck – there was definitely putrifaction in there somewhere – as best I could on the grass, wanting to scream and knowing that I was being utterly pathetic. Patrick voicing his worries about being too old for this kind of thing was haunting me. Was he right? Now we were just plain Mr and Mrs, weren't we? Joe Bloke and his missus playing around and trying to resurrect any past glories?

'Harrison'll be all right if he keeps his cool,' Patrick said absently, consulting a compass. 'That's if he's even here. I don't remember seeing any out-buildings other than in the vicinity of the house, not even huts, do you?'

'No. Patrick, this is a *vast* area for us to search.'

'I have no intention of searching it. We'll go for your original suggestion and set a trap.'

'How, for Heaven's sake?'

'Even if he left most of his armoury behind our Sam probably took his trusty snipers' rifle with him and it may well have night sights. He may have night-vision binoculars, not that he'll really need them tonight. So unless he's really gone to ground in the quarry he'll spot us no bother.'

'But that's madness!'

He grinned at me in the gloom. 'He won't be able to see *who* it is though and he certainly won't be expecting only two people to arrive in order to catch him. We'll just be a courting couple who have climbed in for a nice private roll in the brambles.'

Ye gods. I said, 'I don't like the uncanny way he knew about Aston's trap.'

'Aston was incompetent and clumsy and for all we know surrounded the phone box with men pretending to dig up the road and in ice cream vans. Having said that, this could very well go pear-shaped – we'll then have to make up the script as we go along. If you're forced to shoot him with Ivan the Terrible's handgun then so be it.' After a short silence he added, 'That hard lump in your pocket is the heavy thing that was in your bag, isn't it?'

'I did once divorce you for being a horrible clever-clogs, you know,' I said.

Hand in hand, to a small orchestra of hooting owls, we strolled down the lane that led from the gate which soon merged with the one where the film unit's vehicles had been parked for the first day's shooting. Actually heading in the direction of the house to begin with, we paused now and again, in case anyone was watching us, to put our arms around one another and kiss. They were wary embraces but I found it easy to lose concentration for even with his mind elsewhere Patrick did not just peck my cheek.

About ten minutes later we reached the edge of the trees by the lake and gazed over the water, the moon reflected in it creating a serene silver pathway. Bats swooped and flitted across the still surface and there was a plop as a fish jumped. A breath of a breeze rustled through the reeds. For some rea-son the scene before me was not a thing of beauty – and I usually do find such places spiritually uplifting – at night this place seemed to have the same brooding unsavouriness as prevailed in the hidden valley.

'He's not here,' Patrick whispered. 'In my bones I know he's not in this locality. It's too close to the house and there's no real cover except these trees. Not only that, this man isn't alone, he has a potentially noisy and unco-operative prisoner with him who will be in quite a lot of pain.'

'Just as well you taught Rik a thing or two,' I said, more to cheer myself up about his predicament than anything else. I thought him a bit juvenile but he was charming and good company and loved his parents: it was a bit like something nasty happening to Winnie-the-Pooh.

'Yes, we did touch on kidnap and violent stalkers. One of the things I taught him was to do what he was told if heavily physically outclassed until a one hundred and twenty percent opportunity to have a go presented itself. I suggest we walk in the opposite direction, there's a thick copse with a fallen oak in it above the quarry. We'll go close to the other unused gate on the way and can have a look around there.'

Then, we heard a vehicle. Swiftly, for it was coming in our direction, we left the lane and half-buried ourselves in the leaf litter beneath the low branches of a tree. Lights approached, probing through the woodland on a bend in the lane.

'A smallish diesel of some kind,' Patrick said in my ear. 'A pound to a penny it's one of the estate's Land Rovers. It'll be on some kind of routine patrol.'

We lowered our heads as it went by in a rush of warm fumes and thrummed away into the distance. Then there was silence, but for the breeze in the trees and the owls.

Again hand in hand – this flimsiest of disguises – we walked back the way we had come and passed where we had entered the estate. The road forked to the right, the route

Patrick and I had taken to reach the Hidden Valley when we had first visited Wrotherly, but we did not go that way yet.

I was now going into an area I had not previously entered. The lane immediately became rougher, with holes and ruts and I wondered if large machinery involved in felling trees was responsible. This was confirmed shortly afterwards when we came to a large glade, the ground churned into mud, a stack of tree trunks in the centre.

Patrick enfolded me in his arms. 'In case of a watcher,' he hissed. 'We'll walk over there towards the pile of trunks as though looking for somewhere to . . . ' He kissed me.

'It's too distracting when you keep kissing me like that,' I said afterwards.

'Oh, sorry,' he replied absently, mind on strategy.

It is very difficult to appear casual and lighthearted when you are actually like a cat on hot bricks, expecting to be attacked, or at the very least, challenged by an armed man at any moment. Whether we achieved it or not was of no consequence as there was no one by the woodstack. There was a perfectly legitimate reason to move on; the ground was at least two inches deep in water.

The other entrance lay off to the left a quarter of a mile farther on. This was potentially hazardous as it was approached through a narrow tunnel of overgrown trees, the gate itself invisible from our position at a point where the one-time carriage roads joined.

Patrick took my arm and we went back a few paces to where he had noticed a narrow path, probably made by deer and running roughly parallel to the lane to the gate, which could just be discerned winding through the tall grass and bracken beneath the trees. He led the way, not using his torch, and it was so dark here I could only just make out his outline a few feet ahead of me. We had to stoop low in places where the branches were near the ground. Brambles whipped our faces and tore at our clothes and I felt I was making as much noise as a herd of elephants.

We stopped. All I could hear now was the thumping of my own heart. Patrick then turned to place a hand on my shoulder, a signal to stay where I was, and went from sight. He made no sound and for what seemed an age I stood perfectly still. Then I heard a low, barely audible, whistle and set off in the direction he had gone.

In a dozen paces I emerged from the trees. Patrick was examining the ground by the gate, which even in the dim light I could see was old and in a poor state of repair. The road here had been almost completely buried beneath years of leaf-fall and weeds, the surface, where visible here and there, reflected the wan moonlight as though wet and slimy. It occurred to me that there could be any number of hiding places for a fugitive under the high boundary wall. What chance did two people have of finding him?

'No, he must want what I would have done in the circumstances,' Patrick said quietly, 'a concealed vantage point from which to see if the police are arriving with dogs. He'll have worked out an escape route to use in case he's forced to kill his hostage. I suggest we quickly check the area by the fallen oak and then head for the quarry. It's the only place where you have any kind of overview that isn't close to the house. But that's only a guess – we can't relax anywhere here.'

The lane was still very rough underfoot and we had to be careful that we did not trip. Much as I like owls I was glad we had left them behind as I had thought for a while they were following us and would give away our presence. I could still hear them in the distance when we stopped every fifty yards or so to listen but otherwise there was a heavy silence: the breeze seemed to have completely dropped. I took it that we were abandoning the courting couple ruse.

Again I waited when we reached the fallen oak while

Patrick reconnoitred, concealing myself as best I could. I began to get alarmed as the minutes ticked by and was seriously thinking of starting to search for him when he suddenly returned.

'There are recent footprints,' he breathed, gesturing over his shoulder, 'by the tree. Two men, one wearing shoes, the other boots. They sat on the tree for a while and then went across the glade and into the trees on the other side. We'll follow. No more talking.'

I gave him plenty of space as he sometimes paused without warning to listen and scent the air like an animal. After a little while, in a tiny clearing where a few trees had been felled, leaving the stumps, he stopped and bent down to examine one and I heard a whispered exclamation. He switched on his torch for a couple of seconds, concealing the pencil-thin beam as much as possible with a hand. Then he placed the end of a finger in the fresh blood, for that was what it was, and sniffed. After this he knelt and smelt the ground, repeating the action a few feet away where the vegetation looked as though it had been trampled or flattened. The torch beam picked out more bloodstains and I saw him pick up something very small.

I did not need to be told that this was the place where the tip of Harrison's finger had been cut off, using the tree stump as a butcher's block, and he had been left here, tied up, while Whitaker had delivered it to the police. So where had the actor been imprisoned while his kidnapper had previously secretly watched the phone box?

Patrick started to follow a clear trail of footprints that led away but almost immediately turned round, came past me and headed back towards the lane. Once there he spent quite a while quartering the area, almost on hands and knees, before setting off once again back towards the fork.

'It was a false trail,' he risked whispering. 'We could spend all night looking for the right one so we'll go this way.'

'What did you find?'

'A shirt button. But we can't know for sure that it's Rik's. The other evidence is plain enough; I can smell perfume of some kind on the ground, aftershave, not a scent a woman would use, and I'm pretty sure it's human blood. That's what we could really do with right now, a bloodhound.'

'Show me the button,' I requested. 'It's real mother-of-pearl,' I told him after peering at it in the torch-light. 'He does wear shirts with buttons like this.'

At the fork we took the right-hand path, walking at the side of it as it wended downhill to take full advantage of the deep shade of the pines. As before, every minute or so Patrick stopped to scent the air and listen. The trees began to thin out, we were getting near the quarry. All at once Patrick paused to muddy his hands at the edge of a puddle and smeared it over his face, miming that I should do the same. He stayed where he was, crouched down, smelling the cool air that was gently fanning towards us up the track. Then he rose and we sought the scanty cover of the trees.

We progressed slowly and carefully, using the slender trunks of the pines as cover, and skirted the quarry area we could glimpse down to our right. I think we both heard voices at the same time, or rather a voice, and froze. It seemed to be coming from somewhere in the large expanse of open ground below us but not close by, in the distance. Then there was a cry, as though someone was in pain. The shouting continued for another few seconds and then stopped. We had moved off again when we heard it again, a little louder.

'D'you know what I think that is?' Patrick said under his breath.

'It sounds like someone on a bad phone line trying to make themselves heard,' I said.

'Precisely. I think that's Whitaker on his mobile endeavouring

285

to make his latest ransom demand in an area with a weak signal. I reckon he's had to climb up onto the rocks to make contact.'

Another cry rang out.

'And is sticking pins in his hostage to add a bit of weight to the argument,' Patrick added grimly. 'Come on, before he loses patience. I'm really going to gamble here and assume he's in the more remote corner round to the left – in the area where we filmed the chopper chase.'

Moving more quickly now, we carried on through the trees. At a point where one of the larger rock piles jutted out from the rest and would conceal our approach for a while from anyone in the farthest reaches of the quarry we left the trees to cover the open space near the polluted pools. I detected a strange metallic smell.

We were taking a huge risk. For all we knew Whitaker was concealed somewhere on the rocks we were nearing. If he was wearing dark clothing he would be invisible. At every step of the way I was expecting to be shot and felt weak with relief when we reached the base of the outcrop and began to edge around the lower boulders. This was slow work as the ground underfoot was strewn with stones and it was almost impossible to see where we were putting our feet.

As we started to round the corner Patrick paused and climbed up for a short distance to enable him to look over the top. He remained there for a few minutes, not moving. We had heard no more voices. I was trying not to think about the possibility of Rik having been murdered.

Patrick slid down, even the rustling sound of his clothes against the rocks seeming loud in the dead silence. He took my arm, indicating that we should retrace our steps. To me, this seemed to be a dreadful delay and I held back but he insisted and with a heavy heart I followed him.

Where the rock pile butted against the tree line we went

round it, crossed a dry stream-bed and carried on through the trees, having to go uphill to where they were thicker, thus offering more cover. We seemed to walk for hours, crossed a plank bridge over a watercourse with a strong flow and then came to a barbed wire fence. It was in poor condition and we were able to step over it. Patrick turned sharp right and we headed downhill again.

By now, I guessed, we had reached the point near where the slope we were descending steepened abruptly into the cliffs that bordered the far side of the quarry. Another long outcrop of spoil soon came into view and this had a flattened top covered in crushed stone almost like a road. I then saw that there was indeed a curving ramp leading down from it to the quarry floor so perhaps earth-moving machinery, a crane, had been operated from the top. Scanning the area I realised that where the outcrop finished had been the position from which Patrick and I had been 'ambushed' during filming.

Sitting on this headland, so to speak, were two figures, one hunched over as though tied up.

It was unassailable without our being spotted. Even a cat would be unable to creep up and not be seen. On three sides was the open moon-like expanse of the quarry floor and the remaining aspect was the long, slightly sloping ridge before us now that did not possess so much as a blade of grass of cover.

Should we retreat and then one of us use our mobile phone to inform the police of the two men's whereabouts? Or take drastic immediate action that would possibly be even more risky as far as Rik was concerned? One thing was certain, the two were out of range of hand guns.

I remained quite still and said nothing, not wanting to distract Patrick from his thoughts. Another half minute or so later he moved to place a hand again on my arm to indicate that he wanted to go on alone. He paused to whisper in my ear and then had gone, disappearing from sight between the trees to my left.

'The ghost walks,' he had said. 'Do what you think best.'

I soon discovered what this meant. Not many people, for a party piece, have the call of the Great Northern Diver off to perfection. In Canada it had even fooled the birds to greater efforts of their own. Likely to be heard during the breeding season only off Scottish coasts it comes as a real shock to the average Brit.

The dreadful falsetto wails beat against the cliff walls, the echoes harried by peals of manic laughter; utterly humour-less, mindless, before a long-drawn-out tremulous *ha-oo-oo*. This was still reverberating around, as though the calls were being answered, when it began all over again.

One of the figures had leapt to his feet at the racket, flung a rifle up to his shoulder and started firing, wildly, in the direction from whence he thought it was coming. At the first sign of movement I had been on my feet, gun in hand, safety catch off and running downhill and then along the side of the rock-pile in the opposite direction to that in which Whitaker was firing. Once, I tripped and almost fell.

The terrible row was still going on when I reached where I wanted to be. I had intended to shout at Whitaker to throw down his weapon – there was something that stopped me from shooting him from behind – but had a feeling he would be unable to hear me. Then I saw him, outlined against the sky. He appeared to be highly agitated. Then he lowered the rifle, there was some kind of scuffle and in the next second something large came hurtling down, knocking me flat. I must have hit my head on a rock for everything went fuzzy and the next thing I knew the weight had been lifted off me. A torch beam shone briefly in my face.

'It's that bloody Gillard female,' ground out a harsh voice

288

and despite not being able to see properly because of the sudden glare I knew I was looking down a rifle barrel.

I heard a loud thump and the figure standing over me keeled over. Swearing savagely, he regained his feet and, one- handed, hauled whatever had landed on me away and threw it down again. My vision clearing, I saw him take aim. But not at me, at the bundle.

I shot him, to disable, from almost point blank range.

For a moment, still stunned, the detonation deafening, the flash affecting my eyes again, I thought he had fired at me after all. Everything had started going round and round and there was strange music in my ears, a kind of dance played *con brio*. I could not feel anything.

Did this mean I was dying?

'Ingrid? Is that you?' whimpered a voice. 'For God's sake untie me. I've got my head jammed between some rocks.'

No, I wasn't dying, just felt completely unworldly. I scrambled to my feet, succeeded in removing the rifle well out of Whitaker's reach – although he was lying very still – and blundered over to the shapeless bundle that must be Rik. If this was him he was every way up. I could not shift him so started to haul away a few of the smaller rocks.

'I'm tied up,' Rik repeated. 'Please get a knife.'

'Patrick's got a knife,' I muttered.

Patrick.

Who had been somewhere among the trees where Whitaker had been firing.

Was he hurt?

'Wait there,' I said inanely and lurched around the end of the rock pile. All at once my head hurt like hell. The strange music had reached the second movement, an *adagio*.

There was a brief collision with someone running from the opposite direction who almost had a heart attack, thinking his wife was seriously injured, and then we were freeing Rik, or at least Patrick was. I just sat down on a flat rock like a sack of turnips.

I was trying to piece together what had happened, my very own concerto having reached the cadenza, *allegro,* when I realised that some of the more discordant notes were sirens. Another discovery was that Patrick was sitting alongside with his arm around me.

'You're a bit concussed,' he said.

'You managed to phone then.'

'After walking all the way back up to the lane.'

Another realisation was that we were sharing our rock with Rik and Patrick had an arm around him too. Bruised and battered after twice being thrown down, he was cradling his injured hand, which we found out later Whitaker had stood on to make him scream.

'I think Rik saved my life,' I said. 'He kicked Whitaker's legs from under him even though his ankles were tied together.' My gaze was drawn to the quiet huddle by a boulder. Whittaker was dead but I had not meant to kill him. I did not voice just then what I was thinking; that the action could easily have had the opposite to the desired effect, jerking the finger that was on the trigger, but that did not detract from Rik's courage.

'Patrick?' said Rik.

'Yes, my son?'

'You know what this means, don't you?'

'What?'

'You'll have to do most of the getaway scene tomorrow.'

'I thought that was all down to the stunt team.'

'No, some of it's not dangerous – running about with Jaquie, stuff like that.'

'In about . . . ' Patrick switched on his torch to look at his watch, 'three hours time then.' He sighed.

'What was that dreadful noise? He completely freaked out
– thought it was some ghost or other. So I tried to kick him off
the top.'

'It's a bird called the Common Loon in your new neck of
the woods.'

'Never heard of 'em. So they're over here too?'

'Sometimes,' Patrick said. 'When they feel like it.'

Superintendent Aston arrived, *grandioso*.

Rik spent the night in hospital having his fingertip sewn back
on and the following afternoon hobbled, black and blue, into
the studio as pale, under the bruises, as the boxing glove-
sized dressing on his hand. Martin Longton had progressed
beyond the going up the wall stage by this time and I think
was genuinely please to see him safe, albeit far from sound. It
seemed that kidnap, assault and battery appeared in the very
small print of an insurance policy and a generous amount of
money would shortly be coming in *Blood and Anger*'s direction. It would pay for the delay while Harrison recovered, or
at least until the marks on his face faded sufficiently to be successfully covered by make-up. Meanwhile, a couple of days'
work could be done using the stunt team and the stand-in,
who had come through the rescue effort with one small
scratch.

I had to admit that this made a change for Patrick as in the
past he has been badly injured during various assignments.
Perhaps though, with the prospect of having to turn up for
work after an hour's sleep, he would have preferred to have
broken his leg. I deferred judgement on this for he had not
been over-talkative on the subject.

After a paramedic had shone lights in my eyes and felt the
bump on my head, taken my blood pressure and monitored
my pulse I was spared a hospital check-up and told to go
home and straight to bed. There had been no wish on my part

to disobey the instruction. At least Aston had arranged for someone to take us back to our car.

A couple of days later there was a letter in the *Daily Telegraph* from a birdwatcher living in the vicinity of Wrotherly reporting that he and a friend had distinctly heard a Great Northern Diver somewhere within the estate, presumably on the lake. So far south! Was this as a result of global warming? Word must already have got around for that same morning hundreds of twitchers arrived at Wrotherly's gates loaded with cameras, binoculars and telescopes. They were permitted to enter, no doubt on account of the favourable publicity, but unfortunately the bird had flown.

18

James Carrick was laughing, or rather, trying not to. Although he had been out of hospital and at home for ten days it still hurt a bit too much.

'I simply can't believe that you got the better of a man like that by imitating a bird,' he gasped.

'Nor can I,' Patrick said. 'But according to Rik he was on the verge of breakdown and had been drinking. It had all gone wrong. He'd been found out, his cover was blown and the police were after him. Suddenly he was past it, no longer invincible, no longer the man who could befriend anyone and then kill them at his leisure.'

'He did a runner right at the end of the reconstruction then.'

'So it appears. Rik, who was at the back of the gallery, said he came at him from nowhere, rushed him outside with an hand over his mouth and into the car he and his minder were using – one of the few permitted to be parked directly outside the house. I don't know exactly where the minder was prior to this when he was attacked, shoved in the cupboard and the keys stolen. In the wrong place, obviously.'

'Did Whitaker have a caravan?'

'No. A large estate car. Harrison was locked in it, trussed up, while Whitaker snooped on what the reaction had been to his first ransom demand.'

'So you're on your way home for the weekend. There's more work to do then?'

'We're both needed for more studio filming for at least two weeks. When Harrison's fully recovered. He was lucky. Whitaker had knocked him about in his temper prior to our getting to him, raving that as he'd killed the others he'd kill him too, ransom or not, as such a wimp should never be portraying the kind of man he'd once been. But Rik kept his cool. He told me that what I'd taught him, the mental techniques more than anything, helped. I'm glad about that. And he tried to fight back. The media'll have a field day when the full details come out.'

'Just before the film's released?' James asked dryly.

'Natch.'

'It's almost a shame we'll never know Whitaker's side of the story now he won't come to trial. For example, *did* he betray those men in Northern Ireland?'

'If Ingrid hadn't pulled the trigger we'd be talking about Harrison in the past tense.'

'Thank God she did! I have to say though, I didn't know you were still permitted to carry firearms.'

'I'm not. You'd better ask her about that.'

Not for the first time they were talking about me as though I was not there.

'I took it away from that Russian crook and didn't quite get round to handing it in,' I said to James defensively. 'It's amazingly more effective with serial killers than chewing their ankles.'

'What's Aston going to make of it though? I mean, I know you shot Whitaker in self-defence but is he going to charge you with carrying an illegal firearm?'

'No. He confiscated it and told me not to do it again.'

Patrick cleared his throat. 'Apparently his wife's a great fan of Ingrid's books.'

'But what the hell is he going to put in his report?'

'What would you have put in your report, James?' I enquired.

'I suppose I would have said that the weapon had fallen out of Whitaker's pocket as he came down the rock pile and you snatched it up.'

'Aston's going to do something like that. After all, it

does save an awful lot of paperwork,' I finished by saying sarcastically.

'They found Sonia Lockyer's bracelet at Whitaker's flat with some other things in a locked cupboard,' James said. 'Aston rang to tell me just before you arrived. There was an icon and a miniature painting of some chickens there too. And, as I just said, other things. He'd killed quite a few people.'

'*Other* people,' Patrick commented reflectively.

'Their little treasures,' I whispered.

Three months later, just before Christmas, we went to see *Blood and Anger* for ourselves, having had to turn down an invitation to attend the première as as were abroad on holiday. We left the Plymouth cinema in a kind of daze.

'No, give them their due,' Patrick said. 'You simply can't tell where Rik leaves off and Chris and I take over. It was brilliantly done technically, seamless, and it was silly of me to expect otherwise.'

'No, but I can tell it's you on the staircase.' I said. 'That was funny. But it could have been anyone in bed, which I'm really glad about.'

'But the quarry! That backdrop of brown, barren hills they put in afterwards!'

'Our walzing bit ended up on the cutting room floor,' I observed sadly. I had known it was me in some of the shots but . . .

'Let's go down to the Barbican and have a pint and something to eat,' Patrick suggested.

Arm in arm we went, and later walked along the Hoe, gazing out to sea and yes, we were, in a strange way, very sad. All those people had died for what was, when you really thought about it, a mediocre film.

That night, after we talked about it, I wrote out a cheque, giving the money we had earned to charity.

* * *

An enjoyable Christmas with James, now fully recovered, and Joanna came and went and January set in with raw, dark days when the clouds seemed to brush the cottage chimneys. All the children had coughs and colds, Patrick was writing off for jobs that he did not really want and I could not make any headway with planning my latest novel. Katie had her pony now, Fudge, but because she was particularly unwell at the moment and temporarily unable to help look after him and Polar Bear, at the field and stable we had rented down the road, Patrick and I were doing all the work. I had not been able to nail whoever it was who had, the previous week, put a pair of dirty stirrup irons into the dishwasher.

'The Aga's gone out,' Patrick called up the stairs.

'It can't have done, it's converted to oil now,' I responded grumpily.

'Well, yes, but it's still as cold as a tomb.'

I was not in the mood for cold tombs and suddenly wanted to jet off to somewhere hot and sunny in the name of research and let the others get on with Dartmoor. Then the phone rang so I gladly did a detour to the living room. Ten minutes or so later I put down the receiver and sought out the would-be Aga repairer who by this time was down on his knees, peering into its innards.

'That was David Goodheim,' I told him.

'Oh? What did he want?'

'He asked me if I'd rewritten the film script of *A Man Called Celeste.*'

'I take it you haven't had time,' Patrick said, turning to give me a rueful smile.

'I did get it out the drawer several weeks ago and put it on my desk but I'm afraid it's been there ever since. But he wants it, ASAP. He's going to do it – over here.'

'That's brilliant.'

'Lots of bucks.'

'So I don't have to scrub sewer walls for a while yet then.'

'No, but you could be busy. He knows you were the inspiration and wants you to star in it.'

Patrick stayed where he was, on the floor, uncharacteristically speechless.

'As producers do, he watched all the rushes,' I told him. 'He thinks you're a natural. But you'd have to go to RADA for a while for a bit of polishing up.'

'Practising my man-kissing and things like that.'

'Yes, I'd make sure you needed that.'

There was a pause and then he said, 'Joking apart, Ingrid, I think I'll have to sleep on it.'

'Of course. I told Goodheim that we couldn't possibly give him an answer on that straight away.'

But Patrick remained where he was, staring fixedly at nothing. Suddenly, he said, 'I've slept. There'd be all the ballyhoo and people from *Hello!* magazine banging on the door. Media nerds would try to photograph us in the bath and follow the children to school. Then a tabloid rag would carry headlines that you were having an affair with a footballer while I spent the weekends with an under-age yak. No.'

'No, as in, no?' I carefully enquired.

'Yes, no. You carry on and do the screenplay. But I'm not going to be in it.'

I held out a hand and he took it and got to his feet.

'I'm so glad,' I said, putting my arms around him.